LM KAREN

Shut the Front Door

OAK STREET PUBLISHING HOUSE

To Nick,
Casey's 'One', the best chef I know, and one of my best friends.

Contents

Acknowledgement

This book was so fun to write but it never would have happened if not for Gina and Casey. With great anxiety and trepidation I gave them my first book, Summertime Lilies. Their love of Oak Street encouraged me to act on a half-baked idea to keep the fun going with another, more colorful story. There aren't words to describe what their friendship means to me. Thank you for your encouragement, support, and for loving my characters almost as much as I do.

Thank you to my publisher, who remains a constant in a sea of uncertainty. Who propels me forward and reminds me that 'no one said it would be easy', because it's not. Thank you for making it easier than it would be without your help. Thank you for always having answers to my unending questions. Thank you for all the things. I could not roll the boulder up the hill without you lightening the load. Thank you.

Thank you to my publicist, without whom my first book would have remained stagnant at having sold 26 copies. Thank you for your enthusiasm and pride of me and my work, even when it turns my face deep shades of red. Thank you for also pinch hitting as a second editor, ensuring the finished product is up to standard.

Thank you to my creative director and second set of eyes. I am so appreciative of your enthusiastic ideas and the support and encouragement you provide.

Thank you to Michelle for editing my work and making my writing better. I could not be more appreciative of the effort that you put in on my manuscript. Please join me in a moment of silence for all the repetition and commas she killed in honor of a better, grammatically correct book.

Thank you to Travis, Brandy, Annah, Sheryl, Regina, Erin, Susan, Ramona, and the Crockers for the encouragement, excitement, and support that you've shown throughout this process.

Thank you to Papa for being my number one salesman, shamelessly plying each of his nurses to purchase copies of my book.

Thank you to Dane at ebooklaunch for creating another flawless cover.

Thank you to every single person that has bought a book, left a review, or shared a post. Let's do it again!

Chapter 1

Maddy

Of course, I'm late. I'm always late, no matter how desperately I try not to be late. I jog out to my car from my office building and pretend my cell phone isn't ringing. It should be fine. I'll get to the call later. It's Friday at six p.m.; no one has an emergency on Friday at six p.m. Right? Right. It's fine.

Last December, I moved back to my hometown and joined a local law firm as a partner, practicing mostly family law with some financial and real estate mixed in to fill in the holes of the firm. My brother, Matt, bought a house last year and ended up marrying his next-door neighbor, so I moved in since it was an "abandoned" but newly renovated house. Super convenient while I figure out what I want to do with my life. And bonus, I adore my brother and his new family, including my sister-in-law, Brittany, and her precious seven-year-old son, Grady. Being in close proximity to them couldn't be better.

I race home and smile in relief when I see Brittany's car in the driveway. I run into my house and kick my sensible pumps off, quickly changing out of my business suit into a cute and colorful sundress. I pull my shoulder-length brown hair into a fluffy ponytail, accentuating the beach wave casual look I spent an hour perfecting this morning.

Perfect for a first date.

I grab a pair of completely inappropriate heels and my phone as I run barefoot over to Matt and Brittany's house. I let myself in and immediately start yelling through the house as I hop toward the kitchen first on one leg, then the other, trying to put my shoes on. "It's me! Brittany, I need to borrow your dangly earrings. I have a...." I come around to the kitchen and skid to a halt when I look up to see who is glowering at me.

Detective Derek Masters.

Brittany's brother is the single most attractive man I've ever met. Average height but built like a linebacker, with dark hair and dark green eyes that make him seem mysterious. Also, he's the only man who's ever asked for my number and not called. Not even a text. I try telling myself I'm better off really; clearly, he's one of those men who need a challenge, and getting my number was apparently entirely too easy for him.

I don't remember seeing his motorcycle out front; I usually steer clear when I see his bike. I wonder how he got here. I have become a master at making myself scarce when Derek is around, and the tell-tale sign is always the bike. I hate running into him. It sets me back significantly in my attempt to clear him from my nightly dreams. Avoiding him has become something of a hobby of mine. My insides get all stirred up when he's around, and I need to keep him in the "firmly off limits" shelf in my brain. Best way to do that? Out of sight, out of mind. Mostly. I especially don't need my insides all stirred up right before my date. The only positive is that his eyes are flicking over me appreciatively, affirming my outfit choice of the night.

"Aunt Maddy!" Grady launches himself at me and I almost lose my balance on my stilettos.

"Hey! My favorite guy," I say as I hug him close and kiss him. "Where's Brittany?" I ask the glowering one coolly.

He crosses his arms over his chest and stares me down. "Concert."

I pretend not to notice how attractive his arms and chest look in that position and lift my chin in indifference. "Right. I forgot."

"Do you have a date, Aunt Maddy?" Grady asks innocently.

"I do." Then I cut my eyes playfully to him. "Wanna help me accessorize by raiding your Mom's jewelry?" I ask as if I'm offering him a secret mission.

He giggles and starts toward the hallway. I pull him along, my shoes clomping down the wood floors as we jog to his parents' room.

Grady and I peer into the jewelry box while I survey its contents, eventually holding up two different earrings. "Which ones?" I ask Grady.

He points to the dangly ones and offers matter of fact, "Daddy says you date too much."

"Yeah, well, Daddy is happily married, so he can keep his hypocritical judgments to himself," I mutter with a frown as I hold up another pair for Grady to choose from.

He points to his favorite and asks, "What does hypocritical mean?"

"Tell you what, Buddy, ask Daddy and tell him Aunt Maddy sent you." That'll be a fun surprise for Matt to explain when he gets home. Almost as fun as him wondering how hypocritical even came up in a conversation with Grady. I smile in glee at my own kid sister antics.

I search for a third option when I hear flatly from the doorway, "Maybe he's right."

My eyes narrow in the mirror at the still glowering figure in the doorway. "What's it to you?" I challenge, not waiting for an answer before offering Grady the final pick. "Okay, studs or dangles?"

"Dangles," Grady says definitely. I have to say, the kid has good taste. I like to think he gets that from me.

"Studs," comes contrarily from the doorway.

I eye Derek in the mirror disdainfully, hoping he can't tell I'm

3

checking him out as I put on the dangly earrings and hug and kiss Grady. "As always, thank you to my fashion advisor," I tell him. Just then, headlights flash around the room.

I push past the glowering mass of muscles blocking the door and mutter, "Crap, I'm late."

"Aunt Maddy, can I meet him?" Grady asks chasing after me and sliding to a stop next to the front door.

"Not this time, Buddy. Have fun tonight. Love you, bye!" I kiss him once more and run out the door to catch my date before he gets to my house or before Grady can argue further and insist on meeting him.

I greet my date and allow him to usher me into his car while making polite conversation and casually checking the street to make sure I didn't miss Derek's bike. Nope, not there.

"Madison?"

I jerk my head over to my date. "I'm so sorry, what was the question?"

* * *

Derek

Every time I see Maddy, her beauty hits me in the gut like a roundhouse kick. Her big, blue eyes are framed by long, dark, wavy hair that accentuates her heart-shaped face. Combined, it makes her look like an innocent doe in the woods, only she's the farthest thing from it. She is sarcastic, funny, and wicked smart. She's loud and energetic, her enthusiasm seemingly never waning. Her outfits hint at her personality. Bold, colorful, beautiful. I'm amazed each and every time I see her at how much color she wears. I've never seen so many colors on one woman before, but she pulls it off looking like she stepped out of a catalog. I call myself every name in the book for not calling her when I had the chance. She turned into an ice queen toward me as soon as she moved home, and now we are in some kind of standoff.

I try to focus on the video game Grady and I are playing instead of the fact that Maddy has a date tonight.

"Uncle Derek, I got you again!" Grady calls excitedly.

Crap, he did. Clearly, this is an off night for me. "Good job. Wanna go again?"

"I only get two hours," Grady says seriously.

Screen time is apparently a very serious thing. I smirk. When Brittany and I were kids, there was no such thing as "screen time". It was literally a contest to see who could watch Nickelodeon without moving the longest. "Not when Uncle Derek is babysitting," I say, queuing up another round.

Grady's face lights up and we go again. After the third, or maybe fourth game, I put a movie on because I know Grady will pass out watching it. I don't have the heart to tell him when he has to go to bed. I take my job as a fun uncle very seriously.

When Grady has, in fact, passed out, I pick him up and carry him to bed, tucking him in. I am looking on my phone at the latest sports news sitting on the couch when the door opens.

"Hey!" Brittany greets cheerily as she and Matt come through. "How'd it go?"

"It was fun. We played some video games, ate way too much sugar, and then he passed out during a movie," I say proudly.

Brittany grins in amusement. "Still can't tell him it's bedtime, huh?"

"Cool uncles don't acknowledge bedtime," I explain obviously.

"Thanks for staying. We appreciate it," Matt adds gratefully.

"How was the concert?"

Brittany's eyes light up. "So fun! We had the best time, and then we had dinner and dessert. It was great," she says looking dreamily at Matt.

That's my cue. I get up to leave. "By the way, Maddy stopped by. She and Grady raided your jewelry box."

Matt rolls his eyes and Brittany laughs. "Yeah, she had a date tonight. I guess I should text her to see if she needs saving again," she muses as she digs in her purse for her phone.

"I don't know why we don't just join the two houses. Or better yet, give her the guest room," Matt grumbles.

Brittany nudges him as she types on her phone. "Be nice. She's lonely. I know you love having her here even though you grumble."

Maddy...lonely? This catches my ear and I pause. It seems unlikely that a woman like Maddy, so exuberantly full of life, could be lonely.

Matt gets up and walks toward me as Brittany makes the phone call. "So, you want to come over tomorrow? We are planning to cook out around lunchtime," he offers.

I mentally run through my calendar even though I know there's nothing on it. I get distracted when I hear Brittany giggle and say, "Yes, emergency, right now, hurry," without any urgency at all.

I eye her curiously and Matt just shrugs. "Bad date code. Emergency means it's the worst type of date and she's willing to take an Uber home, urgent means she wants to get away quickly but not pay for her own ride, and help means I'm over it and I just need an excuse to leave." I'm listening to Matt in bewilderment and he laughs, "Don't ask me, man, I just live here. So, tomorrow?"

"Sure. Tomorrow's good. Mom and Dad uncover the pool yet?" It's April, which means it should be happening soon if not already.

"I think they did this week. Still cleaning it out and everything. Maybe next weekend will be our first visit. Grady's ready. Says he wants to learn to swim underwater this year, but Brittany's nervous about it,"

Matt explains quietly so my sister doesn't hear.

It doesn't work. "I'm not nervous about it, I am just a little...hesitant for him to move on from swimmies so early," she clarifies from the couch, having hung up the phone.

I smirk at Brittany's overprotection. "Early? Brittany, we were barely five when we were done with swimmies."

She huffs, not responding.

"She's coddling him," I mutter to Matt, who does not even move an eyebrow. I admire him for his commitment to neutrality. He knows how to pick his battles with Brittany's mama bear.

"I am not!" Brittany protests from the couch.

"Whatever. See you tomorrow," I say as I leave, actually happy about the fact that I have plans. I have been slowly integrating myself into the family more, which is revolutionary for me based on the reclusive ways of my past.

I missed the first several years of Grady's life by not being involved, and it hit me at his last birthday this past summer. He's already seven and I missed it. I hardly even know him. Turns out he's a pretty great kid. I won't be making that mistake again.

I head home with a smile because with any luck I'll see Maddy at the cookout. Plus now I know where to park my bike so she won't notice when I'm at Brittany's and avoid me. It also doesn't hurt she had another crappy date. My gut clenches as I realize there will be other dates and the next one might not be as crappy. My resolve begins to strengthen as I make a game plan. Time to end the standoff. Maddy and I are doing this; I'm making it happen. I need to be ready because something tells me it'll be slightly more difficult to convince her of this.

Chapter 2

Maddy

"It's me!" I call entering Matt and Brittany's house, "And not to brag, but I brought maybe the best dip known to man...don't all crowd at once." I snicker at myself and head for the kitchen, coming to a halt when I see out the window Derek standing at the grill with Matt.

"The dip you made last Christmas?" Brittany asks with her head in the fridge.

I ignore the question and corner her when she turns back to the counter. "What's he doing here?" I try not to sound quite as accusatory as I feel. Based on how Brittany narrows her eyes, I'm assuming I am not successful.

"Matt invited him. I thought you were over that?" she asks suspiciously.

I huff and lift my chin haughtily. "Of course I'm over it, he's just so... moody." I try to make this sound as legitimate as possible.

Brittany laughs. "Yep, that's Derek. He's been better lately, though. He's really making an effort with Grady."

Deciding it's better I keep my eyes off Derek to help keep him off my mind, I turn my back on the window and face Brittany. "What can I do to help?" I offer brightly.

"Actually, there's nothing really. I was just about to go out and play soccer with Grady. Wanna come?" she offers with a glint in her eye.

"Of course," I reply easily, ignoring the glint and wishing I hadn't worn shorts and a tank top today. I wish I had maybe tried a little harder on my outfit instead of choosing to wear my scruffy "at home only" clothes. It's not my fault it's April and already in the 90s. At least the messy bun is appropriately lazy but also cute.

"Grady, ready for soccer?" Brittany calls as we head out to the backyard where he and the sweltering heat are waiting for us.

"Yeah! I want to be on Aunt Maddy's team," he shouts, throwing his arms around my legs.

"Awesome! Me and you against your Mom!" I high-five him and fist bump him with both hands.

"Can I play?" Derek asks. My back stiffens, but I'm proud of myself for keeping my face completely neutral.

Grady loves this idea. "Yeah! Me and Aunt Maddy against Uncle Derek and Momma!"

"You better not hold me back. I'm the undefeated champ," Brittany warns, playfully swatting at Derek.

He snorts derisively. "I think I can keep up."

"Daddy, can you be ref?" Grady calls.

"I'm on the grill, Buddy, but I'll watch from here," Matt replies from the porch.

Once the ball is in the middle of the yard, bounds are laid out and goals are casually marked. Grady shouts "go" and we all rush for the ball.

I reach it first, getting it away from Brittany and Derek and passing it to Grady. I don't rely on my college soccer skills, instead playing the ball rather casually, even more clumsily, than the others.

Grady scores the first goal, which is clearly allowed by all, just to see the excitement on his face. We high five and fist bump in victory and

9

turn to see the playfully grumpy faces on our opponents.

We keep playing, and I have to admit the competition and fun of being Grady's protector makes the tension between me and Derek disappear. I continue casually hiding my skills, choosing instead to make simple movements. I get lost in the game, cheering and tackling Grady to the ground when he finally scores the second goal, which was not so easily won. Grady and I are both laughing helplessly as I help him up and we face off our opponents again.

I take great care to not look at Derek's face, keeping my eyes a safe distance from his. I keep my eyes trained on his legs, strictly for the mechanics of the game and not at all because they are toned and muscular. I don't even want to know how much time he spends at the gym, but reluctantly admit it is paying off.

Grady is on a breakaway when Brittany steals the ball from him and passes to Derek. I try to intercept but miss, almost slamming into Derek in the process. Thankfully, I'm able to avoid direct physical contact, but I miss the ball in the process. Derek scores.

We continued playing until we were tied 4-4. We were playing to five, and Matt has already called a warning that the meat is almost ready.

"Okay, Grady, this is for the game, Buddy. We got this." I pump him up before we face off.

"You're just setting him up for disappointment," Derek taunts me.

I retain my no eye contact policy by lifting my brows at Brittany. "We'll see about that."

I bring it. I pull out my advanced moves for a no-holds-barred, total smackdown of epic proportions. No way am I gonna let Grady lose...or more importantly...Derek win.

I do a fast spin kick, stealing the ball from Brittany and passing to Grady while shielding him from Brittany and Derek with evasive maneuvers. When they get too close, I pull the ball away and call for Grady to head near the goal. He is confused at first, but when he gets moving in the right direction, I kick the ball to him and his face lights up, understanding.

Derek tries to intercept the ball, but I break my no-contact policy just this once and slam into him accidentally on purpose, knocking him to the ground. Desperate times call for desperate measures, and to let Grady score the winning goal, I'm willing to do what needs to be done.

Derek growls in recognition of my intention.

"Oops," I exclaim innocently and jog away.

I catch up with Grady just in time to see him make the goal. I promptly pick him up and parade him around the yard in a vital and satisfying victory lap. I set him down, sharing high-fives and fist-bumps as he declares, "I want to be on your team every time."

"Absolutely. Know why?" I reply with a smile just for Grady.

"Cause I'm your favorite guy!" Grady cheers.

I laugh. "That's right!" I ruffled his hair, foregoing the kiss on his sweaty head.

"Doesn't hurt you played soccer in college," Matt adds dryly from behind the grill.

"What?!" Brittany yells in outrage.

I giggle. "Just through junior year," I correct, then jokingly punch Matt. "Rat." Matt just laughs at my ire, focusing on his grilling.

"Grady, what do snitches get?" I ask playfully as we walk into the house to wash up for lunch.

"Stitches!" Grady cheers, lifting both arms above his head and jogging into the house.

"Words to live by, Matty," I say as sweetly as possible, patting his shoulder as I walk by.

During lunch, it's not as hard as I feared to avoid eye contact with Derek. I focus mainly on Grady and Brittany and let Matt handle Derek. Whenever Derek talks to the whole group, I just become ultra-interested in my food.

That maybe sounds like overkill, but you've never seen his forest green eyes, which are as expressive as his face isn't. They fascinate, dominate, and captivate. I only wish I was being dramatic in describing them. His face is usually frozen in a neutral stoicism, but those eyes. Every time he looks at me, I feel it in my gut, and my only defense is to not look back. It's hard enough being so close to his body, which I can see in my peripheral vision no matter where I'm looking.

Matt and Derek are in conversation back at the grill when Brittany asks me in a low voice, "So, any new dates coming up?"

So aware am I of Derek's body, I notice him stiffen in my side vision instantly from where I sit at the picnic table.

I shrug indifferently and change the subject, preferring not to talk about dating if there's even a remote chance of Derek hearing. Not that I get what he has against me dating. He doesn't want me, so I'm never supposed to see anyone again? He didn't even call. Ugh. Typical caveman behavior if you ask me.

"Aunt Maddy, will you show me the kick spin you did?" Grady asks adorably, using his puppy dog eyes when he really doesn't need to. I would have shown him anyway.

"Absolutely," I reply, jumping up and removing Derek from of my peripheral vision.

* * *

Derek

Well, I can't decide if the fact that she won't look at me is a good thing or a bad thing. Unfortunately, I'm having a tough time justifying it being a good thing, and the list of bad things is steadily growing in my mind. My game plan requires slight alterations given this fact, and I'm trying to regroup.

Brittany has gone inside, and I've just realized Matt has stopped talking. Given we were in a conversation about boats...I think...this means it's probably my turn to talk. I glance up at him and he's staring at me.

"Think you could stop checking out my sister?" he murmurs in a low voice with an amused smirk.

I play my internal cringe cool with a passive shrug. "Would if I could."

Matt chuckles ruefully. "I gotta say, I didn't expect you two to be quite so entertaining."

"Glad you're enjoying yourself," I mutter bitterly.

"Don't get me wrong, I knew it would be fun. Between watching you watching her and watching her avoid you like the plague, I am thoroughly invested in how this will turn out," he says, amusement growing.

Matt's right. She's avoiding me like the plague. I don't really get why. I mean, I just didn't call her. It's not like we had a bad date or anything embarrassing happened. I look back over at Maddy playing with Grady. She's great with him. They clearly have a wonderful relationship, one I find flares my jealous desire to be his favorite. Obviously, I'm not. Not that I blame him. She'd be my favorite too.

Matt captures Brittany on her way out the door to sit with him on a bench near the porch just as Grady jogs inside for a bathroom break. I see my chance and intercept Maddy before she gets to the bench, deciding that maybe poking the bear will be worth it.

"You gonna teach him to cheat too?" I tease in a low rumble.

Her surprised eyes find mine, then quickly look away. "I don't cheat."

"Felt like an illegal foul to me," I return, watching her avoid my gaze.

She snorts. "Gonna cry foul because of an accidental bump? Didn't take you for a sore loser." She cocks her head and squints at my face. "Or maybe you're just soft."

I grin. Poking the bear is definitely worth it. I take a step forward. "I think you know that's not the case."

She flicks her eyes across me and shrugs. "I don't know what else to call it when the big, bad detective can't take a little brush in a friendly soccer game," she states sounding bored, but I notice she takes a step back.

She returns to looking at the ground and I decide to go for broke. "Tell you what, Maddy, you can throw your body against mine anytime."

Maddy's eyes fly up to mine and her mouth opens in surprise. I can't help but feel like I've won this round as she stares up at me in silence, blushing slightly as Grady runs back to her. Maddy turns away and I saunter over to the bench to sit next to Brittany, feeling her gaze but not acknowledging it.

"I need to know what you said. I've never seen Maddy speechless before," Matt asks with a grin, then an "oompf" as Brittany elbows him in the ribs.

* * *

Maddy

I cannot believe he said that to me. I also can't believe he made me break my no eye contact rule.

I inwardly sigh. It was worth it though. Those eyes.

I check my watch and cringe. I really should get some work done before the afternoon is over. I finish up with Grady and head toward the house. "Alright guys, I'm out. It's been fun." Hugs all around, save for one notable exception, then I follow Brittany into the house to get my remaining dip, also known as dinner. I collect my bowl and snag a bag of chips to go with it as I head for the door. I don't normally pilfer chips from my brother, but the only consumable thing in my kitchen is bottled water, and I'm not eating dip with a spoon. If I get away quickly enough, I can count this visit in near proximity to Derek a success despite his best efforts to corrupt me. I jog across the yard to my house, plopping myself on the floor in the living room and opening my laptop on the coffee table once there. It takes maybe ten minutes for me to have legal papers scattered everywhere, smudges of dip on half of them.

I am an hour deep into legal work when there's a knock at the door.

"It's open," I call distractedly, expecting Brittany or Grady.

"Always keep your door unlocked?" I hear from a deep voice behind me.

My head whips around to find Derek standing behind my couch.

"Didn't know you wore glasses," he mentions, staring.

I take them off and frown at him. "What do you want?"

His face remains impassive, but his eyes flicker in amusement at my tone. "Not safe to leave your door unlocked."

I snort and put my glasses back on, turning my back to him and returning to my work. "Believe me, I understand that now."

He chuckles, clearly enjoying getting a rise out of me. Maybe I should play this cool.

"Anything else?" I ask shortly when he doesn't say anything.

"Go out with me," he demands in a low rumble.

"No," I respond immediately, not turning or putting down my papers. Instead, I type some on the computer. Probably gibberish, I have no idea really.

"Why not?" he presses stubbornly.

"Had your chance. I'm over it," I say as indifferently as possible while initialing the top of a legal page for no reason whatsoever. I'm honestly impressed with myself. Somebody call me an agent because I'm taking these skills to Hollywood.

Now, this next part is a little my fault, but mostly his fault. I just want the Lord to understand this before I get to judgment day and He wants a good, Christian girl like myself to explain my actions.

I am so focused on keeping my focus off of Derek, I do it a little too well. He crouches beside me and grips the wrist of the hand holding my pen before I hear him move at all. For a bulky guy, he's very stealthy. I meet his gaze in surprise, and I fall deep, I mean deep, into those eyes. My heart races and I can't look away. His touch lights my skin on fire, and his gaze flips my belly inside out.

"Your heart always race when you do legal work?" he asks smugly, and I belatedly realize his finger is on my pulse for a reason.

I snatch my hand away and try to salvage my remaining coherent thoughts. "Just when strange men enter my home and accost me," I say coolly, turning back toward my laptop again. I take a deep breath and gather myself. I will need to sanitize my brain before going to bed tonight, his touch and his eyes being a lethal combination. I feel his intense gaze watching me closely as he rises. I hold myself together with the tiny thread that is now my willpower while he walks to the front door.

"Maddy?" he rumbles, turning before he leaves.

"What?" I respond with as much annoyance as I possibly can.

"I don't accost beautiful, fascinating women. I hunt them." He reinforces the promise with a purposeful stare before walking out and shutting the door with finality.

And then I learn what heart palpitations feel like.

"Holy Moses." I breathe, putting my hand on my pounding chest trying to catch my breath. I get up to take a shower and then dress for a run to the grocery store because, let's face it, I'm not getting any more work done tonight.

* * *

Derek

I take the long way home, riding my motorcycle through back roads and country lanes. The only thing I know for certain, other than my own feelings for Maddy, is that she is definitely not over it. I get that she wants to play hard to get, and I'm okay with it. It makes it fun.

Admittedly, my game plan has taken a little hit since she flat out refused my invitation. Things could be worse. All in all, I would say that last interaction was a rousing success. At least now she knows I'm coming for her. Now I know her feelings too. She can deny it all she wants, but her eyes don't lie.

Twice in one day I've seen Maddy speechless. I need to start prepping because I don't expect it to be that easy again. She'll come out guns blazing, and if she doesn't, I'll be disappointed.

Chapter 3

Maddy

I am walking with Matt, Brittany, and Grady to Brittany's parents' house to swim when I come to a complete stop.

"Brittany," I groan in frustration. I specifically asked earlier if Derek would be here and she evaded the question, saying she thought he had to work but wasn't sure. But what's currently sitting in his parents' driveway? Derek's bike, plain as day.

"Huh," she says nervously, speeding ahead, "I guess he was able to make it."

"Uh huh," I mutter, smelling a setup. The betrayal when family turns on you cuts deep. Standing still on the street, my fight or flight reflex kicks in and I contemplate leaving.

Matt drops his arm across my shoulders. "Come on, Mads. I'll protect you. Besides, can't let 'em see you blink." He pulls me toward the house.

Ah, the old Knight family motto to the rescue once again. Strangely enough, it gets my back up. It's how our Dad trained us from infancy. I pretend to make myself busy behind the others as they greet Gran and Pop, and of course, Uncle Derek.

"Maddy, don't you look darling. I love that color," Gran greets hugging me.

"Thanks, Gran. They called it rose but I think it's more fuchsia," I say lightly. "Thanks for including me."

Gran keeps her arm around me. "You come whenever you want, you are family now."

"Thanks," I reply cheerily. "As such, I was wondering if you would give me the secret family recipe for those brownies you served last time." I flash a cheeky grin and Gran laughs.

"Aunt Maddy! Come play with me!" Grady calls, and dang it, I can't tell him no. That little kid, with his sandy brown hair, brown eyes, and freckles, has my heart. I put my bag down and that's when I remember what I'm wearing. I wore a modest two-piece tankini that's more sporty than sexy because Grady likes to play, but it's still a two-piece. I look across the pool and see Brittany is in a similar two-piece, so I push my insecurity aside. I'm not being immodest.

"Aunt Maaaaaddy!" Grady beckons desperately.

I set my shoulders and make up my mind, deciding not to let Derek, of all people, ruffle my feathers and get me all worked up. Besides, maybe if I ruffle his feathers a little, it'll throw him off long enough for me to make an escape. Can't let 'em see you blink, I chant to myself. I pull my cover-up over my head and slip out of my sandals, reaching to put my hair up in a bun while I approach the pool.

"Aunt Maddy, get in!" Grady calls before Matt tackles him in the water.

I walk into the pool, pleased that out of the corner of my eye I see Derek hasn't moved a muscle. If my distance vision can be trusted (and it can—I wear reading glasses to avoid the strain of tiny legalese only), I think there is a vein pulsing in his neck.

I roundly ignore him and stalk Grady, catching him as he tries to swim out of reach, and take turns tossing him around with Brittany and Matt, Gran and Pop watching from the deck. I spend the next two hours looking everywhere but at Derek's bare chest. *Everywhere.* I even dunk underwater in a desperate situation or two. Not that any of this actually keeps me from seeing it, it's just a dire attempt at keeping my thoughts pure even though I'm human with 20/20 vision. When I have successfully worn Grady out and reached my bare-chested Derek limit, I notice the family is getting ready to make sandwiches for lunch. I see my opportunity and take it.

"I should probably get going actually," I announce, toweling off and pulling my cover-up on.

"No!" Grady shouts in agony.

I smile indulgently at his dramatics. "We'll do this again soon, Buddy. I have some work I need to do." It's a lie. I've told a falsehood to my seven-year-old nephew. Does it get any lower? My only defense is self-preservation. Darwin wouldn't have gotten anywhere without it, and my instincts tend to be stronger than most.

"At least stay for lunch, dear," Gran insists.

"Thank you so much, but I can't impose. I really should get going. Next time though!" I call with a wave as I quickly leave the backyard.

I don't consider myself safe until I'm back at my house, securely behind the door. I'm starving but go to my room to take a shower first. Unfortunately, the only things I have in the house to eat are Pop Tarts and the dip I made last Saturday. Guess I'm having dip for lunch.

* * *

Derek

"You have your work cut out for you with that one," Dad comments wryly.

I watch Maddy speed walk down the street and smirk. True. You know what they say, the harder you work, the greater the reward.

I eat lunch with the family, then spend another couple of hours with Grady in the pool, trying to earn back some of the cool points he has shamelessly given Maddy. Somehow, I don't think I earned any from her, though. I take a shower at my parents' house and change so I don't have to ride home in a wet bathing suit. On the road, I decide to take a little detour. I cut my engine and I head up the street, not sure how tuned into my bike Maddy is.

I try the doorknob gently, and it's unlocked. I push the door open and pray to God she's not naked.

In fact, she's in exactly the same position she was in the last time I walked in on her, sitting on the floor, surrounded by papers, typing away on her laptop. I creep up until I'm right behind her couch and I say, "Not safe to leave your door unlocked." I grin at her startled jump and spin.

"You can't just walk into somebody's house! What is the matter with you?" she yells in outrage.

"You can if they leave the door unlocked," I respond flatly.

Her look of pure hatred makes me fight back another grin. "I leave the door unlocked for Grady, not that it's any of your business," she returns icily, then turns back around to straighten the papers, which went flying when I startled her. "What do you want?"

"Come to dinner with me." It's more of a statement than a question I'll admit, but Maddy, she's stubborn. I don't know how much of an option I can really give her. She seems to need the push of a command more than the imploring of a question.

She heaves a sigh and stands up, pushing her glasses to the top of her head. I try not to show my excitement; this is going to be good. She faces me but doesn't come around the couch. "What are you doing?"

"Asking you to dinner," I state obviously, although I feel certain I'm walking into a trap.

"Why?" she asks in a long-suffering tone.

I pause. This is a weird trap. "Because I want to take you to dinner."

She shakes her head woefully. "Wrong."

I can't help it, my eyebrows shoot up. "Then by all means, please enlighten me."

She eyes me disdainfully. "You want me to agree to go to dinner and then you'll ditch me, like the phone number thing. You said yourself, this is about the hunt for you. Sure, it's interesting to you now, but when I give in and go out with you, you'll find me boring or high maintenance or too chatty or too much work and you'll ditch me to chase the next semi-interesting pair of legs that cross your bike."

"So, you like my bike?" I tease with a smirk.

Now she looks pissed. She picks up a throw pillow and it comes flying at me. She misses by at least a yard and I don't even flinch. She looks like she is going to go for another when I say, "I'm kidding."

"No, you weren't," she replies acidly.

"You're right, I wasn't," I admit freely. The fact that she and I disagree on the most important part of her tirade does not surprise me, however; it is mildly entertaining. I knew she liked my bike.

"Please leave now," she demands with one hand on her hip and the other pointing at the door.

I cross my arms over my chest and plant myself where I stand, noticing her eyes linger on my biceps. Nice to know she likes those too. Time to deploy the second part of my game plan. "I didn't call you because I was an idiot. You lived in Atlanta, I lived here. I was going through a thing, but now I'm over it and I'd like to take you out to dinner."

Her eyes narrow and her arm drops from pointing at the door. "What kind of thing?"

"A thing with an ex, okay?" I offer reluctantly. Like I said, idiot. I get it now, but I'm not saying it again.

"I'm still not going out with you," Maddy insists defiantly.

"Why?" I demand with both curiosity and amusement.

"Because what I said before is still true. I know your alpha male, too-cool-for-school, bike riding, leather-wearing, scowling tough guy type. The second we go out, you'll lose all interest, and honestly, I don't have time for that." With finality, she crosses her arms.

I eye her up and down, my gaze lingering on her figure as I gather my thoughts. "This is a weird position for me to be in because usually I'm the one ending a relationship before it starts," I start with a growing grin. "But I think there is a strong possibility you are wrong." Not about me—she's pegged me right on the head—but she's wrong about my motivation and our potential, clearly.

Maddy snorts as she turns her back on me to take her seat on the floor. "As Grady mentioned oh so eloquently, I date a lot, and I'm never wrong. Don't let the door hit you on the way out," she grumbles, returning her focus to her papers and effectively dismissing me.

I walk around the couch and crouch down beside her. I see her stiffen but not look up, so I use my finger to gently turn her face to mine. "This isn't over," I warn.

At her stunned expression, I leave, firing up my bike loudly and riding out of the neighborhood. When I get home, I pull up her number on my phone and call it.

"Hello?" she answers hesitantly.

"Hi, Maddy, this is Derek."

I hear her deep sigh and it sounds like she's rolling her eyes. I grin. "What do you want?" she asks with supreme irritation.

"I'm sorry it took so long for me to call you, that was my mistake, but I was wondering if you would like to have dinner sometime?"

She hesitates, then quickly demands, "Are you mocking me, Derek Masters?"

Geez. You try to do things exactly the way they say they want it. "You said you wanted me to call. I'm calling," I explain although I would have thought it's obvious.

"I said you missed your chance," she clarifies with irritation.

"I said you were wrong," I reply stubbornly.

"Don't call me again, Derek, I'm busy." Then, she abruptly hangs up.

I shake my head at the phone. Yep, I have my work cut out for me with this one.

Chapter 4

Maddy

"I'm calling on all your big brother protective mode-ness. What kind of brother would you be if you didn't help me?" I plead.

Matt laughs, my frustration growing. "Mads, I would, but it sounds like he's being a perfect gentleman."

"How can you say that? Stalking is not gentlemanly," I argue to more laughter. I grumble at him but stop talking when Brittany comes through the door. She looks from my disgruntled face to Matt's amused one and grins. "What has Derek done now?"

"He has called every night this week!" I tick off his infractions on my hand. "He sent flowers to my office, and then stopped by asking me to lunch. When I said no, he had lunch sent from my favorite deli. He texts me randomly throughout the day and has even sent candy. I keep saying no, but he won't back off," I finish in exasperation. I don't mention it's also completely disconcerting that he knows all my favorite things. Halfway through the week, I started wondering if I was battling some kind of Jedi master.

Matt reasonably offers a suggestion. "Maybe you should just go out with him. If your theory is correct, he'll lose interest and leave you alone."

I narrow my eyes. "Now it's the principle of the matter. I will not be bullied into dating someone."

Matt snorts. "He's not bullying you, Mads, he's wooing you."

I frown. I will not allow myself to be wooed. Not by Derek Masters. No matter how much I like it.

Brittany is suspiciously quiet through all this. I look at her but she avoids eye contact. My lawyer senses tingle. "Brittany?" I ask suspiciously.

"Yes, Maddy?" she answers innocently.

Suddenly, pieces start falling into place and I stare at her in shock. "You've been helping him," I accuse. She looks overwhelmingly guilty. "Traitor!" I cry pointing at her.

"I just told him your favorite flower, and your favorite lunch place, and maybe your favorite chocolate, that's it I swear!" she defends, holding her hands up in surrender.

I stalk out of the house with her apologies following me. Stabbed in the back by my own friend. Sister, really.

Oh, the agony!

I retreat to my house to stew in peace and continue living in denial. I can't afford to admit the truth; that I want to say yes to Derek too much. The fact that it hurt when he didn't call shocked my system and indicates I needed to steer clear of him or certain heartbreak looms in my future. If there is one thing I know for absolute certain, Derek Masters is a heartbreaker. Nope, I will strengthen my resolve and continue protecting my heart against Derek's assault like there's no tomorrow. After all, if I end up falling for Derek, there may not be a tomorrow.

* * *

It's Friday night and I don't have a date.

I know.

I decided to take the night off what with all the drama going on lately. It is surprisingly exhausting to constantly rebuff suitors. Or suitor in my case. Just the one. However, I don't let this keep me from imagining I know exactly how Scarlett O'Hara must have felt. I do happen to know that Matt and Brittany are going out tonight, but they didn't ask me to watch Grady. That means either Derek is doing so or they are taking him to his grandparents' house.

When I don't hear a bike come down the street, I rest easy. Deciding to be "I don't have a date" comfortable, I change into yoga pants and a t-shirt and put my hair in a messy bun. I am microwaving popcorn when I hear my door open.

"Aunt Maddy?" Grady calls mournfully.

"Yeah?" I come around to the front, surprised to see him.

"Can I play with you?" he asks using the best puppy dog eyes I've ever seen. He's giving me his best. Big brown eyes, sparkling just a little, looking up through his thick lashes, and tilting his head just so, giving me the full effect of his freckles.

"Your Mom and Dad gone?" I try to ascertain who is responsible for him tonight, although I'm certain his presence gives me the answer.

He nods dolefully. "And can Uncle Derek play with us too?" he asks hopefully, not sparing one single ounce of pitifulness from his huge brown eyes. Geez.

"So, Uncle Derek is babysitting?" I press, avoiding the question.

"Yeah, but he doesn't know how to build a fort-like you do." He hugs my waist and props his chin on my belly woefully.

I laugh, then take a long look at the freckles and puppy dog eyes. "Fine," I sigh.

Yes, I've just allowed myself to be emotionally manipulated by a seven year old. We all have things we aren't proud of and I don't appreciate any judgement.

Grady instantly beams. "Better come to my house, I have pizza!" he yells excitedly, grabbing my hand and tugging me toward the door.

I allow him to pull me along, already annoyed. Derek's smug expression at the front door of Brittany and Matt's house isn't making it better. "You don't get any points for this," I mutter to him bitterly.

"All's fair in love and war," he replies unrepentantly.

I bite back a huff of amusement, wondering which this is. I feel certain our answers would be different.

"Aunt Maddy, can you show Uncle Derek how we do forts? He can't make them like you."

Now it's my turn to look smug. "Where do you want it, in the living room or your room?"

"My room!" he cheers, taking my hand and practically dragging me to his room.

When Derek joins us, he asks, "You don't drape the sheet across the cushions?"

I look at Grady sadly. "Amateur," I say with a thumb pointed over my shoulder at Derek. Grady giggles. "The key to any good fort construction is height. I go more of a string-and-hammock style in the hanging of the sheet as opposed to a more rudimentary prop cushion method," I instruct coolly. I make the mistake of looking at his eyes. For the passive blank that his face stays, his eyes are always so expressive, and right now they are dancing with amusement, and what appears to be...respect.

I look away and continue to help Grady run string and then drape sheets across his room. I carefully avoid Derek and move around the room helping Grady build a masterful fort. We turn out the lights and make shadow puppets on the wall of the sheet until he hauls in some toys, then we discuss at length who the better superhero is. When I look at my watch, it's an hour and a half after Grady's bedtime. I tap my watch at Derek, but he just shrugs. Chicken. "Okay, Grady, time for bed."

His face immediately crumples. "Aw! Thirty more minutes and I won't complain?" he implores.

I see that ploy coming from a mile away. My Dad has recently taught him the Knight art of negotiating, so let's see how good he is.

"Bedtime now, one chapter of your book, but no complaints about bedtime or brushing your teeth," I counter.

His nose crinkles in thought. "Three chapters and you stay till I fall asleep, but I get to complain a little."

I consider this discerningly. "Two chapters, I'll stay till you fall asleep and massage your scalp, but no complaining."

"Deal!" Grady says and shoots to the bathroom to brush his teeth. He's played me again, but I'm okay with it. Dad would be proud.

I start picking up toys when I hear a husky chuckle come from Derek. "You are absolutely amazing."

"Negotiating is a skill Knight children learn early," I say by way of explanation, avoiding his gaze.

Grady races back in and hands me his book. I climb in bed with him, and Derek moves to leave.

"Uncle Derek, stay. Will you read a chapter?" he asks, giving Derek the puppy dog eyes.

I am snuggled in bed with Grady, reading the first chapter with one arm around him running my fingers through his hair. Derek sits on the floor on Grady's other side, and when his turn comes to read, he props one arm up and reads in his signature deep, rumbly growl. Honestly, I am ready to fall asleep myself by the end. I could curl up and take my own little nap inside that throaty sound.

It never takes Grady long to fall asleep, so by the time Derek is done with the second chapter, he is full out, clinging to me. Derek puts the book away gently and starts Grady's white noise machine before flicking on the night light while I gently try to disentangle myself from my nephew without waking him. This in and of itself should be an Olympic sport; it's a cross between acrobatics and a gymnastics floor routine.

When we close the door gently and walk into the living room, I survey the mess and say, "Ok, well, good night." I walk toward the door quickly, chanting I can make it, I can make it, I can make it to myself.

I don't make it. Derek grabs hold of my hand. I knew this was likely coming, but one can always hope.

"Stay. Come on, hang out for a minute. You caused half this mess you know," he teases.

I grin and try to extract my hand from his, the electricity from his touch making me tingle. "I know, but I'm not babysitting tonight." I'm still inching toward the door.

"Stay," Derek entreats, tightening his hold on my hand. His eyes get bigger and sparkle just like Grady's. Dang it.

Ok, time to change tactics. "Just curious, how does it feel to know a seven-year-old has more game than you?" I taunt, yanking my hand away from his and making a play for the door again.

Derek smirks, blocking me. "He's family. I like to think he gets a little of it from me."

I give him a pitying look. "He doesn't." I move around him, already confessing my lie to the Lord and asking for forgiveness.

"Thirty minutes and I won't complain," he offers, mimicking Grady.

I look back at him doubtfully. I can't help it; I love to negotiate. "Ten minutes and you never call me again."

"Thirty minutes and I'll clean this mess up without insisting you help," he counters.

I narrow my eyes. "Fifteen minutes, you clean the mess up, and you stop asking me out."

Derek takes a step closer to me. "Fifteen minutes and I'll clean the mess, final offer."

"Fine."

He grins victoriously, and I sit on the opposite side of the couch from him, trying to avoid being near him at all. "You're great with Grady," he says comfortably.

"It's easy, I love him. Plus it's a chance for me to annoy my brother doing little sister-type things, so win-win."

Derek smiles. "No wonder you and Brittany get along so well."

I glare at him. "We do, but we won't if you keep using her and Matt for your little crusade."

"You won't punish them. Besides, it's not their fault. I have the goods on Brittany," he adds smugly.

"You shouldn't underestimate me," I warn. It's a typical male mistake.

Derek leans forward, inching toward the middle of the couch. "And you shouldn't underestimate me."

I scoot further away from him. "Can you not just give this up? I'm not going out with you. Even if I did at this point, it would only be to prove you would lose interest. This game has to be exhausting for you."

"No game. You'll give in eventually. Besides, I haven't even deployed my biggest asset yet," he says with calm self-assurance, still inching closer to me on the couch.

I laugh at his arrogance. "What are you waiting on? It can only go up from here."

"Don't worry, I'll show you when you're ready," he replies with confidence.

I roll my eyes in irritation and check my watch with faux boredom. He's so close now that my body heat officially enters the danger zone.

"You are telling me you would rather go on awful dates than to go out with me, at least once?" Derek contends doubtfully.

I lift my chin defiantly. "At least I have hope when I start on the date with the guy. It's not my fault they are all duds."

"You wouldn't have hope on a date with me?"

He sounds...hurt?

I avoid his eyes because they are staring into mine quite deliberately. "I just know how it's going to end. Even if you don't lose interest after the first date, how many will it take before fresh blood in the water draws you out to hunt again? You are my brother's brother-in-law, and it's just better for us to not complicate things," I say firmly, nodding once. That was good. Legitimate even. Perfectly believable.

I should stick to this story. Admitting I'm so close to losing all self-control and dignity in his presence, and that it would take nothing at all to fall in love with him so completely it would crush me when he leaves, is definitely not an option. Derek stares at me for so long I finally look into his eyes. Through the layers of arrogance, determination, and confusion, I see the hurt. I can't look away. I'm drawn in and get lost, everything else falling away.

I am vaguely aware he moves closer until he is right beside me. Still, I can't remove my eyes from his. My heart is racing as his body heat bleeds into mine. After I'm not sure how long, his lips touch mine, firm yet coaxing.

I return his kiss. Immediately and exuberantly. I should be ashamed really.

My hands climb up his muscular arms and wind around his neck. One of his hands grips my waist and the other he places to the side of my head, holding my lips to his. His silky-smooth lips move with mine, and the sensations are overwhelming. I part my mouth a bit more, and his tongue sweeps into my mouth, dancing with mine. For a moment, all I can think of is his taste, his touch, the feel of him under my arms. My mind is completely consumed.

"Well, this brings back horrifying high school flashbacks," Matt's voice floats flatly above me.

I pull away from Derek with a gasp, the spell broken. I have no idea how long we've been kissing, but our bodies are more molded together than separate at this point, and I'm half horizontal on the couch. I launch myself up and as far away as possible from Derek, looking from him to Matt with wide, horrified eyes as the full weight of what's just happened hits me in waves. Crushing, consuming waves that tell me I am one hundred percent correct in every single fear I've ever had of Derek Masters.

I'm sure I'm turning red as a beet from mortification as Brittany walks in to find me standing flustered and looking desperately for my dignity.

She looks from me to Derek to Matt. "What's going on?"

Matt grins, "It appears your brother and my sister are making out like teenagers on our couch."

Brittany's eyes widen and she immediately looks to me, mouth open. My fight or flight instinct kicks in. I duck my head and sprint toward the door. "He's responsible for the mess, I tucked Grady in. Goodnight!"

Yep. I'm a runner.

I leave the house relatively calmly, but as soon as the door closes, I sprint to my house and close the door. Leaning back against it, I cover my face with my hands, breathing deeply to keep the tears at bay.

This is bad. Very bad.

I am not dating Derek. For all the reasons I have previously stated out loud, and for all the real fears that reside deep in my heart as well. Unfortunately for me, despite my best efforts, I'm pretty sure Derek Masters just ruined me for all other men. How could I have let this happen? I'm not supposed to let 'em see me blink and I just folded like a twenty-year-old card table at the local community center. I stayed strong for so long. I didn't even crack when he wooed me with chicken salad from my favorite deli. And I love chicken salad. I was prouder of that than all the other attempts combined.

I am contemplating the purpose of ever dating again when there's an insistent knock on the door. "Maddy?" Derek's voice cuts through the wood.

Geez, that voice is going to haunt my dreams. The voice, the lips, the feel of his hands...I groan. "Go away."

"We should talk," Derek insists.

I lock the door for the first time since moving in. "I told you already. I'm not going out with you. Go away."

"Maddy, come on," Derek says, sounding frustrated. "How can you say that?"

How can I say that? He ruined me and now he's mad? Oh no, he has no right!

I unlock the door and open it to face him angrily. "We are practically family, and when it ends, because it always ends, it will make things even more awkward. You had it right the first time. Don't call. Stop asking. The answer is no." I state this firmly in my best lawyer voice, adding an extra layer of ice for good measure.

I move to close the door, but his arm catches it. "Madison Knight, you are an infuriating woman."

I look and, sure enough, his nostrils are flared and he looks ready for a fight. Seriously? "Let go," I demand, tugging on the door.

"Never." Derek's body closes in on mine as he pushes through the doorway and pursues me while I back away from him. The fox is officially in the henhouse, people. "You cannot possibly stand there after what we just experienced on that couch and tell me you don't want to do it again. You can't stand there and tell me the future like you are some all-knowing czar. You're not. So, get over yourself," he growls angrily.

My mouth drops open and I gasp, "Get over myself? Who is the one with such a wounded ego that you are hunting down the one woman in the universe who's dared turn you down? You even send your nephew to do something you couldn't!" I emphasize my point by bouncing on the balls of my feet, pointing at him, and raising my voice.

"Don't flatter yourself. You're not the first to say no, but you will be the last. I used Grady tonight because you are so thick-headed and stubborn and I got tired of beating my head against a wall. The only reason you keep bringing it up is because it worked!" he finishes loudly.

"You are the most egotistical man I've ever met!" I shout.

"And you are the most stubborn, pig-headed woman I've ever met," he shouts back.

We stand right in front of each other, breathing hard and shooting daggers, but in the next moment, he grips my face and kisses me with such ferociousness I don't think I'll ever be the same. He's claimed me. Like it had a mind of its own, my mouth thanks him for it, kissing him back with equal ferociousness.

"So you guys good? We heard shouting," Matt asks with amusement at the open door.

For the second time tonight, my brother has walked in on me making out with Derek. Heaven can have me; I'm done here. I pull my lips from Derek's and drop my forehead to his chest, hiding my face in embarrassment.

"Geez, man, you are killing me," Derek groans.

Matt laughs. "You look fine to me. Goodnight you two."

I splay my hands on Derek's chest and push him backwards through the door. He doesn't fight back, walking backward easily, with a look of steely determination on his face. I avoid his searching gaze and close the door without another word. I walk back to my room and press my fingers to my lips, reliving every detail of those kisses until I fall asleep.

Chapter 5

Derek

I'm starting to officially get ticked. Stubborn woman won't return my calls, texts, or even emails. Who even emails socially anymore? Desperate people, that's who. Won't see me when I stop by her work and won't answer the door when I go to her house. I can't figure out how she knows when I'm coming, because her door is always locked when I get there yet Grady and Brittany say it's still unlocked when they try it. She has become some kind of ninja at avoiding me.

Seems like she's doubled down on this whole not dating me thing. I would think at this point I'm coming across as pathetic, however, my efforts seem to make her angry more than anything else. Madison angry is passionate, and that passion is a good thing, so I'll take it how I can get it. I feel like maybe this is a roundabout way of getting there, but we'll end up where I need us to be sooner or later.

It's been two weeks since that night, and all I can think about is how smart and witty she is, how her lips feel on mine, and how attractive she is when she's yelling at me. I cut the engine on my bike and walk it the rest of the way to Brittany's, parking it on the side of the house where I know Maddy won't see it. I trudge through the door, calling out a greeting, and walk in on the family eating some kind of casserole at the kitchen table.

"Want dinner?" Brittany asks, motioning to the empty chair known as "Aunt Maddy's seat".

"Where's Maddy?" I ask directly. It's Friday night, and I'm done messing around. We are settling this now. I have never worked so hard on one woman, and if I weren't absolutely certain Maddy is worth it, I would have given up long ago. My game plan has officially been chucked. I'm winging it from here on out.

Brittany looks at Matt with panicked eyes and he nonchalantly replies, "She's on a date."

I freeze, sure I heard him wrong. "She's what?" I grind out, willing my head not to explode.

"On a date. With some lawyer," Matt repeats, casually avoiding Brittany's elbow. "Come on," he tells her playfully, "remember earlier when I wanted to go to a movie and you wanted to stay here? You were right about staying, this is more fun," he says gesturing at me with a grin.

"Matt, we promised," Brittany chides.

"What exactly did you promise?" I ask tightly.

Brittany eyes me and doesn't say anything, so I switch my focus to Matt. "She doesn't want us to talk to you about her anymore." He takes another bite of the casserole. "But I've never respected my sister's privacy, so whatever."

"Where is she?" I ask again.

Matt looks at Brittany questioningly while Brittany studies her plate. My blood pressure is rising by the second.

"I know," Grady offers brightly, cutting through the tension. "I didn't make any promises."

I breathe in relief and cross the table to kiss his head. "You are my favorite person in the entire world, Grady. Where is she?"

"First, I want you to take me to a baseball game. A big one," he says with calculation.

I look at Matt and Brittany in shock, who appear extremely amused and not at all like they are going to help me. "Okay, you little extortionist. I'll take you to a game."

"On your bike," Grady adds. I look at Brittany and she shakes her head no.

"One minor league game and a trip to the toy store where you get three things, whatever you want, we go in the car," I offer, the ridiculousness of the situation lowering my heart rate.

"Five things," Grady counters.

"Deal," I say immediately. Don't tell Grady, but if he asked for ten things I would have agreed. Thank God he doesn't realize exactly how much I need this information as the art of the deal is based on supply and demand. Hello capitalism and welcome to America.

"Dinner at Luigi's, and they were planning to go to a movie after," Grady announces.

"What movie?"

"I don't know, but it's at the big theatre with all the colors."

"Thanks, Buddy." I kiss his head again and glare at my sister and her husband, who look more proud and amused than they have a right to. "You two should be ashamed for raising a blackmailer."

Matt corrects, "Negotiator."

I leave without another word, cranking my bike and riding straight to Luigi's.

Thankfully, they are still at the restaurant when I get there. I spot Maddy immediately, looking absolutely gorgeous in a cobalt blue dress that matches her eyes. I don't know who she's with, but he's slightly balding from the back and is in absolutely no way worthy of that dress. My blood pressure rises again as another wave of anger hits me. I can't believe she'd rather be out with this guy than me. I stalk up to her table and watch her eyes widen when she notices me.

"Did I not make myself clear?" I ask calmly. Relatively calmly. I mean, as calmly as attainable in my current state.

Her mouth drops open and her eyes dart around nervously. "Are you really making a scene right now?"

I nudge the lawyer over without a word and sit down saying, "Well?"

Maddy sniffs and tosses her hair. "I don't know what you're talking about." She levels a glare at me. "But I'm fairly certain I made myself clear," she replies in warning.

"Um...do you need a minute?" the guy beside me asks awkwardly.

"Actually, I can take it from here, thanks for playing," I say tightly without removing my eyes from Maddy.

Her mouth drops open indignantly. "I am on a date. Who do you think you are? You can't speak to him like that."

I lean forward over the table. "I just did. Besides, the only person you are supposed to be on a date with is me," I respond with just as much attitude. I'm getting real tired of her stubborn streak. Canyon is more like it. We've passed streak; it's more like a stubborn canyon.

"I told you I'm not dating you," Maddy says through clenched teeth. Her words protest, but the challenge issued in her eyes is very clear. That's the thing about Maddy. Her words say one thing, but her body says another. I get the feeling she's not exactly lying. She wants to believe herself, but when it comes down to it, she doesn't. That's exactly why she needs a little nudge. Except gentle nudging doesn't seem to get through to Maddy, so here I am with a battering ram about to shove.

"And I told you, that's not an option. Now, tell this nice man you have an emergency and let's go," I demand more angrily than I intended. She has a knack for chipping away at my self-control.

"That's okay, I think I'll just..." he stammers, inching away from me.

"Donald, stay," Maddy urges, starting to apologize, but I snort, interrupting her.

"Donald?" I ask derisively.

Maddy straightens her back. "Now you are just being mean." She shifts to talk to Donald again. "I'm so sorry about this. It seems I may need to handle it, though, so maybe we can get together another time?"

Donald nods wordlessly and lets himself out from other side of the booth, heading straight for the door.

"Don't count on it, Donald," I taunt as he goes.

Maddy turns up her glaring, crossing her arms over her chest. "I hope you are happy. You were mean to a perfectly nice man. What, have you resorted to intimidation tactics now?"

I shrug. "You don't return my calls, texts, or emails, won't see me. Then I go over to Brittany's and have to hear from Grady that you are on a date? Too far, Madison," I say gravely.

"Snitch," she grumbles, although she has the decency to look embarrassed.

"Have you eaten?" I question.

"What does it look like? No, we were very rudely interrupted before we got our meal."

"Good." I stand and put some bills on the table, then hold out my hand. "Come on."

Maddy tilts her chin defiantly. "I'm not going anywhere with you."

Nope. No more asking nicely. I lean over the booth and put my face close to hers, talking low and slow. "You are either walking out or I'm carrying you out, but we are leaving here together."

Her eyes widen and I can tell by her dilated pupils that it's from excitement and not from fear. She takes my hand wordlessly, and I pull her out of the booth and out of the restaurant. I draw her up beside me on the sidewalk and put my hand on the small of her back, escorting her to my bike.

"I can't ride on your bike!" she squeaks as we approach the curb.

"Why not?" I ask in confusion.

She stutters, "I'm in a dress. And heels." The fear in her eyes is very clear, and it's not about the dress or the heels. I sigh. Why is every single thing work with this girl?

She is backing up from the bike, so I drop my helmet on the handlebars and follow her until her back is against the building. I put my hands on the brick on either side of her and lean in, capturing her bright blue eyes with mine. They widen and I can see the pulse pounding on her neck.

"Your dress and heels aren't the problem, Maddy," I refute in a low rumble.

"Oh?"

I'm pleased with the hypnotized look she has when she looks into my eyes. "You're afraid that once you climb on that bike, it'll be all over, but you're wrong."

"Oh?" she repeats breathily.

"It was all over the moment I saw you. It was a done deal the moment we sparred, after the moment our lips touched, and it's never gonna be the same." I feather my lips on her right cheek before taking her eyes with mine again, which takes a second because it takes a while for her to open them after my kiss. "Come with me. Give me this a chance. Let me show you why some guy that chooses a cliché restaurant for a first date with a woman like you is so totally wrong and why it'll only ever be right with me." My eyes are locked on hers, imploring her to agree.

"Okay," she whispers, eyes wide.

"Ma'am, this guy bothering you?" comes from behind us.

Geez, can I not catch a break here?

"Very funny, Green," I growl, my eyes cutting behind me. Cackling laughter follows, getting further away as the beat cops from my precinct continue their patrol. If those guys have broken the moment I have with Maddy, bones will break. I push up and take her hand, pulling her back to my Harley. I take off my leather jacket and hand it to her before putting my helmet on her head.

She frowns. "I don't really have the hair for this tonight."

"It'll be windblown anyway," I point out.

"True." She eyes the bike. "Where do I put my feet?"

I show her and she nods as the bike roars to life. Then she hops on, tucking her dress around her legs, and puts her arms around me.

"Good?" I ask above the engine. When I feel her nod, I pull away slowly from the curb and feel her arms tighten.

All worth it, for this moment, right now. Maddy wrapping her arms around me and putting her trust in me makes every single bit of effort worth it.

* * *

Maddy

He was right. I was ruined for all other men the moment I laid eyes on him. Much less the moment we first kissed. Now he's ruined all other modes of transportation for me too, and I'm sorry, but that just makes him selfish.

The wind buffets around me deafeningly; it's all I can hear. It feels like I'm flying, and I never want to stop. With my arms wrapped around Derek's hard chest, I have to use every ounce of self-control I have to not feel him up in the process. Truthfully, I fail a couple times, but he doesn't seem to mind. I have no idea where we are going, but I hope to goodness we never get there because this is heaven.

He pulls off the road in the middle of nowhere, seemingly on a dirt road in the woods, and I wonder absently if he's planning to kill me and stash my body. I dismiss the thought because he would probably have to tell Grady I wasn't coming home and he can't even tell Grady when to go to bed, so I have that going for me. As the bike eases to a stop, I lift my head to see a small restaurant surrounded by trees. We are in a gravel parking lot, and it looks fairly busy. Color me curious.

Derek shuts off the bike and extends his hand to help me off. "Well?" he asks, eyes shining.

I want to lie, but I can't. I pull the helmet off and smile widely. "It was amazing," I admit.

He smiles broadly. "I knew you'd love it."

I try running my fingers through my hair to smooth it, but it feels like a total mess.

"Here, let me." Derek combs his fingers through my hair, smoothing it somewhat, before gazing into my eyes and saying, "Gorgeous."

I playfully punch his shoulder and remove his leather jacket, although I miss its scent and warmth immediately.

He drapes the jacket on his arm and takes my hand. "Come on."

"Where are we right now?" I ask, looking around.

"Technically, we are on the South Carolina side of Hill's Lake."

"Technically?"

He grins. "There is some debate about where the state line actually is back here in the woods." He opens the door and the scent of oregano fills my nostrils.

"Derek!" A round, matronly woman calls to us as we step through the door.

"Hey there, May. How are you?" He greets her warmly with a hug.

I watch in awe because I've never seen Derek this personable before. His face is even...friendly.

"Same as always, and who's this?" she asks, eyeing me curiously.

"This is Madison," Derek introduces proudly, taking my hand and gazing at me before presenting me to her like I'm a prize and she's the winner.

I offer my other hand to May. "Nice to meet you. Friends call me Maddy."

"Nice to meet you, Maddy." She gives Derek a not-so-subtle wink and says, "I suppose you want your regular table?"

"Please." He flashes her a devastating grin I feel in my gut.

May leads us to the back to a booth in the corner, asking about Brittany and Grady as we go. We sit down, and May walks away after handing us two menus, telling us to choose wisely or she'll choose for us.

"So," I start, gazing at my menu, "Regular table, huh? This where you bring all the ladies?"

Derek clears his throat and I glance up at him. He looks uncomfortable. "Actually, I've never brought a date here."

I'm surprised by this because I'm fairly certain Derek has no issue convincing girls to go out with him. "It's nice," I say, "and Italian's my favorite."

Derek frowns, his tone going sarcastic. "Well, you were all ready for Italian earlier, so I figured I should keep it similar."

"Poor Donald," I remember sadly. He really was a very nice man.

Derek snorts. "He'll live."

"We were very rude," I say regretfully.

Anger flashes across his face. "Why did you go out with him, Madison?"

I look away from his eyes because I can see the hurt in them, and also I don't want him to know how affected I am hearing him say my full name. Instead, I look down at the table. "I was trying to prove to myself that I could date someone other than you."

Derek chortles. "With that guy?"

I wince, then snicker. "Not my finest decision making, I'll admit." I pause before remembering a question I wanted to ask at Luigi's. "So

44

how did you know where I was?"

Derek tilts his head back and laughs. It is a glorious sight and sound. "Grady. You would have been so proud. I was pumping Matt and Brittany for information and they weren't spilling."

"Good." Glad my threats were at least taken seriously.

"Then Grady says he knows where you are and that he didn't make any promises. He proceeds to tell me he'll tell me what I want to know if I take him to a baseball game on my bike."

I laugh. He's right. I'm so proud.

"I negotiated him down to a minor league game and five toys at a toy store," Derek admits sheepishly.

"Five!" I laugh. "You were had. I could have gotten it to two."

Derek leans in, whispering, "I didn't put up much of a fight, to be honest."

I put my menu down and stare at him. It's baffling to me that he is trying so hard to win me. I honestly don't get it.

"What are you thinking about so hard?" he asks, putting his menu down too.

I shake my head. "Just trying to figure you out."

"Not much there to figure out," he replies simply.

I narrow my eyes. "That's what you'd like me to think."

He smiles and then points out the window. "We should come back later in the summer. You'll be able to see the lake out here."

"I would love to see that," I say with a soft smile.

"We'll do it then," he agrees.

I take a breath to shake off the feelings that promise gives me. "So is this date all you hoped it would be? You fought pretty hard for it," I challenge him.

He leans back and watches me carefully. "Yeah, well, we could have gotten here without me having to fight quite so hard. You are the most stubborn woman I have ever met."

"I know my own mind. I know what I want, and I fight for it," I answer unrepentantly.

He shakes his head. "Wrong, try again."

My back straightens and my cheeks flush. He's calling me out, and I've never been one to back away from a challenge. "Just because my answer wasn't what you wanted it to be doesn't mean it's not what I want." Even as I say the words, I know he won't buy it. I'm not even sure I can attempt being that believable anymore around him.

He smiles knowingly. "You know what I think, Maddy?" he leans forward, "I think you are fighting this so hard because you are just as gone as I am."

I swallow and those heart palpitations return. Dang. Apparently that's a hard no at being believable around him.

"Why would I do that?" I'm like a double agent, slipping behind enemy lines trying to see how much he knows.

He leans back and his eyes flick over me, assessing. "My guess is you've been hurt before, but I intend to find out for sure."

Good luck with that. I'm locked up tighter than a Kardashian's iCloud account. It's not fun to be so easily read, however. I feel heat fill my cheeks and it kinda ticks me off. Change of subject is needed immediately. I give myself a mental pep talk to not let him see me blink. "Okay, so," I shrug indifferently, "let's date. Typical first date question. What made you become a detective?"

Date. Derek Masters. I'm dating Derek Masters. The twenty-eight-year-old me sitting in the booth is terrified, but the twelve-year-old version of me in my head Lizzie McGuire cartoon-style is doing backflips and a happy dance.

He sits back. "I was an angry kid. Shorter than my entire class growing up, didn't hit a growth spurt till college."

I grin. "Your family *is* pretty short."

He playfully frowns at me. "Still taller than you, though," he replies smugly.

"Except in heels," I retort.

"Nope, same height in heels," he states. "I knew I wanted to do something active, and after what happened to Brittany, I guess being a cop just appealed to me."

I digest this and hesitate before asking my next question. "If you don't mind telling me, what happened to Brittany?"

His brows lift in surprise. "You don't know?"

"I never asked, she never said," I explain.

Just then the waitress comes over with our drinks and takes our orders for our meal. When she leaves, Derek says, "I don't think she would mind you knowing. She was drugged and raped."

I gasp. I, like everyone else, assumed she made some mistakes and the dead beat left her. "I had no idea," I stammer.

"I think Brittany and I are both pretty much over it now. Well, now that she has Matt. It messed me up for a while though."

"How?" I ask curiously, propping my chin in my palm and watching him closely. My curiosity grows when he shifts uncomfortably in his seat and looks nervous.

He huffs out a breath and grins wryly. "I could use a drink before having this conversation." I watch him take a sip of his drink as he gathers the words. He looks more at the table than at me as he talks, only glancing up every few minutes to gauge my reaction. "I was an angry kid, and I guess what happened to Brittany just tipped me over the edge. I felt guilty I didn't protect her. So I started the program at the academy and was good at it. No one thought anything about perps coming in a little more banged up than they probably should have been. I had a lot of unspent aggression, and I drank pretty heavily for a while." He sighs and straightens, then looks me in the eye. "But a few months ago, I rededicated my life to Christ, got back on the straight and narrow," he finishes proudly.

I smile encouragingly. "That's great. What prompted that?" My lawyer senses are tingling and telling me there's more to the story.

His gaze darkens. "I lost a good friend on the force. Not even to anything violent, but to disease. Then, Lily, our cousin, died, again by disease. I don't know, it just spooked me I guess. That we never know what's gonna happen, and the only one in control is God."

"I get that."

He looks relieved, like he was scared to tell me, that I would reject him. Now that it is over, he seems lighter. I watch his nervousness disappear and his cockiness come back. "So why a lawyer?" he asks.

"I love to negotiate." I add indulgently, "And maybe I wanted to wear power suits and yell things like 'I want the truth!' at a witness."

Derek gazes at me in admiration. "You do mostly family law, right?"

"Yeah, sad divorces mostly, custody battles. Although I do get to do adoption cases. I'm working on Matt and Brittany's right now. Should be final in a few months."

"Really? That's great," he says with surprising enthusiasm.

I grin mischievously. "Want to hear a secret?" He leans in, brows raised, eyes dancing. "Financial law is my favorite. Don't you dare tell my dad," I add quickly.

"Why is that a secret?" he asks in confusion.

"Because my Dad pushed me to do financial law and I resisted, flexing my independence. But you know what? I love it. I love spreadsheets. I love loopholes. I love beating the system," I admit with a sigh of longing.

Derek gazes at me with an odd expression. "So why family law?"

"Family law lets me use my powers for good. I can keep families together or do my best to make sure kids end up with the right parent. Financial law isn't the same," I say with a wrinkled nose. "Besides, I get to dip my toes in the financial waters every once in a while at my current firm, so I'm happy."

Derek slowly smiles in wonderment. "You are something else, Maddy."

"Back atcha," I wink.

We get our food, and after the prayer and a few bites, I decide to liven things up a bit. "So," I say around a bite, "run me through a Derek Masters first date."

He narrows his eyes warily. "What?"

I roll my eyes. "I know you date a lot. Run me through a typical first date. We are at dinner, what's next?" I look at him expectantly. "This is really good by the way," I mention, gesturing to my pasta.

His eyes flick from his plate to me and back. "What makes you think I date a lot?"

I can see the corners of his mouth twitching. "Please don't insult my intelligence," I answer wryly.

"I would never." Somewhat sheepishly, he continues, "To be honest, I gave up dating when I rededicated my life."

I cock my head to the side. "You said you were doing a thing with your ex and that's why you didn't call me. That wasn't so long ago."

He shifts uncomfortably in his seat. "Look," he rushes out, "I only dated so I could take women home. I'm not super proud of that. My ex wasn't someone I was in a relationship with, it was...mutually beneficial. I broke it off when I rededicated. Then I met you and wanted to get to know you, but then she called and made it this big thing." He shrugged. "I felt like I owed it to her. She didn't get the whole rededicated thing, so I broke it off. Again. Now I'm dating you."

I take all this in, watching him closely. "You are a lot more work than I thought you'd be."

He laughs a deep, throw-your-head-back belly laugh. "Same to you, Princess."

"Other than the...end of the night-thing... continue. What does a typical first date look like for you?" I ask curiously.

He looks uncomfortable again. "Dinner and a movie."

"You don't look like the dinner-and-movie type," I argue, searching his face to determine the source of his discomfort.

"It serves a purpose. Wouldn't do that on a date with someone I really liked, however," he says with an awkward shoulder lift.

"Why not? I like movies. Donald was taking me to dinner and a movie," I challenge.

"You take a girl to the movies for three reasons: either, one, you don't like her and don't really want to talk to her; two, you're boring and you don't know what else to do; or three, you want to hold her for two solid hours in the dark. For those reasons, a movie is a strictly fourth date only because that's when it's okay for me to hold you for two hours in the dark."

My eyes widen at the heat in his eyes. I swallow in an effort to dampen my now dry mouth. I lean back and smile, gathering myself. "You look like a 'let me show you how male I can be by doing an activity I'm really good at' type."

He smirks. "Maybe. Although I prefer to think of myself as not being one dimensional."

I'm learning if there is one thing Derek Masters is not it's one dimensional. I let the topic drop as we finish our meal. We discuss our favorite hobbies, what we are currently doing at work, and potential summer plans.

While he pays the check, I ask, "So what are we doing after this?"

"You'll just have to wait and see," he answers with a grin.

I take another sip of my drink. He's having fun with this, and so am I. I call gun range, but I don't want to say it out loud because he probably won't do it then, and I'm a really good shot.

"It's not what you're thinking," he predicts, narrowing his eyes.

"You don't know what I'm thinking." But something tells me he does.

"It's not the gun range," he says smugly.

My mouth drops open. "How did you know I was thinking that?" It is truly terrifying how well he can read me.

"Ah, that would be telling. So what do you think of Mays?" he asks, gesturing around.

I smile, glancing around the restaurant. "I love it. I want to come back. Best shrimp alfredo I've ever had."

He looks supremely pleased. "Good." He stands and offers me his hand. "Come on, let's go."

I take his hand and we leave, waving goodbye to May before we go. With every step, my excitement mounts at the thought of getting back on his bike. He hands me his jacket, and this time I leave my hair tucked in, having learned my lesson earlier. I put on his helmet and get on behind him, not hesitating to scoot close and hold on tight.

"Good?" he calls above the engine.

I nod, then he starts down the lane. When we get on the road, he starts slow, as he did before. This time, though, he goes faster and faster until I truly feel like there is nothing else in the world but me and Derek and the wind. It's a little scary, but a lot exciting, and holding onto Derek, I know he won't let anything hurt me at all.

Chapter 6

Derek

Maybe I get a little carried away with the speed, but I can't help it, I can tell she is enjoying it. I slow it down after a while, though, because I'm not in any rush and I want this ride to take as long as possible.

I navigate the bike through town, excited to see her reaction to our activity.

Once again, she's pegged me. I am an activity guy who likes to show off for a date. I would never tell her this, but it would've been the gun range if she hadn't guessed it. She's awfully astute, and I like it. She keeps me on my toes because I want to keep her on hers.

"Putt-putt?" she laughs as I cut the engine in front of the attraction.

"You look like a girl who likes to have a good time," I say getting off the bike. "Can't imagine a better time than putt-putt." I hold out my arm to help her off and she removes the helmet and jacket. This time her hair is in much better shape than before.

She laughs heartily, and it makes me want to do anything possible to hear it again.

"I love putt-putt! I want a pink ball," she calls, trotting ahead of me to the window.

"You gonna be okay in those shoes?" I ask, doubtfully eyeing her stilettos. They look good but painful, not necessarily putt-putt appropriate.

"Absolutely," she replies dismissively. "Excuse me, do you have any pink balls?" she asks the teenage kid behind the counter.

The pimple-faced degenerate looks like he's about to come back with a dirty comment but catches my no nonsense glare over her shoulder. He just about swallows his tongue before he turns beet red and hands her a pink golf ball wordlessly.

Maddy hops in excitement and picks a club, testing the height while I pay, then choose my own club and ball. Despite her absurdly high heels, she trots excitedly ahead of me and lines her ball up at the first green.

I come up behind her and stand unnaturally close. "Want me to help you with your form? I'm very good at putt-putt," I say into her ear. I'm pleased with the shiver that runs through her body.

She grins slyly over her shoulder at me. "I'll let you know if I need help."

With that, she takes a swing and lands a hole in one, throwing her hands in the air and laughing in victory.

"Good shot," I say, impressed. Is there anything she isn't good at?

I line up my shot, and to my delight, I, too, make a hole in one. I look over at her trying not to be so smug, but I can't help it. It's all I have by way of a victory dance.

"Good shot," she cheers, turning to trot to the next hole.

"Tell me something you're bad at," I call after her.

She turns and looks at me oddly. "Why would I do that?"

"I'm starting to wonder if you are superhuman," I tease.

She laughs. "I would tell you, but that would take all the fun out of you figuring it out for yourself."

"Is that a challenge?" I ask with the intention of sounding intimidating yet realizing it may have come out more excited than anything else.

She eyes me with that amused smirk and says, "You look like you can handle it."

Yeah, I can. I can handle anything she throws at me. Even Donald can attest to that.

We go through the putt-putt course, and we are about halfway through when I miss my second shot.

She cringes, slightly delighted. "Oops. That puts me in the lead by two."

"You're keeping score?" I ask in surprise.

"You're not?" she asks in an equal amount of surprise.

I shake my head. "I never do."

"Is it because you usually win and dates don't like that?" she asks knowingly.

"Actually, I've never brought a date here either. Growing up, Brittany was a bit of a sore loser. It was more fun to come and play without keeping score," I explain.

"You are a good brother. Matt always kept score and was a sore winner." She cocks her head. "But then, so was I, I guess," she admits with a grin.

"No!" I say with mock astonishment.

She laughs and saunters over to me. "You should know, I always keep score."

I hit the ball and sink the put. "That's fine. With this game, even if I lose, I win."

"How's that?" She tilts her head adorably, looking at me curiously.

"Because I'm here with you," I say obviously, coming to stand directly in front of her. Her eyes widen at my nearness and her breath catches. I can't resist her a minute more; she's so stinking cute with her excitement, her victory dances, and that smart mouth that always surprises me. I brush my lips over hers, lightly at first. I deepen my kiss a little, not a lot, just enough for her to remember those other kisses before I pull back. I linger over her lips, a breath away, considering going in again when children's squeals interrupt my thoughts.

Maddy pulls back and blinks rapidly, seemingly trying to focus. "Trying to tip the score in your favor?" she asks huskily.

I cup her face with my hand and brush my thumb along her cheek. "This between us isn't a game, Maddy. The score will always be the same."

I pause just for a second, to make sure she's heard me before I brush my lips lightly over hers again. I don't feel it's the appropriate time to mention I'm keeping count of how many times I can make her speechless. That's something just for me.

* * *

Maddy

I win putt-putt. I was nervous for a minute because his kisses threw me off my game so much, but I rallied and took him in the end.

True, he made another hole in one on the very last hole, and I jumped up and down and cheered for him. I couldn't help it. An energy like electricity zips through me every time his green eyes watch me, when he smiles at me, or when he touches me. Anywhere. At any point in time. He could step on my toe and I swear my foot would light on fire from his touch.

"Can we do the arcade? Pleeeease?" I beg with an enticing smile.

"Sure. Want me to win you a teddy bear?" he teases.

I snort derisively. "Please, if I wanted a bear, I'd get one myself. No, I love an arcade. Not that I'm proud of this, but the more violent the game, the more fun it is," I say with a huge smile.

He puts his arm around my shoulders and tugs me into the building. "Who am I to keep the lady from what she wants?"

It's a relatively small arcade and fairly crowded, it being a Friday night, but we end up playing every game. I get a few looks, being that I am incredibly overdressed, but I don't care. I'm having fun. So much fun. It doesn't hurt that all the teenage boys are checking me out, not because of my outfit, but because I can beat their high score on Diablo Immortal.

Well, maybe a little because of my outfit.

It's fun to watch Derek glare at them threateningly when they get too close or their looks get too long. Teasing and flirting with Derek is incredibly addicting. Not only that, but he is almost as competitive as I am, and it's fun to watch him concentrate on impressing me.

"That was so fun," I sigh in contentment when our last game credits have been spent.

"It was." He looks at me oddly before taking my hand. "Come on, night's not over yet."

I grin and follow him to his bike, excited for another ride. I could definitely get used to this. I eagerly put on his jacket and helmet as he starts the bike, climbing on behind him. I never want this night to end.

He drives downtown to a small café on the river. "Ice cream?" he asks when he shuts off the bike.

I pull the helmet off. "Always!" I get off the bike and wait for Derek and can't help but lean into him when he puts his arm around my shoulders.

We go into the café and pick out our ice cream and cones, then Derek suggests, "Let's eat on the boardwalk."

I follow him down to the boardwalk over the river, and we walk while munching on ice cream until we find an open bench. We sit down and Derek puts his arm around me. Once again I lean into him. Why not? I might go back to fighting this tomorrow, but tonight, I'm giving in.

"This is literally the best ice cream I've ever had," I murmur as I take my first bite of cone.

Derek grunts in agreement. "The family is Mennonite, and I don't know why, but they always make the best ice cream."

There is a half-moon reflected in the river, and we can hear the cheers from the minor league baseball stadium just across the bridge. "This is nice," I comment as we sit and enjoy the evening.

"Where does it rate on your emergency scale?" he asks me, suddenly.

"My what?" I reply in confusion.

"That emergency thing you and Brittany do," he explains and I laugh.

"Matt thinks I'm crazy, but it's important to have a system," I justify.

"So, where does this date rate at?"

I consider this for a moment. I have a rating for good dates, obviously, but I've never had one this good.

"Actually, hold that thought, this is going to take it over the top," he says pointing toward the minor league baseball field just across the river. We have the perfect view as fireworks begin exploding in the sky. My mouth drops open and I look back at Derek. He is smiling as he watches me.

That's when it hits me. I'm his. Ruined forever for all other men. Even if this crashes and burns, I'll still never be able to replace the feelings I get when I'm close to him. It's in my nature to be slightly overdramatic and emotional, but even I can tell when I've been permanently altered.

When the fireworks are over, I turn to look back at Derek, whose smile still plays on his lips.

"Wow." It's all I can say.

His smile widens. I cup his face and kiss him, deep and slow. When I pull back, I grin because his lids are fluttering. It's nice to know I'm not the only one affected by our kisses.

"I was wrong," I admit softly.

"Oh yeah?" he asks, eyes on my mouth.

"Grady doesn't have more game than you," I answer before covering his mouth with mine again.

I am still going slow, just enjoying the feel of his lips on mine when someone near us cuts into my euphoria. "Twice in one night, Masters?"

Derek pulls back and cuts the cops near us a death gaze. "Keep moving, Green."

More laughter as they walk away.

"Is this going to be our thing? Being interrupted at awkward moments?" I ask with a wry grin.

He ignores my question and captures my lips again. I'm not complaining, and I'm not holding back. Our other kisses were either light and feathery, or hard and urgent, and this is...perfect. Just right. I shiver as his tongue traces my bottom lip, feeling it all the way to my toes.

He pulls back and rests his forehead on mine. "I guess I should get you home," he says reluctantly.

I'm disappointed too. He gives me his jacket and I pull it on, following him to the bike. I get on behind him and scoot in close, tapping his shoulder as he starts it. He turns his head and I put my mouth near his ear and say, "Take the long way." He smiles and nods, carrying us off into the darkness.

Take the long way he did. Almost an hour later, we pull up to my driveway and it is still too soon. I don't want to get off, don't want to let go, don't want to leave him. I am still holding on when he cuts the engine. It takes me another minute before I finally get off.

I hand him his helmet slowly and take off his jacket, immediately missing it. Derek puts a hand on the small of my back, walking me to my porch.

"Thank you, I had a great time," I say sincerely, then with a mischievous grin. "Despite the fact you crashed my original plans."

He leans in close and I stabilize myself against the door. He rubs a thumb across my cheek and whispers, "Any regrets?" I can't find words when his eyes are this close, so I just shake my head no. He smiles and kisses me lightly before pulling back and saying, "You never gave me a rating."

I huff in breathy laughter. "That's because my ratings don't go that high."

"I'll take that," he says before kissing me again.

I like to think I see extreme reluctance on his face as he takes a step back. "I should go before I do something we will regret," he says as if it's causing him physical pain.

I nod regretfully.

"You're coming swimming tomorrow with the family?" he asks hopefully.

I cock my head considering this. I'm not sure so much contact this quickly is a good idea...mostly for my own sanity. "I don't know. I have to get some work done. Mom asked me to come shopping with her...so I'll have to see tomorrow morning."

"Come," he says with a smile and eyes that say the same thing.

Oh, heavens. I have to look away now or I'll never be able to tell him no ever.

"We'll see," I say with a shy smile. "Thanks again. I had a great time."

"Me too. I want to see you again soon," he says pointedly as he backs away, and I'm not sure if it's a promise or a warning. Honestly, I'm okay either way. I open the door and walk inside, and after giving him another smile, close it.

"And lock your door," I hear from the other side.

I laugh, ignoring his demand and peek out the blinds as he walks to his bike, puts his jacket on, (did he just sniff it?), smiles in my direction, and then shakes his head at the house. I walk dreamily through my home and fall backward onto the couch, hugging a pillow to my chest and staring at the ceiling thinking about how life as I know it is over.

"Maddy?" I hear Brittany come through the front door a few minutes later.

I pop my head up in surprise. "Brittany?"

She pads in wearing her pajamas and eyes me with a smile. "Good date?"

"Oh, my gracious, Brittany. Mind. Officially. Blown," I gush, hugging the pillow as she sits down on the chair across from me. "I'm totally screwed," I admit miserably.

"Tell me," she demands with curiosity.

"What are you even doing up? What time is it?" I ask in surprise.

Brittany blushes. "I heard the bike and I snuck over. I wanted to hear how it went, and I wanted to be here if...it didn't go well."

"You're a good friend," I say sincerely, touched by her thoughtfulness.

"I love you," she replies in explanation.

"I love you too." Then I take a deep breath. "Stop me if I gross you out or anything...but whoa. He totally crashed my date. Thanks for not spilling by the way. He told me he got it from Grady." I pause at Brittany's laugh.

"You would have been incredibly proud. He played Derek like a violin. I can't wait to tell your dad."

I giggle. "He told me. He scared my date away and then demanded I leave with him, which I eventually did."

"Derek always did have the subtlety of a sledgehammer," Brittany replies fondly.

"He took me to May's for dinner."

Brittany looks impressed. "May's! He pulled out the big guns. I can respect that," she says with a nod of approval.

"It was perfect. We had a great dinner, the food was amazing. I can't believe you've never taken me there before," I accuse.

"Actually, I'm not sure Matt's ever been. We'll have to take a family trip soon," Brittany mentions thoughtfully.

"Then he took me to putt-putt."

Brittany laughs. "Putt-putt? I thought his thing was the gun range?"

My head pops up. "I knew it!" I cry. "He said it wasn't, but I totally called it," I say smugly, laying my head back down. "We had a great time. I totally beat him. Then we did all the games in the arcade. After that, he took me for ice cream on the river where we watched fireworks explode over the baseball stadium," I finish dreamily.

"Wow. That is quite a date," Brittany says, impressed.

I sigh deeply and stare at the ceiling. Memories from the evening fight for my attention.

Brittany chuckles. "You've got it bad, girl."

"I really do," I groan, "It's not normal."

"Since when have you ever worried about being normal? I thought your goal is to be fabulous?"

"You're right. The question is how fabulous is it to be completely head over heels for someone after the first date?" I ask uncertainly.

"You're overthinking it. Stop worrying. Just let it happen," she replies easily.

I stay silent. Am I? Should I?

"Coming swimming tomorrow?" Brittany asks.

I throw my arm over my eyes. "No. I can't. It's too soon. He's too much. No way can I be half naked with him so soon after he was kissing me like that."

I hear a choking sound. "Better not let Matt hear you talking like that," she says with an eventual giggle. "Seriously, Maddy, don't run from it. Just let it happen."

"Well, Mom does want me to come shopping with her and I do have work to do, so it's not like I am just making up excuses," I justify weakly, except I know that's exactly what I'm doing.

"Isn't it?" Brittany challenges.

"Stop." I throw the pillow at her. "It's never been this bad before. Let me do my thing. I'll come over and play with Grady after church Sunday. But don't tell Derek," I instruct, pointing at her.

She crosses her heart. "Won't tell a soul. Not even Grady."

I breathe out in relief, "Thanks."

Brittany gets up and stands over me. "You know he's gonna find you, right?"

"I'm not hiding," I contend.

"Aren't you?" Brittany asks seriously.

"Yes," I whisper. I absolutely am. It's my only defense. She can't take this away from me.

Brittany sighs. She starts to walk away, and then she stops and turns back. "I get it. I do. I'm not here to pressure you, and I'm here for you and to support you no matter what. Just..." she pauses to consider her words, "Just be careful with him, okay? He's had a tough few years, and he's finally got himself together, and...he likes you a lot."

I reach for Brittany's hand. "You're the best sister, to both of us, that we could ever ask for, and I love you."

"I love you too, Mads," she says affectionately before letting herself out.

Chapter 7

Derek

I am disappointed the next day when Maddy doesn't come swimming. I could tell from her reaction last night she wasn't coming, that she needed a minute. That's okay. I can give her a minute if she needs one. Besides, Brittany won't tell me, but I'd bet dollars to donuts she's planning to spend tomorrow afternoon with Grady to curb his disappointment at her not being here today. Might be fun to just pop by tomorrow and see what they're up to. I send her a picture of me and Grady in the pool and text that we miss her. I think it should be noted, I have never texted anyone like I have Maddy. As far as I'm concerned, texting should be used for one-word questions and/or answers. It's worth breaking my habit, though, when she responds immediately with a smiley face with hearts for eyes.

Me: What are you up to?

Maddy: Shopping with Mom.

Me: You should get a leather jacket.

It takes a little longer for her to respond but I am not disappointed.

Maddy: I prefer sequins.

With this, she sends a picture of her rocking a short dress that is nothing but colorful sequins.

Me: Wow.

Maddy: I usually get my fashion advice from Grady.

I show the picture to Grady and then type out his response.

Me: Grady says "Aunt Maddy looks pretty" which personally I think is an insult because you are gorgeous. He also thinks you would look good in a leather jacket.

Maddy: I can't borrow yours anymore? *frowny face* *crying face*

Me: I'm torn...I'm thinking about safety, but you do look good in my jacket.

Maddy: You keep the helmet, I take the jacket?

I chuckle.

Me: I'm getting you your own helmet.

Maddy: Can it have sequins?

Me: It can have anything you want.

Maddy: Gotta go, Mom demands my full attention.

Me: Have fun. See you soon.

I toss my phone up on the deck and glance around. Everyone is staring at me except Grady.

"What?"

My parents just share a look and head into the house for snacks.

"Something distracting you, bro?" Brittany asks with a wicked glint in her eye.

"Shut up," I say and head toward Grady to play with him.

A little while later, Grady is eating a snack on the deck while me and Matt lounge in the pool, my thoughts squarely on Maddy.

"It means a lot to Brittany and Grady that you're coming around a lot more. And to me," Matt starts quietly.

"I'm enjoying it too. I'm just sorry it took so long for me to come around."

"Brittany told me about some of the stuff going on..." he starts hesitantly.

"I gave all that up when I rededicated," I interrupt.

"No, I know, I'm just saying...I'm glad you'll be there for Grady. If he ever struggles like you did, I hope you'll help him come out on the other end."

I hadn't expected that. "You know I will."

He stays quiet for a minute, but I have a feeling he's not done.

"Maddy's special. Not just because she's my sister, but just because she's...Maddy. I am glad she's found you. I don't think I could've found anyone better for her."

Wow, that means a lot. "Thanks, man."

"That's why I feel I should tell you..."

Crap, here it comes. Why do all these conversations go the same way? Why can't they just stop at the good part? Why is there always a secondary bad part that negates the good part at the beginning?

"Maddy is a force of nature, you know."

"I noticed," I reply with a smirk.

"She gives all of herself to every single thing. All that passion and energy she has, she can't help it. She just tackles everything with the same excitement and enthusiasm, which is great, but it makes failure that much more difficult for her. She loves freely and fully, with everything she has. Just like she does everything else. Just like with everything else, she falls harder when it doesn't work out." Matt pauses before continuing, seemingly lost in thought. "Anyway, I'm sure you've worked most of that out already. I say all that to say this. She's been hurt before. I don't know what happened and by whose hands, but she was hurt and it took her a long time before her light came back. It crushed her spirit. She was never really the same person after."

I was afraid it was something like that. Hearing that hurts, but it makes sense. "I'm very sorry to hear that."

"It was in undergrad. I'm just letting you know because she might...
be hesitant," he explains.

I snort. If by hesitant he means it takes months of asking, hundreds
of dollars in gifts, borderline stalking tendencies, alleged misuse of
my detective's badge, and intimidation tactics with the implied threat
of kidnapping to get her to agree to go out with me...yeah, I guess you
could call that hesitant.

I do not share my thoughts. Instead, I repay him in kind. "For the
record, I'm glad Brittany found you too. You've been great to her and
to Grady, and I'm thankful."

He nods once and we don't speak again. Not until Grady jumps back
into the pool, effectively ending relaxation time.

Chapter 8

Maddy

I'm not necessarily trying to avoid Derek, I'm just...unintentionally unavailable...on purpose. Not one to be deterred, he texted every day and called every night for the entire week. Honestly, I enjoyed doing only that. I've decided to take Brittany up on half her advice and let it happen by actually answering the phone and responding to his texts. I find it is nice to get to know him without becoming overwhelmed by his presence. I know the second I am in the same room with him I will be completely overtaken by him again, and I want to make sure I like him for him, and vice versa, and that it's not just physical. Turns out, based on the research I've done the entire past week, I not only like him for him, I'm completely in love with him.

No one is more concerned about this than me.

I know Derek wants to take me out tonight because it's Friday night, and I don't think I can put him off any longer. I was able to tactfully avoid spontaneous dinners and a couple of lunch invitations during the week, but tonight I don't have a credible excuse. My only hope was if Brittany and Matt needed me to babysit, but I've already asked and Brittany just laughed, saying, "Not a chance, go out with Derek."

I procrastinate going home until I'm officially running late...as always. I consider feigning illness or a work emergency, but then I remember what it feels like on the back of his bike and decide to be a risk-taker.

I get home and fly through the house, picking out a hot pink mini skirt loose enough to get on and off the bike easily and a sleeveless white top. I put my hair in a low, helmet-friendly side pony. I am still mulling over shoes when I hear my doorbell.

"It's open!" I yell as loudly as possible, then, "I'll be right there!"

I pull on a pair of nude stilettos that are particularly uncomfortable but extremely attractive and proceed down the hall accessory free.

"You really should lock your door, Princess," Derek scolds as I come into the room.

He is incredibly attractive in jeans and a black button-down. I can't help but appreciate his hot gaze as it travels up and down my body. A pet name? Geez.

"Why on earth would I do that? Then insanely handsome men wouldn't be able to get to me," I flirt.

Big mistake. Huge. He prowls toward me like a lion, and my stomach drops down to my stilettos. "I would get to you, it's all the other men I'm wanting to keep away." The fire in his eyes says what his lips don't. He pulls me into his arms and presses his lips to my exposed neck. "Mmm, I like your hair like this," he rumbles.

I shiver with pleasure and smile. "It's helmet-friendly," I present proudly.

He chuckles. "I missed you this week."

I melt against him and surrender my lips to his. I missed him too. Too much. My hypothesis was to employ "out of sight, out of mind" to cool my feelings for him, but it turns out "absence makes the heart grow fonder" is an expression for a reason.

He pulls back and hands me his jacket. "Per your request."

I grin maybe a little too huge. "Thanks, although I feel bad you don't have one, since it is a safety issue and everything," I admit guiltily.

"It's fine. We'll get you one eventually, and until then I'm not gonna crash. Not with you on the bike." He pulls me out the door and waits. I shrug the jacket on and go for the bike.

"Maddy, lock the door," he insists grumpily, standing still beside it. I roll my eyes. "It's fine." I wave him off as I stand next to his bike. He stands in indecision for a frightening period of time before finally grumbling and getting on his bike.

I climb on behind him and feel home. I dreamt about this all week. Literal dreams about being on his bike, with him. I mean, I dreamt other stuff too, like his lips and his growl, but it was mostly about the bike.

"Up for a ride?" he asks over the engine. I nod enthusiastically and cuddle into his back, settling comfortably into my happy place. An hour later, he pulls into the outdoor amphitheater outside of town, and I'm actually disappointed that we made it to a destination.

"I thought movies were a fourth date option only," I accuse stepping off the bike.

"In movie theatres, yes, but not at the amphitheater, under the stars. Totally different date with interaction and a certain...whimsy," he justifies, then glances me. "But...if you'd rather not...."

"No, no!" I rush, "This is good." There's just something about hearing the word "whimsy" come from the dark, mysterious Derek Masters whose facial expression is permanently stuck on impassive.

"I need to make a quick stop. Hang right here for a second." He jogs toward the concession stand. I watch him bang on the door and exchange a few words before coming back with a picnic basket and blanket. He takes my hand easily. "Where do you want to sit?"

I look at the completely empty lawn ahead of us and unceremoniously take off my shoes. I point to the perfect spot centered in the middle of the screen. I hope no one crowds us when they start arriving. Derek spreads out a thick quilt, setting the picnic basket on top.

"You have really put some effort into this," I say, impressed.

"You ain't seen nothing yet." He sits down on the blanket, patting the spot beside him. I grin and drop down next to him, tucking my legs under me. "For the lady," he says as he hands me a bottled water.

I giggle, replying, "Thank you, kind sir."

He then unpacks the contents of the basket, which are not from the concession stand but instead from a local deli. My favorite deli, with that chicken salad. I have a serious chicken salad weakness. "Wow."

He wiggles his eyebrows goofily and then pulls out an assortment of movie candy.

I laugh. "You thought of everything! Do you mind me asking what we are watching?"

He leans in. "Singin' in the Rain."

"That's my favorite movie!"

"I know. Little birdy told me."

"I didn't know it was playing here tonight! How did you know?" I ask curiously because I keep an eye out for these things.

He shrugs nonchalantly. "I called in a favor."

My mouth drops open. "You did all this for me?"

He looks at me with an expression I can't identify. "Of course I did. Why would that be hard to believe?"

I look away in embarrassment. "Because no one has ever done anything like this for me before."

He doesn't respond. He just wraps his arm around my shoulders and pulls me back against him, kissing my temple before handing me a sandwich.

* * *

Derek

After a full week of Maddy avoiding me, I finally have her in my arms on Friday night. We are watching her favorite movie at the outdoor amphitheater and the night couldn't be more perfect.

"I hope you don't share Grady and Brittany's affinity for going to sleep halfway through the movie," she says. "As my pillow, that would be extremely inconvenient." As if to demonstrate, she backs up and leans deeper against my chest.

I wrap an arm around her waist and hold her tight. "You definitely don't have to worry about that, Princess."

"I like that," she says shyly.

"What?" I ask, hoping it's my arm around her waist or my lips on her ear.

"Princess," she responds as my lips travel from her ear to her jaw.

"Seems fitting," I say against her skin.

She sighs lightly. "You're making it awfully hard."

"What?" I whisper against her jaw.

"For me to guard my heart," she says hoarsely.

I lift my head and look into her eyes. "Why would you want to do that?"

The energetic, strong outer shell of Maddy breaks away, and I can see the vulnerability so clearly, as if she were a child. I can see her soul. Her eyes are clear and open, waiting for me to read them. So full of fear and conflicting emotions. So certain I'll leave. So certain this is fleeting. The desire to believe me, but the fear if she does. "Because if I don't, I'll be crushed when you leave me," she whispers.

I take a moment before saying lowly, "Madison." Her eyes dilate, and I make a mental note she likes it when I say her full name. "I'm not going anywhere. Not without you."

I thought she understood, feels the same intensity I do. I know she feels it; I can see it on her face. She's mine, and I'm hers, and that's just it. Maybe she's not ready to admit what this is, and that's fine, but she's crazier than I thought if she thinks I worked this hard to get her to go out with me just to leave her.

She stares into my eyes, clinging to my words like she would a life saver; as if it's what she needs to hear more than anything. That's until her eyes shutter and she shuts down, covering with a flirty grin. "Ten bucks says you'll run screaming by fall."

I don't crack a smile, even though I know she is trying to lighten the mood. Instead, I continue staring into her eyes, begging her to see what is there. "Give it your best shot, I'm not going anywhere," I promise seriously, then crack a grin. "I'll collect at Christmas, along with an apology and your declaration of undying love."

She smirks just as the movie starts and reaches forward for some candy, occasionally leaning back further to pop something in my mouth, and it's the most comfortable way I've ever watched a movie in my life. She takes me up on my comment to interact through the movie, narrating it for me and telling me her favorite parts. She even sings along to a few of the songs, and nothing has ever been more adorable.

When the movie ends, we don't move for several minutes.

"I don't want to go," Maddy complains.

"We can come back," I comfort, not making any effort to move her.

"But then the date will be over," she says glumly.

"Maybe, but there's always tomorrow," I counter optimistically.

"Don't you ever wish you could freeze time?" she asks thoughtfully.

"Not really. There's always something better coming. Like the feel of your arms around me on the ride home. Or the feel of your lips on your doorstep."

She shivers, and I know it's not from the cold. My lips find hers in the sweet and slow way we were kissing last week, feeling like nothing in the world is more important than this woman, at this moment.

She pulls back and sighs, laying her head against my neck. "I don't ever want this night to end."

But something sounds off about the way she says it. Not happy, but... melancholy. "You could sound more excited about it," I say dryly.

"I wish you could understand. How hard it is."

I kiss her forehead. "It's not hard, Princess. Nothing's been easier."

She groans low in her throat. "Stop! You are making it worse," she cries in frustration.

"You gonna make me wait another week to see you again?" I ask in amusement.

"No," she replies sullenly, "Grady guilted me something fierce last week for not coming Saturday, so I have been properly punished. Learned my lesson and will not repeat," she says bitterly.

"That's my boy," I say with an unapologetic grin. "In that case, I better get you home."

I pull her up but can tell she doesn't like it. We clean up the blanket and basket and take them back to the concession stand. We walked arm in arm back to my bike, slowly.

I give her my jacket and watch her shrug it on, grinning as she subtly sniffs it. I take the long way home and enjoy the feel of her body pressed against mine, her arms around me, and her chin resting on my shoulder.

Chapter 9

Maddy

Not gonna lie, Derek's good night kisses don't really say good night. They say, "I claim you as my own," and by the time the door shuts and my heart returns to normal beating, there's still no way I'm going to bed anytime soon.

I run a bath for myself as I think back through the night. Another perfect date. But I have discovered maybe the only bad thing about riding on the back of Derek's motorcycle is bug hair.

I lay back in the hot water and close my eyes, considering Derek's words. He likes me. He wants to keep me. He says he's not letting go.

But will he?

He seems sincere.

Unbidden and without approval, memories flood me like I'm watching a movie behind my closed eyelids.

Trevor.

Trevor Daniels was my first and only love. We met freshmen year of undergrad, and I was so taken with him, I immediately fell head over heels. I watch the good times flicker in my memory. The magic. The perfect night at winter formal when we danced under twinkle lights and he kissed me and told me how beautiful and special I was.

More sweet memories. Dates that made me feel precious, fun with friends, and watching him walk toward me in the quad with a huge smile on his face. Then, once I was sure, deeply positive that I was going to love this man for the rest of my life, the relationship started to change.

Trevor disappeared for days on end with no contact. Yelled at me for "flirting" with his friends. Told me I was being clingy and overemotional.

Several memories are the hardest to think on because I turned a blind eye for so long. Walking in on Trevor cornering my roommate with a predatory smile and the fear in my roommate's eyes. More than one waitress made to feel uncomfortable at his outrageous flirting when he thought I wasn't looking. Finding him at a bar leaning into different girls until he happened to notice my presence.

Then, the darkest memories. Trevor laughing at me and calling me stupid, telling me he never loved me, and I was just a momentary distraction...and not even a good one. Breaking up with me and spreading wild rumors about me to all our friends, forcing me out of his social circle. My roommate rolling her eyes and telling me I should've known better as I skipped class to cry my eyes out.

I open my eyes as the memories dissipate. She was right. I should've known better.

I consider Derek. My feelings for Trevor can't hold a candle to my feelings for Derek. I'm in deep. I have stronger feelings for Derek's eyes than I did for Trevor's entire person during the whole relationship. Derek isn't the same as Trevor; even I can see that. He is kind, sincere, and a Christian. He doesn't just want my body, he wants me. Right?

My mental picture of Derek with hearts and rainbows drawn around his head starts to cloud as doubt and fear seep in.

He is recently rededicated, but before that, he was quite the ladies' man. What if he is sincere in the moment but later loses interest? How can I know he is feeling as deeply as he says he is? How can I know that he won't drop me in a few months when he gets bored or finds a new shiny thing to play with?

I have never been one to have low self-esteem, but it's not a secret that men have never stuck around me for long. I have long since pictured my life alone, and I'm happy with it. However, I did become almost addicted to dating. Though I never anticipated meeting someone who could actually change the future I'd decided for myself, I still enjoyed the distraction. At least my escapades make for good stories.

But now...Derek.

Derek has broken the mold. Shattered my dreams. Put every fantasy I've ever had to shame. Instantly changed my future, making the only acceptable possibility being with him.

I guess the issue isn't guarding my heart against getting hurt at this point. I'm so far in it's unavoidable that I'll be crushed. I guess the issue is trying to prevent my heart from being completely decimated. Honestly, I'm not even sure that's possible, but maybe, if I keep my distance and stick to the once a week dates for a while, it'll give me a chance to see if he really means it when he says he isn't going anywhere. My mind clears and I resolve to not give in.

Space. I need space.

* * *

I am supposed to go swimming with Matt's family today, but instead, I get up at the crack of dawn and drive to Atlanta. I text Brittany and Derek that something with work has come up, and I have to go see a client, then I turn my phone off. Cowardly? Absolutely. In my defense, I am deep in panic mode.

The further away I get, the more tears stream down my face. Brittany told me not to fight it, but I don't think she understands. I can't fight it. It's already done. That leaves me one defense; and y'all already know I'm a runner.

I spend the weekend in Atlanta, catching up with old friends and doing marginal paperwork to assuage my guilt over lying to everyone by saying I am here for a client. I don't enjoy lying but I think of it as self-preservation. I finally turn my phone back on Sunday afternoon before my drive home. I am not surprised to find multiple messages from Derek, Brittany, Matt, and even Mom. As if turning my phone on sends some invisible beacon to my loved ones, it immediately rings with a call from Brittany.

"Hey there!" I answer casually as if I haven't been hiding out ignoring all their calls and texts like the yellow-bellied coward I am.

"Girl, you are in so much trouble," she says unhappily with heavy emphasis on the last words.

I wince because I have no doubt she is telling the truth. "I know. I'm sorry."

"Grady was beside himself you didn't come swimming. Derek was beside himself you cut your phone off. And Matt was beside himself that you seemed to have disappeared from the planet with barely a word to any of us," she rants.

I feel terrible. I really do. I'm a terrible person. I also feel kind of great, though. It's nice to feel so loved and wanted. "And you? Were you beside yourself?" I ask impishly.

Brittany huffs. "No, I get it. I mean, did it feel great to have my best friend, sister really, ignoring my calls and texts? No. Was it awesome to be stuck at home with three cranky, needy men by myself? No. Did I miss you? Yes. But hey, I get it."

"Not much for a guilt trip, are you?" I ask flatly.

"I said I get it, but I didn't say I was okay with it." The humor in her voice is clear.

"Thanks, Brittany. I owe you," I say with a smile.

"You on your way home?" she asks, her tone lightening.

"I am hurtling through time and space as we speak," I answer, although I'm still not sure I'm happy about it.

"You better stop by when you get home. And, if you want to be assured of a warm welcome, you should bring ice cream," Brittany warns.

"I thought Grady couldn't have ice cream after dinner anymore?"

"Not for Grady, for me! Weren't you listening? I spent the weekend with three cranky, whiney men. No one deserves ice cream more than me," she declares without an ounce of teasing.

I laugh. "You got it, sister. See you soon!"

I stop at the grocery store on the way home, appropriately repentant. I don't even head into my house when I pull in the driveway, just go straight over to Brittany and Matt's, ice cream in tow.

"Hey, guys!" I greet as I walk through the door. Just as anticipated, Matt, Brittany, and Grady are gathered on the couch for movie night. "Hey! You're watching *Trolls* without me?" I object.

"Aunt Maddy!" Grady yells as he runs at me, throwing himself in my arms. Always awesome when he does that.

"Serves you right, worrying us all weekend," Matt grumbles without moving from his place on the couch.

"Aunt Maddy, why were you gone all weekend?" Grady asks me, brown eyes big and sorrowful.

"I was out of town, Buddy, I'm sorry. I missed you. Tell me what you did." Distraction is the name of the game folks.

While Grady gives me a play-by-play of his entire weekend, Brittany puts the ice cream in the freezer and Matt glares at me from the couch.

"Get comfortable, we are unpausing the movie," Brittany announces when she returns to the couch. Grady and I snuggle up on the chair and ottoman while Matt and Brittany stay on the couch, and we finished watching *Trolls* together. True to form, Grady falls asleep about half an hour in. I savor holding him while he sleeps, enjoying the feel of his small body pressed against mine. The trust and adoration of a child should never be taken for granted, and I can't adore this little boy anymore if he were my very own.

When the movie ends, Matt kisses Brittany's temple and they get up from the couch. Matt picks Grady up from off me and carries him tenderly to bed, Brittany trailing him. The picture they make touches my heart in a way I never thought possible. I've always loved my brother but watching him be a great dad is indescribably awesome.

When they return, Brittany makes a bee line for the kitchen and Matt relaxes on the couch, eyeing me again. "So, Mads, did you have a good weekend?" he asks sardonically.

"Despite your mocking tone, yes I did," I say haughtily. He thinks he knows so much.

"Liar," Brittany calls from the kitchen.

"Agreed," Matt adds with a frown.

I ignore the fact that I did indeed have a crappy weekend. "Do you two just want to tell me what's going on with me?"

"No, no, we would much rather ask you questions and have you lie to us," Matt replies with a healthy dose of sarcasm.

"Point taken. You drop the attitude and I'll be as honest as I can," I promise solemnly.

Matt's eyes narrow. "Done, although I recognize the loophole you gave yourself, counselor."

I wink. Can't get anything past this one.

Brittany brings Matt and me a bowl of ice cream before sitting on the couch and snuggling into Matt with one of her own.

"Thanks, baby," he murmurs, giving her a sweet kiss before starting in on the bowl.

"So, talk," Brittany says plainly as she lifts the spoon to her lips.

"I just needed some space. Things with Derek are great but...intense. I just needed a minute to clear my head."

"If he's so great, why do you need space?" Matt asks suspiciously.

"Because she's scared," Brittany answers for me.

Matt's annoyance gives way to tender concern. "Freshmen year?"

"Freshmen year," I confirm. We have never spoken about Trevor before, but Matt knows something happened and I know he knows.

"Your freshmen year or hers?" Brittany asks Matt in confusion.

Matt looks to me, silently asking me to fill in the blanks.

"I fell in love my freshmen year of college." I heave a sigh. "Long story short, I fell hard, he was a crappy person, dropped me like a hot potato, broke my heart."

Matt's eyes narrow. "She's being flippant, but she was a shell of a person for at least two years after that."

Brittany gazes at me with concern as she processes my and Matt's words. Finally she says, "You're worried about picking the wrong one again."

Her words send a chill through my heart. How does an ocean of insecurity and fear get summarized in one neat little sentence? It is embarrassing to admit, but in the interest of being as honest as possible, as promised, I nod wordlessly.

Brittany hands her bowl to Matt and crosses over to my chair, cuddling next to me and taking me into her arms. "Oh, Maddy."

After a few minutes, and a successful bout of holding my threatening tears at bay, I say, "I'm fine, I just needed a minute to clear my head."

"And?" Matt asked.

"And what?" I ask in confusion.

"It clear?" he presses.

I consider his question. I didn't really decide or resolve anything, I just ignored my feelings for two days. Matt's expression grows increasingly disappointed the longer I deliberate the question.

"I don't know," I answer honestly.

Brittany grips me tighter. "Oh, Maddy," she says again, this time her voice of pity is tinged with disappointment.

Geez. I hate being such a girl.

"You aren't acting like a girl, Maddy, you are acting like a coward," Matt says sternly.

Not realizing I have spoken aloud, I am surprised at his words and tone. Is it too much to ask for a little sympathy?

"I think what Matt is trying to say, and could maybe say with more kindness," Brittany starts with a pointed look at her husband, "is that it's okay to be scared as long as you're honest. With yourself and with Derek."

"Buck up buttercup and face it head-on, just like anything else," Matt pipes in from the couch.

"Easier said than done, I would say," I mutter.

Matt rolls his eyes. "Of course it is. That's why it's worth it. That's how it makes you better."

I stare at him. "Is that how you got over it after yours?"

Matt was engaged in college, but the girl dumped him and ran off with his friend. Our situations are similar enough in that we both fell for and trusted the wrong people.

Matt nods, smiling fondly at Brittany. "Absolutely. We went slow. Talked, got to know each other. It was scary, sure, I mean, she had scars, I had scars, but what we have together is real. What we have together was worth the risk. I had to trust her, but I had to trust myself. I'm older, wiser, and I'm not prone to surrounding myself with disingenuous people any longer."

Brittany gets up and goes to him, sitting across his lap and kissing him. "Well said."

"It was," I agree wholeheartedly, turning his words over in my mind.

He gives me a pointed glare and, removing the easiness from his voice, goes back to tough love. "Look Maddy, at some point you need to let go of what happened. That was freshmen year. That's why I don't get what's going on right now. You are the fiercest fighter I know. A force of nature that bows to no man. Yet you are running away to Atlanta instead of facing your fears and running right over them like you always have."

I can't stop the tears from falling; I had no idea he thinks so much of me. He's right. This isn't me. I don't give in to fear. "You're right. This isn't me." I sit forward in new determination.

Matt nods and adds emphatically, "That's right. Nothing and no one scares my sister."

I bob my head, catching his confidence. "Nothing. No one. I'm not a freshman anymore. I'm a grown woman. I have good judgment. I can do this."

"Yeah, you can. No more running. No more hiding. Straight through, it's the only way," Matt coaches forcefully, pointing at me.

I continue bobbing my head, creep to the edge of the chair. "Straight through," I echo with resolve.

"Good. Glad that's settled," he finishes easily, nuzzling Brittany's neck, who is watching us with amusement. "Ready for bed, baby?"

She nods and kisses him, getting up from his lap and walking over to give me a hug. "You are awesome, and I love you. Don't shut me out again," she demands with a pinch.

"I love you, Mads," Matt says, bending to give me a hug.

"Love you, Matt. Thanks."

As I leave Matt and Brittany's and go home, I consider Matt's words. He is right. Certainly, the fear isn't gone, but I have new confidence in myself. Things are different now. I'm different now. I'm not a starry-eyed freshman surrounded by frat guys and sorority girls. What I have with Derek is worth the risk.

When I get home, I call Derek. I consider waiting until the morning, but I'm still riding high on Matt's locker room pep talk and I don't want to waste the overconfidence. Although he has every right not to, he answers.

"Hey there," I call cheerily in greeting.

"Hey, are you home?" he asks sleepily.

"Yeah. I'm sorry, did I wake you?" I should have thought of that. I should be a more thoughtful person. Sometimes I just get so excited and in my own head and I just jump in with two feet without thinking at all.

"No, I was just about to head to bed," he says without inflection.

He isn't offering much here, but I kind of deserve it I guess. I decide to ride the wave of overconfidence I am feeling and jump in with both feet. "I'm sorry I didn't respond to your messages this weekend. I turned my phone off while I was in Atlanta."

Silence. Should I wait? Say something?

"Wouldn't have been very effective hiding if you answered your messages," he grumbles.

The overconfidence starts to wane a little. "Yeah, well, it was very effective hiding, not really effective of anything else, however."

"Oh yeah?" he replies mildly.

Is it just me or does he sound bored?

"Yeah, so, no more hiding," I boldly state. I hope I can live up to that. I've kind of gotten carried away with my new can-do attitude and maybe made a bigger statement than I intended. Dang Matt and his pep talks!

"Oh yeah?" At least he sounds marginally more interested.

"Yeah," I state lamely.

Okay. That's all I got.

I feel dizzy. What just happened? What am I doing here? This was a terrible idea. Matt is stupid and doesn't know anything and I should have never listened to him. What was I thinking? Is this like that time he tried to convince me that mud was chocolate pudding?

Derek sighs heavily, seemingly releasing some of his tension. "So, what did you do while in hiding? I assume shopping was involved?" he asks in a lighter tone.

I gulp in surprise as my spiral of panic recedes. "Absolutely. You know me, a sucker for anything shiny and colorful," I say in relief.

Matt is a brilliant, brilliant man.

Chapter 10

Maddy

The next morning, because God has a sense of humor that we as mere mortals will never understand, I am assigned to an audit for a client in Atlanta for the next week at least, probably longer. I pack for the week, just in case, and I drive right back to Atlanta, staying in a nicer hotel than before at the expense of the office.

Breaking the news to Matt and Brittany is hilarious. They all but require a notarized note from my employer proving my story. Derek isn't as suspicious, but still very growly at the news.

I spend the week threading through the financial statements of a small company and working my way through an IRS audit with them. Derek texts me every day and calls me every night. It is unexpected and...nice. He texts me first thing in the morning to start the day, again usually sometime around lunch, and then when his shift ends. Then he calls around ten at night because that's when I am done with work.

I know. TEN AT NIGHT. But it's not forever. I feel certain if I just keep telling myself that I'll be more okay with it.

I would never tell him this, and I'm barely admitting it to myself, but I live for those messages and phone calls. To know he is thinking of me, at least a fraction of the time I am thinking of him. This time of getting to know him and just spending time talking to him has done a lot to quiet my fears.

Every night we talk a little longer. The first night I cut it short at thirty minutes, but every night it goes a few minutes more as we talk about our day, our interests. Around the middle of the week, we start discussing our dreams, our goals, and our favorite memories. The phone calls get so long by the end of the week that I'm not getting much sleep by the time we hang up.

It is with great disappointment on Friday that I give him the bad news.

"Hey, Princess. How was your day?" It's how Derek starts all our conversations. Every time he calls me Princess, I want to collapse in a puddle and declare my undying love to him. You can understand how this might be problematic.

"Long. How was yours?" I ask in a disappointed breath.

"Good. Got a case wrapped up. You sound tired, you okay?" he asks in concern.

I smile. I am tired. I'm exhausted actually. I've been working eighteen hours a day and then spending half the night talking to him or dreaming about him. It's catching up to me in a big way.

"I have bad news," I start, not really wanting to admit to myself how disappointed I am. "Looks like I'm going to be here another week, maybe two."

He is silent for a minute before asking, "Not coming home for the weekend?"

"No, we are working every day until this thing is done. Weekends included."

Ugh. I know. It's the worst. But it's not forever, it's not forever, it's not forever.

The audit, of course, won't be taking place on the weekends; the IRS are federal employees after all. My client, and myself for that matter, need to be one hundred percent prepared for every question and contingency, and that means working on weekends. The only solace I find is that this also requires three employees from my client's firm to work the same hours. Does that make me a terrible person? Don't answer that.

I hear him sigh. "Well that sucks. I miss you," he says softly. Sweetly. The heart palpitations I'm getting all too familiar with kick up.

"I miss you too. Going to the pool tomorrow?" I ask, picturing him flexing as he plays with Grady, bare-chested, droplets of water glistening on his chest. I stop the train of thought right there before I need to pray for forgiveness.

I hear him smile. "Yeah. Mom and Dad are headed to the beach house soon, so this is the last weekend before they are gone."

"I forgot they leave for the summer," I mention sadly. I'm missing their last weekend.

"Yeah, we've done it for as long as I can remember. The house was my grandparents'."

"That's nice. Wish I was there to send them off," I say wistfully, because I do. I'm kicking myself for missing last Saturday, and the Saturday before.

"Me too. Wish you had been there last Saturday. I don't know who missed you more, me or Mom. She loves visiting with you, and getting fashion advice," he says in amusement.

I smile. "Yeah, I regret missing last Saturday too."

Derek hesitates. "Wanna tell me why you ran?" he asks gently.

I freeze. We haven't talked about the why of it. I didn't exactly offer to bare my soul to him and he didn't exactly ask, so I just...didn't. I fight the urge to cower in a corner and deny any knowledge of recent events and instead face this thing head-on. Cause apparently that's what I do. Or so I'm told.

I take a deep breath and start pacing my hotel room. "We had a great date Friday night," I start.

"Yeah..." he replies hesitantly.

"It was great. So great. Everything was...great." Although I mean this with all my heart, I know that my choice of adjective is lame.

I hear him smile despite my lack of vocabulary. "Great."

I cringe at myself. I'm being such a girl. Power through. That's what I do. Don't blink. I clear my throat and straighten my shoulders. I got this. "I just needed space, I think. It was so great it was overwhelming."

"I'm not going anywhere. If you need space, you can have space," he says sincerely. "I would prefer it if you didn't go a hundred and fifty miles away every time you need space, but we could work up to that if you like," he finishes lightly.

I smile. Of course, he's understanding. Because unicorns are real and there really are pots of gold at the end of the rainbow.

"Maddy?" he asks when I remain silent.

"Yeah?"

"How much more space do you need?" he asks. He sounds a little worried maybe?

I sigh in melancholy. "At the moment Derek, I wish I was in your arms," I say honestly. "But I can't promise I won't freak out again." I feel the need to clarify because, honestly, I can't tell if it's self-preservation or self-sabotage at this point.

"That's okay, Princess. I'll be here when you're done freaking out," Derek says smoothly, sounding relieved.

I smile, and for the first time, I don't wonder if he's telling the truth.

"So, what's on the agenda for tomorrow?" he asks me.

"Same. Get up. Go to work. Come home. Talk to you."

"I hope you get done early tomorrow at least. After all the hours you've put in this week."

"Might as well get the work done. I don't have anything else to do," I mutter.

Derek exhales dejectedly. "Another week, huh?"

"Maybe two," I match his tone.

I can't help it, but I yawn. The week is catching up with me.

"I should let you go get some sleep. You're tired," Derek says regretfully.

I hate that idea. "No! Talk to me," I plead, crawling into bed anyway.

"What do you wanna hear?" he asks, and I can tell he's smiling.

"Tell me about your favorite family memory of growing up," I request with another yawn.

"That's not hard. It's definitely the time we were at the zoo and a monkey hit Brittany over the head with its huge hand. Greatest moment of my life." He replies with amusement.

"Tell me about it," I demand, wanting nothing more than to hear his voice.

And just like that, I fall asleep with Derek's hypnotizing rumble in my ear.

Chapter 11

Derek

The first week sucked. The second week was torture.

Maddy has been in Atlanta for two weeks now, working eighteen-hour days and straight through the weekends. Making do with phone calls for two weeks didn't seem that hard until she confirmed it would be an additional week yesterday. I have listened to her voice grow more and more tired for two weeks, and I'm over it.

I haven't seen her. I haven't looked into those gorgeous blue eyes. I haven't touched her. Haven't hugged her. Haven't kissed her in two weeks, and I'm done.

I was partially glad for the distance the first week because it was clear she needed it, and honestly, the distance helped me control myself. Now, she sounds less like she needs space and more like she's miserable too, and for that reason, I'm on my bike heading to Atlanta.

She told me last night she was taking Saturday to sleep late and watch movies, and it sounds like music to my ears. It's a two-hour drive, but I get up at dawn to make it. I want to have some time to stop and put together a little something after finding her hotel.

My first stop is to the hotel's front desk to get her room number. I feel a little bad flashing my badge, but not for long. I walk down the street and get her favorite coffee, along with some breakfast Danish and muffins, and take it all back to the hotel and proceed up to her room.

I realize belatedly maybe I should've checked my hair or something. I've had a helmet on for two hours, but then I remember I don't care. I knock on her door and hear silence. I knock again, and I finally hear muttering and movement. It's clear she was serious about sleeping late.

My mouth drops open when she opens the door. She's in a tank top and shorts; she has bedhead and sleepy eyes. She's the most gorgeous thing I've ever seen. It hits me in the gut, just like it always does, and dang if I don't want to wake up to that every morning.

Her eyes widen in surprise and I smile widely, hoping I made the right call. I laugh when she flies at me, wrapping her arms around my neck. I would hold her, but my hands are full, one with a bag of baked goods and the other with our coffees.

"Hey, Princess. Up for company?" I greet.

She doesn't say anything, she just kisses me, hard.

Okay, now these things in my hands really need to go. I kiss her back and walk her backward into her room. I kick the door closed behind me and set the things down on something behind her before taking her into my arms and really kissing her.

After a few minutes, she pulls back suddenly and says, "I just realized I have morning breath," with great consternation.

I laugh and pull her head back to mine, giving her a long and slow kiss, the kind she can feel to her toes. When I pull back, I lean my forehead against hers. "I missed you."

"I missed you too," she says without opening her mouth much.

I grin. "Go on, brush your teeth. I brought coffee and pastries, though, so easy on the toothpaste."

She beams at me, saying, "My hero," before giving me a quick kiss and turning to the bathroom.

* * *

Maddy

I look at myself in the mirror and cringe. Bedhead...and not the cute kind. He's seen me in a tank top more times than I can count, but my shorts are a little too short, so I try to make sure they are pulled down and covering everything.

I brush my teeth and put my hair up in a bun, then wrap the hotel robe around me before going back out and facing Derek.

Derek.

I can't contain my joy that he is here. I fling the door open and scan the room until I find him, unpacking a bag of pastries at the table by the window. He's ditched his leather jacket and is in a plain, black t-shirt that stretches over his chest and biceps perfectly. I bounce over to him and wrap my arms around him from behind.

He came.

He spins in my arms and pulls me into a tight hug. "No more space?" he asks, nuzzling my hair.

I squeeze him tighter. "Nope." I can't describe how good it was talking to him every night on the phone. It was the quality time I needed to get to know him and calm my fears and anxiety, but with my fears successfully calmed, I'm ready to move on, or at least be in the same county.

He lets me go. "I brought coffee and Danish. I wasn't sure what you liked, so I brought a little bit of everything."

My eyes glance over the spread on the table. Carbs. Precious, wonderful, delectable carbs. "Yum," I say as I pick up a cherry cheese Danish and the coffee cup. "What do you want to do today?" I ask around my food, before taking a sip of coffee.

"Whatever you want to do. Just hanging out here is fine with me. I know you wanted to rest today," he mentions.

I eye the bed and determine hanging out in my hotel room is not the greatest option. I trust Derek implicitly, but I don't see the need to tempt myself unnecessarily. And that's exactly what it would be, even though curling up and watching movies all day sounds magnificent. When I glance back at him, he's watching me, and I can't name the emotion his eyes contain.

"Don't trust me?" he asks. His face is, as always, carefully blank.

He thinks he's so big and bad. He knows nothing. I get up and, in a dangerously risky move, I sit on his lap and put my arms around his shoulders. "You don't scare me, but for the record, I should scare you." His eyes widen in surprise before lighting on fire, then he takes my mouth in one of those all-consuming kisses he's so known for.

He suddenly pulls back and pushes me off his lap gently. "Right." He clears his throat. "So staying in is a bad idea," he says to his coffee cup.

Point made, I go back to my chair. "We could take a walk in the park across the street, go see a movie, or hit some of the tourist stuff in town. Although, the tourist stuff will probably be crazy busy on a Saturday." I take another huge bite of Danish and sipped my coffee while Derek chews and thinks it over.

"Why don't we walk around the downtown market for a little while, do some shopping? We can decide where to go from there," he suggests.

I haven't been to the market in ages. "Perfect."

And this can't be stressed enough, he is. He's perfect.

We finish breakfast and I mentally run through the clothes I have here. Mostly all work clothes, but I think I have a casual but cute outfit I kept in my suitcase from my first weekend here.

"Thanks for breakfast," I say as I snag a muffin. Ah, the carbs.

His smile couldn't be more attractive. "Had to make sure I was welcome. I know how you value your sleep."

I grin and chew. It's true. I don't think sleep can compare with Derek, though, but I do not tell him this.

I sip my coffee as he begins to clean up. "If you're done, I'll go downstairs while you get ready. I need to run a quick errand," Derek says, grabbing his leather jacket. I don't ask what kind of errand because I'm certain if he wanted me to know he would have told me.

"Meet you downstairs in half an hour?" I ask.

He bends to kiss me softly before saying, "Half an hour."

Swoon.

I watch him walk out the door with a determined stride, and I kick it into high gear. I have to shower and get dressed with full make-up in half an hour. Why do I always think I can do that? Spoiler alert: I can't.

Forty-five minutes later, I enter the lobby, proud of myself for keeping it under an hour. I scan the room until I find Derek, who is moving toward me while his eyes roam my body. The look of appreciation in his eyes affirms my outfit choice of leggings, a flowy tunic, and boots. I bought these boots last weekend specifically for riding on his bike.

"Nice boots," he says with a growl, placing a hard kiss on my mouth. I grin when he pulls back and takes my hand, weaving his fingers with mine. "Bike's parked out front."

He pulls me through the lobby and hands me his leather jacket when we come to a stop beside his bike. I put it on and again consider getting my own. Honestly, it's just a matter of time before I break down and do, but I want to soak in as much time wearing his as possible.

If driving on country roads on the bike is exhilarating, driving in the city is its adrenaline-charged, nerve-wracking cousin. In one word: terrifying. Derek easily weaves through traffic until we come to a stop right outside the market, but getting side-swiped by a fellow motorist was a real and present danger in my mind the whole ride. Parking for the bike isn't an issue, so that's a positive, and I decide my freak out isn't worth mentioning to Derek.

"You okay?" he asks with downturned brows when I tug his helmet and jacket off.

I nod somewhat jerkily and take a deep breath. "Good. You?"

He smirks. "You know, I know the difference between you holding on for balance and you bruising my ribs from fear."

I lift my chin. "You almost always ask questions you already know the answer to and it's annoying."

Derek laughs at this and gets off the bike. "You're just annoyed cause that's the thing you do, and you don't like that other people do it too."

I eye him. He's good. Very good. Can't resist that grin, though.

Derek presents his arm. "Shall we?"

I look him up and down one more time to make a point (that does not have to do with the fit of his jeans) and take his arm with a grin of my own.

"I haven't been here in ages. This will be fun," I mention as we stroll through the sidewalk vendors on our way to the main avenue where the more upscale stores are located. The market is a large shopping area with shops and restaurants lining the street. Picnic tables with umbrellas dot the sidewalk, particularly outside the restaurants. Between the shopping and the food, it's a popular destination for locals and tourists combined.

"Did you used to come here a lot when you lived in Atlanta?" Derek asks with interest.

I shake my head, remembering my time here. "Not really. I worked a lot."

"Every weekend?" Derek asks knowingly.

"I mean, not every minute of every weekend, but yeah, pretty much," I admit.

"That why you decided to move home?" he asks casually.

"I missed my family. With Matt marrying Brittany and precious Grady, I wanted to be closer. I was tired of being alone," I explain easily. I can feel Derek watching closely, so I intentionally get distracted by some scarves on display outside a shop's open doors. "Ooh, look!"

I finger through a few before taking Derek's hand and lacing my fingers with his and moving on. Derek's scrutiny is unsettling to say the least. Mostly because he sees me more clearly than any other person on the planet. I love that about him until I don't.

"What do you think about going in there?" Derek uses his chin to point to a leather boutique displaying belts and jackets in the window.

"I guess it was only a matter of time anyway," I mutter as we walk over.

"You can still wear mine you know, it's just that now you'll have your own too," he rationalizes.

I pout and follow him into the store. "S'not the same," I complain with a sniff.

Derek holds up a jacket and asks, "What do you think?"

I scrunch my nose in disgust. "You're not serious right?"

"What? This is a good option, very functional," he says inspecting the lining.

"I don't have a lot of functional in my wardrobe, Derek," I reply dryly. He smirks. "I've noticed."

I roll my eyes just as a salesman walks up. "Can I help you?"

I let Derek answer because this is his crusade. "We are looking for a leather jacket for her, something she can wear on the back of a motorcycle."

The salesman looks Derek up and down and then me.

"Something that doesn't look like that," I clarify, pointing to the jacket in Derek's hand with distaste.

The salesman offers an experienced grin. "Ah, a lady with distinguished tastes."

I smile while Derek frowns and puts the rejected jacket back on its rack.

"Follow me, I think we have just the thing. I'm Brad by the way," the salesman says as he turns and walks to the back of the store. There he hands me a jacket to try on. "Small, right?" he asks eyeing my chest.

"Medium," I correct. His eyes flicker to mine in amusement, but he switches out the jacket in his hands for a larger size. My chest tries not to take offense to his assumption.

He helps me into the jacket and I zip it up, turning toward a mirror. I scrunch my nose. "Too T-Birds."

The salesman nods and takes the jacket back, and I look at Derek in the mirror. He is glaring at Brad in a very amusing way.

"Try this." Brad hands me another jacket.

I put it on and zip it. It fit better, but I still shake my head. "Too many zippers."

Brad taps his lips with a finger, looking me up and down before taking the jacket and saying, "I'll be right back."

I turn to Derek and put my hands on his hips, capturing his eyes with mine. "You're adorable," I say with a grin and a peck on his nose.

Derek's brows lower and he frowns. He opens his mouth to say something, but Brad comes back.

"This just came in. I haven't had a chance to display it yet, but I think this might be what you are looking for," our shopping host says as he holds out the jacket.

I narrow my eyes at him. "That looks small," I say without amusement.

He smiles patiently and requests, "Humor me."

SHUT THE FRONT DOOR

I let him help me into the jacket and it fits like a glove. I zip it and the clean lines and cropped cut are perfect.

I do my mirror thing, eyeing myself from every angle before looking back into Derek's eyes, which are no longer trained on Brad but on me.

"What do you think?" I ask.

He smiles and there's heat in his eyes. "Gorgeous."

I look to Brad, who has a pleased but smug smile on his face. "Thanks, Brad! It's perfect."

"My pleasure," he coolly replies.

I take it off and follow Brad up front to pay for the jacket until Derek nudges me out of the way.

"Derek..." I start in confusion.

"I got it," he says, handing Brad a credit card.

I don't make a scene, but I will address this. I didn't even ask the price of the jacket and, given where we are, I know it's expensive. I have always had an independent streak. I can't help but protest any authoritative male in my life who tries to financially control me in any way, though I admit I may have become oversensitive to this issue throughout the years. Derek takes my hand as we exit the store, carrying the bag in his other hand and looking particularly pleased with himself.

"Derek," I start carefully. It's a fine line between independence and ungrateful.

He puts an arm around my shoulders and draws me close to his side as we walk. "Yes, Princess?" He kisses my temple and I consider swooning for a minute.

"You shouldn't have done that," I say with concern.

We are strolling along the shops again and he pauses to look in the window of a toy store. "Do what?" he asks distractedly.

I stop in front of the toy store and turn to face him. "You shouldn't have bought that for me, Derek. I am perfectly capable of buying my own jacket," I say firmly.

He looks at me in confusion. "I know. I wanted to."

"It's too much, Derek, you shouldn't have done that." It's more than being capable of taking care of myself, it's also partially about the money. I don't want him spending a ton of money on me when it's not that much money for me and it might be a lot of money to him.

His eyes narrow as he asks stubbornly, "It's not too much. You needed a jacket, I got you a jacket. What's the problem?"

Uh oh. Am I straddling the ungrateful line?

I take a breath and eye him, suddenly uncertain of doubling down on my position. "It's too expensive for a gift, Derek. You should have let me get it."

His lips press together and eyes me for several seconds. "You aren't the only one with money, Maddy. Relax." His face is expressionless, but his voice is cold.

This worries me. I have bungled it, and I tried so hard not to. I try backpedaling.

"That's not what I meant. It's just a lot for a gift," I argue, hoping he can read the intention in my face. He's so good at reading me. He reads right through my thoughts and get to the point every time. I'm hoping he can also see pure intentions.

Derek crosses his bulky arms over his broad chest, and I try to peel my eyes away from the incredibly attractive picture he presents. I remind myself now is not the time to get distracted, but my man is HOT.

"Would it be too much from your parents, or from Matt?" he asks seriously.

My head jerks as my eyes reluctantly leave his chest and move to his. "What?"

"Would you consider the cost if it were from your parents or Matt?" he repeated.

I search my mind in confusion. "Of course not, but you're..."

"I'm what?" he asks, deceptively lowly.

"You're not my family," I explain pointedly.

He cocks an eyebrow at me, then blows out a breath, dropping his arms. "Look, you needed a jacket, I got you a jacket. It's not a big thing. Let's just drop it."

I eye him carefully, suddenly wanting the same thing. I made my concerns known, he clearly isn't trying to control me in any way, and I don't want to make a big thing of this. This doesn't feel like something we should spend our time arguing over when he made the trip all the way here just to see me. I feel silly making nothing into something. I walk into him and wrap him in my arms, pressing a kiss to his lips. "Thank you."

His arms fold over me and he kisses me back gently. "You're welcome." The earlier tension is gone and replaced by warmth again. "Come on, I wanna look at stuff for Grady. His birthday is coming up."

I smile and follow him into the toy store, shaking off the uncomfortable feeling of Derek spending so much money on me.

Derek nods toward a display of Legos. "What do you think?"

I eye them in indifference. "Typical birthday gift."

"What do you mean?"

I turn to him dramatically. "I've been meaning to talk to you about this." I very seriously put my hand on his shoulder and look forlorn. "You need to step up your uncle game. It's shameful, really." I shake my head sullenly. "You don't get Grady something any kid from his class could get him. You need a gift that will blow it out of the park and make you a legend."

Derek grins, now getting it. "I'm open to suggestions."

I lean in as if telling him a secret. "My general rule of thumb is to start with anything the parents would hate. Also, anything another parent would get is immediately off the list."

"I have so much to learn from you," he says with admiration.

I smile cheekily. "Yeah, you do. It's okay, I'll show you the way," I reassure him, patting his shoulder.

"What are you getting him for his birthday?" he asks with interest.

I dramatically put my hand to my chest. "How dare you?" I wag my finger in his face. "Don't try to copy my paper, Derek Masters. But if you are exceptionally nice to me, I'll help you with your gift."

Derek chuckles. "Deal."

We stroll through the toy store and I point out possible options to give him ideas.

"So what you are saying is," Derek starts, "consider anything that can cause a mess, that's incredibly loud, or that he can shoot at his parents repeatedly."

I nod yes. "Good places to start, all of them. I'm currently trying to get Grady interested in drums so I can give him a drum set for Christmas, but he doesn't seem overly enthusiastic about it."

I watch Derek laugh and admire his attractiveness. He puts his arm around my shoulders and pulls me toward the exit. I wrap my arm around his waist as we continue strolling through the market. I idly wonder if anything will ever feel as good and as right as Derek's arm around my shoulders, me pressed against his side.

We go into a couple other shops before Derek turns to me. "Break for lunch?"

"Sure. Where?" I smile and follow willingly.

"There are few restaurants this way." He points with his chin and tugs me along.

We pick a BBQ place with a borderline inappropriate name. Why people think that clever puns on "butts" is an appetizing name for a restaurant, I will never know. We sit outside under an umbrella and people watch as we eat.

"You look like you are thinking of something awfully hard over there, Princess. Care to share?" Derek asks, popping a french fry into his mouth.

I blush. "I like to people watch. I like to make up stories about them sometimes," I admit in embarrassment.

Derek slides his chair near mine and, going along with the game, asks, "Who are we looking at?"

I gesture to the left. "That couple over there. It's a first date."

Derek watches them for a moment. "Definitely first date. How do you think it's going?"

I watch them for several moments before answering, "She likes him, but he doesn't like her."

Derek turns his head to me. "What makes you say that?"

"See how she's leaning in? She's practically hanging on his every word. I bet she has their kids' names picked out. But he keeps sitting back and looking at his phone. My guess is he has another girl he's really interested in. That or he's checking the stats of a basketball game or something."

Derek's lips twitch in amusement. "Okay, what about them?" he asks, nodding to the family sitting a few tables over from the couple.

"It's a family outing. Dad works in one of these tall buildings doing something in middle management and likely boring while Mom is a stay-at-home in the burbs. Probably northwest Atlanta area given their outfits," I judge.

"Wow. You are good at this." He sounds impressed.

"People are rarely original," I say sadly as I gaze around at the others in our surrounding area.

"I think you are pretty original," Derek says, nudging me with his shoulder.

I smile. "Thanks for thinking so." I turn and gesture to a couple to our right. "Your turn."

We sit and people watch for a while before spending another couple of hours strolling through the market. We walk hand-in-hand, sometimes with his arm around me, sometimes not, but almost always touching. The market is flooded with people despite the warmth of the day. There is a constant stream of people milling around and walking in and out of the stores that line the sidewalks. The sun is bright and hot as it reflects off the stone storefronts and concrete sidewalks.

"I should get you back," Derek eventually says, reluctantly. "Let you rest for the rest of the day before you get back to work tomorrow."

I frown. I know he has to leave, but that doesn't mean I have to like it. "Yeah, probably," I mutter in disappointment.

We head back to the bike and Derek hands me my new leather jacket to put on, handing me also his helmet to wear. "Should I take it a little slower this time?" he asks as he gets on the bike.

I shake my head and hop on behind him. "I trust you."

He weaves in and out of traffic the same as before until we are back at my hotel. He pulls up to the entrance under the overhang and cuts off the bike but doesn't get off. I reluctantly dismount and take off his helmet and toy with the chin strap before handing it back. I don't want him to go. "Thanks for coming. It was a great day," I say peeking up at him through my lashes.

Derek tugs my hand to pull me toward him and put his other hand on my waist. "I like you in that jacket, Mads."

His voice is thick and growly. I look up to his eyes and inch closer, pressing my lips to his. When we part, I keep my forehead on his and try not to embarrass myself by panting in his face. I am doing my best, but my heart is racing. "Call me when you get home?" I ask pitifully, trying to delay his exit.

He smiles affectionately. "Absolutely."

"I'll miss you," I whisper. I try to keep the words in, but they slip out in a rush.

Derek's hand squeezes my waist. "I'll miss you too, Maddy. Come home soon, okay?"

I kiss him again before watching him disappear into the busy street ahead.

I glumly turn to walk into the hotel and find a group of older ladies watching me. They look as if they've just finished lunching in the hotel restaurant. Some of them look interested and a couple disapproving.

"Try not to look so sullen, dear. Frown lines will be here before you know it. Besides, he looks like he'll be back," one of them says as I pass.

I snicker and continue through the hotel lobby, proceeding to my room. When I let myself in, I find a huge gift basket on the table consisting of a variety of bath products, movie candy and popcorn, and a few chick flick movies. I pull the card from the front of the basket and read it: To help you rest and relax until I can see you again. Love, Derek.

I fall backward on the bed and clutch the card to my chest.

Love Derek.

He has no idea.

I do. I so do.

Chapter 12

Derek

"Masters, you're with that new lawyer, right?"

I pull my gaze from the report I'm working on at my desk and look up at Green and Barnes coming toward me as they walk through the bullpen, the beat cops we'd run into on our first date. I narrow my eyes. "Why?" I ask suspiciously. I'm not real into office gossip.

Green smirks, sensing a fish on a hook. "It serious or is it just, you know?" He makes a lewd gesture with his hands, and my suspicious gaze becomes deadly.

"Get lost, Green, I'm busy," I growl, going back to my report.

"It's just that," he starts, casually leaning against my desk, "her assistant called to file a report of harassment against her, and if you're together...." He lets the pause linger.

My head snaps up and I jump out of my chair. "What? What happened?" I don't even try to contain my murderous expression as I take my gun out of my drawer and put my jacket on.

Green holds up his hands. "Easy man, she's not even in town."

I inch impatiently toward Green. "I know that. What happened?" I ask through clenched teeth.

Barnes steps in. "She does family law. Seems she helped a mom get custody of her kids and the dad is threatening her lawyer now. He has sent some angry letters, but today he stopped by Ms. Knight's office. The assistant wasn't scared but wanted to get it on record."

"You filed the report?" I confirm with Barnes.

Barnes nods in the affirmative. "And we left our direct contact information with the assistant."

I've always liked Barnes.

"So...I guess it's serious then?" Green persists waggling his eyebrows like a creeper.

Never liked Green though.

"Shut up, Green." I grab my keys and turn back to Barnes. "If you get a call, I want to know. I am your first call, got it?" I wait for him to nod before grabbing my helmet and heading for my bike. I ignore Green's comments at my back as I go, something about being whipped. I drive like a bat out of hell to get to Maddy's office, taking my frustration out on the traffic.

I drive straight to Maddy's law firm, which is in an office building in town, and nod at the receptionist at the large round desk in the lobby on my way to the elevator. I've already made friends with her, and she seems to like me, so she doesn't bother to stop me, especially since she's on the phone. She is the first friend I made in my courtship of Maddy. Never underestimate the receptionist; they hold the keys to the kingdom...or office building as is the case. I proceed past the law firm's front entrance and down the hall past dozens of non-descript doors until I reach Maddy's office. I stop in front of her assistant's desk. Macy is the second friend I made in my pursuit of Maddy.

"Took you long enough. I filed the report this morning," Macy states dryly, though with a twinkle in her eye. Macy is a middle-aged woman, who, if her hair was whiter, would bear a remarkable resemblance to Mrs. Claus. She does not have Mrs. Claus's countenance, however.

"Why didn't you call me?" I ask pointedly, not hiding my displeasure.

"I asked for you at the station, but you were out. I don't have your direct number," she explains pointedly.

I hand her my card. "Call my cell, Macy. Anything happens ever, call my cell, and then call the station."

"I assume you'd like to see the letters?" she presumes flatly.

"And to hear your account," I reply, holding steady with her stare.

Macy reaches for a folder. "I made you copies of the letters as well as my detailed account of the encounter right here."

I smile, impressed. We could use her at the station. Sensing my thoughts, as any good assistant does, Macy frowns. "You can't afford me."

I smirk and head to the chair beside Macy's desk to look through the file. It's very organized, the date the letters were received all stamped in succession. There are five, one a week since the ruling, each getting gradually more aggressive. I read Macy's account of the encounter, as she calls it, and it seems as though he was fairly calm, although anxious and jittery.

I close the file. "What do you think?"

She lifts a brow. "About what?"

"About him. What do you think about this guy after your chat this morning?" I inquire, watching her closely.

She considers this. "He was very calm. That's why I insisted on reporting it. It was too calm. The letters are one thing, and if he came barreling in here screaming, that's another thing entirely. We get that sometimes and it's always quickly diffused. They just need to scream and yell some. But this guy, he's up to something," she says definitively. "I'm glad Maddy is still in Atlanta."

I nod once because I agree on both counts. "She's lucky to have you. If you need anything, call me," I remind as I stand. I head back down to the lobby where the security office for the building is located. I have a serious conversation with their pathetic excuse for security guards, threatening each of them within an inch of their lives. Once they are looking contrite enough for me to feel better, I give out my business card and collect the manager's card, planning to call the owner of the company as soon as I leave.

I stop at the round receptionist desk on my way out. "Hey, Shelly."

"Hey, Derek. You hear about this morning?" she asks knowingly.

"Yeah. If you need anything now, you call me okay? I'll get here just as quick as I can with the cavalry," I promise seriously. Shelly's a good girl. I don't mind pledging her my protection.

She smiles and blushes. "Yeah, that Officer Green said that too."

I roll my eyes; I bet he did. I lean over Shelly's desk, propping my forearms on the raised edge. I'm about to do something I never do. Green's been asking for it, and I owe Barnes. I lower my voice like I'm telling her a secret. "You don't need to mess with Green, Shelly."

Her eyes widen. "Really?"

I shake my head. "Green is...not really into relationships. Now Barnes...he's a good guy." I can't resist putting in a good word for Barnes.

She smiles. "He caught my eye, but he didn't come to speak. Only Green did."

"That's because he was being respectful of Green," I explain, letting her in on the unspoken male dynamic.

"Oh." Understanding dawns across her face.

I give her my card. "You call me if you need me, and I think I'll send Barnes over here every once in a while to check things out."

Shelly smiles and gives me a little wave. "Thanks, Detective."

I walk out the front doors, immediately calling Maddy.

She answers sounding out of breath. "Just a second, I'll be right back, Drew. Derek? Hey! What's up?"

"Why didn't you tell me you were getting threatening letters?" I demand.

Silence.

"Drew, I'm taking ten," she says away from the phone. I hear her heels clicking on the floor and wait patiently until she is happy with her location. "Because I frequently get threatening letters and it is always nothing," she replies in a warning tone.

I take a deep breath, not allowing myself to express my anger in the way I want to. "What do you mean you get threatening letters frequently?" I ask calmly. Well, as calmly as is currently possible given the shade of red I'm turning.

She huffs in impatience. "I mean that people need someone to blame other than themselves when their kids get placed with the other parent. I would have let you know if it was serious."

I am upset that she hasn't told me what I consider vital information, that she isn't taking this seriously, and that Green, of all people, knew anything about this before I did. I cling desperately to my self-control for maybe the first time ever because I love her, and I don't want to show her that side of myself. Yet.

"Some guy coming to look for you at your office is serious, Madison," I say evenly, keeping a tight lid on my anger.

"Macy said he was very calm. I was going to mention it tonight, but I don't think it's anything to worry about," she says defensively.

"Macy told me he was up to no good," I reply shortly, emphasizing Macy's name. "Macy knows enough to know the calm ones are much more dangerous than the screaming ones," I continue, trying to get my point across.

I can hear her suck in a breath. "You went to my office?"

The lid keeping my anger in check is starting to slip. "Yes, Madison. Of course I went to your office. I heard from Green there were threats against you. I went to figure out what's going on and have a very serious conversation with the sorry excuse for what you people call security in that building," I explain harshly.

Maddy gasps. "Derek! They do their jobs. Leave them alone, this is nothing. It'll blow over in another couple weeks when this guy moves on. Is Green the one that interrupted us on our date that night?"

I growl, ignoring her efforts to distract me. "You don't know that this'll blow over, and if this guy got to your office, they aren't doing their jobs."

"Derek," Maddy says in warning.

"Don't worry, they are going to do their jobs from now on," I promise darkly.

"Derek." Maddy puts on the lawyer voice I love. She thinks it makes her sound authoritative, but it just makes me think of her as an angry kitten.

"You are also going to start locking your door, Madison. I'm not kidding around anymore," I demand firmly.

"Derek, enough!" she huffs. "I don't have time for this. Everything is fine. This happens all the time. You are blowing things out of proportion. I have to get back to my meeting; we will talk about this when I get home. And don't accost any more security guards," she scolds.

"Nothing more to talk about, Princess. I'm just telling you how it's going to be."

"I would love to break down that sentence into the fifteen different ways it's insulting, infuriating, and false, but I don't have time right now. I'll call you tonight." Her voice has gone hard and she hangs up.

Fine. I'll let her cool off. In the meantime, I'm taking care of business.

Instead of calling the owner of the security company taking care of Maddy's building, I decide to go to their office. He happens to be a friend from high school, and I'm not looking to cool off. In fact, I'd like to put this righteous indignation to good use.

* * *

"Derek!" I'm greeted when I get to the security company.

"Hey, John. Good to see you," I say as I walk into his office, returning his handshake.

"You come by to finally accept my offer?" John asks with a gleam in his eye. He's been trying to hire me for years.

"Nope, I came by to berate you about the embarrassing excuse for security in Maddy's building," I say seriously.

John's lips quirk. "First tell me about Maddy, then we'll get to your insulting my life's work. I take it you're seeing someone?"

"Madison Knight," I explain impatiently.

"The new lawyer in town?" John asks, placing her name.

"That's right," I grunt, accepting the bottle of water he offers me.

"That's great, Derek! It serious?" The gleam in his eye is irritating. He's been urging me to settle down for years. I use my irritation to hold onto my anger and remind myself why I'm here.

I glare. "Yup. Sure is. And I'd like her to stay alive long enough to make it to forever if you could bring it upon yourself to help with that," I reply sarcastically.

John blows out a breath. "The one, huh? Congrats, man. I'm happy for you. Tell me what happened."

I go through what I know, showing him the folder from Macy. I start pacing as I pelt him with questions, "Why didn't your guys know about these and spot him when he entered the building? Their response time is entirely too slow. Seventeen minutes, John. Where were they coming from, Mars? This man is actively threatening her, and he walked right into her office," I end on a shout.

"Calm down, Derek," John soothes.

"Don't tell me to calm down. She could have been hurt, and your so-called security was completely useless," I thunder. It feels good to finally release some anger.

"Derek," John starts, "I understand your frustration. The contract we have on that building is not very involved. They want minimal security."

I growl in frustration.

"Listen, I'll ramp up security and put a few of my more qualified guys down there. How's that?" John offers.

"Define ramp up," I say tightly.

John considers this. "Hourly patrols, actively monitoring threats, someone stationed in the lobby, you know...the works."

I stare at him. "What are you doing down there if you aren't doing that already?"

"Monitoring the cameras mostly." I shake my head at his shameful admission, and he holds up his hands in surrender. "Hey, don't look at me, it's all they want to pay for. We offer more, you know that."

"Thanks, John. Can I get some stuff to ramp up her home security too?" I ask, calming down.

"What do you need?" he asks.

I consider this for a moment. I will set her up with a security system subscription but there is one thing I need that I'm not sure exists.

"She doesn't lock her door," I say with embarrassed frustration. John's brows quirk. "I know. It drives me nuts, but our nephew lives next door and she wants him to be able to come and go as he wants to."

"Our nephew?" he asks in surprise.

"Her brother is married to my sister," I explain lightly.

"Brittany's married?" John says with consternation.

"Yeah," I say, suspicious. I don't like that he doesn't seem happy about it.

"I didn't know. Huh," he says, staring into the distance. I watch him and think back through my memory. I guess he always did pay special attention to Brittany. He catches me watching him and shakes it off. "I think I have just the thing," he says with a faint smile.

He takes me down to their warehouse, and I get to play with some of their more sophisticated toys. I also get a couple more job offers from John before he shows me what he's thinking for her door.

Chapter 13

Maddy

It's been a long week. After a tense Monday with the threatening father who showed up at my hometown office in my absence and scaring Macy, an uncomfortable conversation with Derek the same night about boundaries, and working round the clock to finish the audit the rest of the week, no Friday in the history of the world has been more deserved.

I make the two-hour trek from Atlanta back home early, the result of me pushing to make sure the audit is wrapped up Thursday night. I want to get home and get ready for my date with Derek tonight. After three weeks of only phone conversations and one weekend visit, I'm more than ready to see him. I can't deny I've treasured this bonding time with him though. Time to just talk to him, get to know him, and feel comfortable with him. I wouldn't trade this experience with him for anything.

Just after lunchtime, I pull into my driveway and notice a small sign in the flower bed in front of the porch indicating an alarm system that wasn't there when I left. I decide to ask Matt about it after I take a shower. I don't want to do anything else right now but unpack and get ready for tonight. I haul my stuff to the porch and stop dead in my tracks as I reach for the knob.

There is no doorknob. My front door doesn't have a doorknob. There is a number panel where my doorknob should be.

Derek.

My mind says his name like a curse. I stomp and let out a sound of frustration, which probably would have been more intimidating if it wasn't so high-pitched.

I call Matt, knowing he won't answer the phone because he is a middle school teacher and in school, but I leave a scathing message referencing female independence, personal space, and boundaries in the scariest voice I can muster.

I stomp back to the car and head straight to the police station where Derek works, seething the entire way. Visions of myself relaxing in a luxurious shower and taking my time primping for my date tonight slip away as I whip myself into a nice little frenzy. Fortunately, the patrol officer who harassed us on our date catches sight of me in the parking lot and, seeing I am visibly angry, gleefully decides to let me past the front lobby and reception desks and straight to their open bullpen where Derek's desk is located. I'm sure this is primarily for his personal amusement, but the rage I worked up on the way doesn't care.

I follow the smirking officer back toward Derek's desk, seeing the exact moment he catches sight of me. He is on the phone and does a double-take. I see instead of hear him say, "I need to call you back." He can clearly see I am upset but decides to ignore it and smile.

That's how we are playing this?

Fine.

"Hey! You're back...early," he starts in false excitement but slips when he adds that last word.

So, he had a plan I messed up. Good.

"I got home today and can't get into my house. Wanna know why? Because there is a number panel where my doorknob should be, Derek."

I say this in a hard but calm voice that is impressive given how my insides are quaking.

Derek glances nervously around. "Maybe we should go into the conference room...." He tries to take my arm and usher me toward where I assume the conference room is located.

"Why is there a number panel where my doorknob should be, Derek?" I demand, refusing to be moved.

His eyes flick around while he continues to try and guide me into said conference room.

Hoping to make him as uncomfortable as possible, I stay planted where I am and raise my voice. "I cannot believe after our conversation about boundaries you broke into my house and switched out my doorknob without my permission!" I punctuate my words by throwing my hands up and watch as Derek's composure cracks.

"I wouldn't have had to do that if you agreed to lock your door. Which, by the way, I didn't have to break down since it was unlocked. I just waltzed in off the street like any psycho could do."

"It's my house! I'll lock it if I want to!" I yell. "You have no right to change anything about my house without my permission!" I continue, the crowd officially discarding their ambivalent eavesdropping, gathering around instead to watch in interest.

Derek raises his voice to match mine. "Don't be stupid, Maddy, you need to lock your door! Especially when there are men coming after you."

"Did you just call me stupid?" I ask in a dangerously low tone, narrowing my eyes. I know he didn't, but I can't help it. I'm fired up and willing to yell at him about anything and everything at this point.

I ignore the snickers and comments from the crowd behind me.

Derek narrows his eyes to match mine. "No, but you are making stupid decisions when you don't lock your door. It's basically an invitation for madmen to come and attack you."

"The only madman who has ever come through my door without knocking is you!" I yell bouncing on the balls of my feet for emphasis.

"You gonna tell her about the security at her office and the system you installed at her house?" I hear from behind me.

"You WHAT?" I shriek.

Derek holds his hands up. "Now Maddy..." he starts in a calming tone.

"I CAN'T believe you! What is wrong with you?!" I shout.

"Maddy..." he says trying to quiet me.

"Don't you Maddy me! I can't believe you! I very specifically said I did not want a security system!"

"Maddy..."

"Undo it," I demand in a low growl.

He looks surprised, "What?"

"Undo it. All of it. Everything you did while I was gone, undo it all," I demand.

"Absolutely not," he says fiercely. "Whether you are too stubborn to admit it or not, you need that stuff and I'm not undoing a single thing. Matt and I did what we thought was best at HIS house, and I stand by it." He crosses his arms and squares off in front of me, making it clear he's not backing down.

"If I'm stubborn, at least I'm not overbearing and obnoxious," I say coldly.

Derek's eyes shoot fire and he opens his mouth to speak, but someone to our left cuts him off.

"Ms. Knight. Lovely to see you. Why don't you step into my office?" Chief Pearson calls to me in a friendly voice.

My eyes don't leave Derek's while I return Chief's greeting stiffly. "Chief," I begin following him to his office, still gazing at Derek. "This isn't over," I poke Derek's chest and mutter as I pass him.

"You can say that again," he grumbles and turns to follow.

I go straight into Chief Pearson's office and sit in one of his guest chairs. It is with extreme pleasure that I watch him close the door on Derek and leave him, open-mouthed, outside the office.

"How are you, Madison?" Chief asks me warmly, sitting in the chair next to mine.

"Been better," I admit crisply.

"I heard. Why don't you tell me about it?" he invites. Chief Pearson, with his tall frame, military haircut showing his salt and pepper hair, and perfect posture can pose a very intimidating figure. Fortunately, whenever I have interacted with him, he has been in grandpa mode. He makes a very jolly grandpa.

I sigh, relaxing into the chair, then gaze at Chief Pearson adoringly. I've always liked Chief Pearson. I helped his daughter and son-in-law finalize their adoption a few months ago. They were a great family to work with. Normally, I don't emotionally spill my guts to virtual strangers, especially clients, but I'm hanging on by a thread. A thread from the unraveling rope I'm at the end of.

I tell him about my three-week work trip to Atlanta, the heinous audit I just finished, and how excited I was to get home. I go over the threatening letters and the brief visit my assistant, Macy, had from an angry father this week. Then, I get to Derek's overstep. Major overstep. He basically pole-vaulted over the line of appropriate behavior. "I mean, trespassing is a thing. I could press charges," I finish, knowing very well I legally can't.

Chief Pearson chuckles. "He had the property owner's permission, Maddy. You can't press charges. Though I'll say, that would be entertaining to watch."

I grumble and cross my arms.

"You're a reasonable person. You know Derek is just trying to protect you. What's the problem?" Chief asks me softly.

I open my mouth, but nothing comes out. He watches me closely as I struggle to find the words. "It's not about the stuff. We talked about it and agreed to handle it when I got home. Then he totally ignored me and went and did what he wanted to anyway," I say defensively.

"Now, I'm not defending that. You need to work that out yourself, but maybe he did that because you were blowing it off? You know this guy is dangerous, Maddy. Derek is protecting you the best way he knows how. He was pretty proud of that keypad door he got you," Chief adds gently.

"He was?" I ask, feeling the first twinge of guilt.

Chief nods. "So you wouldn't have to carry a key and Grady could still come and go whenever he wanted."

Tears threatened to fill my eyes. "Oh." That was pretty sweet, I guess.

"It's what we do, Maddy. We serve and protect. Derek has always been a little more of a bull in a china shop, but his intentions are good." He pats my shoulder in comfort.

"What are you, a relationship guru now?" I ask with amused sarcasm.

Chief booms laughter, and then I laugh with him. "I like you Maddy, and I feel it's my duty to assist with issues concerning my most valuable officers."

"How's the new family?" I ask, referring to his new granddaughter. His face lights up. "Splendid. Laila is growing like a weed."

I smile fondly. "Good." I stand, saying warmly, "Thanks, Chief."

To my surprise, he pulls me into a brief but reassuring hug. "You need anything, you call me, you hear? Maybe try to keep from making such scenes in the bullpen? It riles everybody up," he adds with a wink.

I blush and nod. "Will do. Thanks, Chief."

I leave Chief's office and walk stiffly by Derek's desk on the way out, avoiding his eyes at all costs. Though I don't look at him, I know he follows me out of the station. As soon as I'm free of the doors, Derek takes my hand and walks with me to my car. I consider pulling away, but I love the feel of his hand in mine, and I think I have successfully caused enough of a scene today.

When we reach my car, Derek pulls me into a bear hug, squeezing me tightly. "That wasn't the welcome home I imagined," he says into my ear.

I huff. "Me either."

"I'm just trying to protect you, Maddy. I'm sorry I didn't talk to you before installing the stuff at the house," he says contritely.

"We did talk, Derek, and we agreed to wait until I got home," I say plainly.

"It just seemed like you weren't taking it seriously. I thought if I went ahead and took care of it and you didn't have to worry about anything, you wouldn't mind as much," he explains helplessly.

Flimsy, but I'll take it. I blow out a deep breath. "I'm sorry. I maybe overreacted."

Derek puts his forehead to mine. "I can't have anything happening to you."

My breath catches. The sincerity in his voice makes those all-too-familiar heart palpitations startup. "Just...can we talk about things before you take them into your own hands like that?"

Derek smiles and kisses me deeply. He pulls back to growl over his shoulder as a cheer goes up at the doors of the station. I giggle and give the crowd a brief wave as he opens my door for me. "I'll follow you home and show you all your new toys," he says hesitantly.

I nod, and, I'm not trying to be a stickler here, but notice he didn't exactly agree to my request.

Chapter 14

Maddy

We arrive back at my house, and Derek excitedly shows me all my new security "toys" as he calls them.

"See, everyone gets their own code, even Grady. That way you don't have to carry a key. If one of our codes is used to open the door, the security system automatically shuts off when it opens." I nod along, irritated I can't find one thing to complain about. He walks through the security system in detail, pointing out motion sensors and entry sensors, even the smoke and carbon monoxide sensors. I find this all a little much, but I am surprisingly pleased with how simple it is to operate. Admittedly, I zone out toward the end. I don't find home security quite as titillating as the average person, I suppose. I consider what Derek's told me so far and try to come up with something to object to as he raves about this system that can apparently do everything but actually take out an intruder. Unfortunately, I come up empty.

The system is delightful and I hate it.

"So, what do you think?" he asks with excitement when he finally finishes.

The look on his face is so cute, like Grady looks when he picks me a dandelion and presents it to me proudly like it's a rose. I begrudgingly admit, "It doesn't sound awful."

His face falls slightly before he smirks. "I'll guess I'll take it, considering the circumstances."

He starts moving toward the kitchen and I follow, watching him open and close cabinet doors. I lean against the bar and prop my chin on my palm. "Whatcha doin'?"

He opens the fridge and the freezer and peers in with a frown. "Where's all your food?"

"I've been gone for three weeks," I answer obviously.

He eyes me over the open fridge door. "Yeah, but there's absolutely nothing in here except two bottles of water and coffee. I mean, not even ketchup. No herbs, no dry goods. Nothing. How do you cook?"

"I don't cook," I say simply.

His eyes light as he walks over to the bar. "Have I finally discovered the only thing Madison Knight isn't good at?"

It's not the only thing, but he doesn't need to know that. "I said I don't, not that I can't." He eyes me with amusement. I really can't cook. I mean I can't even make toast appropriately, but I'm not prepared for him to think of me as anything other than completely capable yet.

"You're in luck, Princess. It just so happens I can cook. Why don't we go to the store real quick, pick up a couple things, and I'll cook us dinner?"

I don't resist being pulled into his arms. It's really the only place I want to be anyway. You would too; they are great arms.

"Why don't you go to the store while I shower? I'll be ready by the time you get back," I suggest because he's close and I can smell myself. Not in a good way.

He shakes his head gravely. "No can do. You've been away for three weeks and there's no way I'm letting you out of my sight tonight. Come with me. You can shower while I'm cooking."

I frown. "I wanted to watch you cook."

He considers this. "Tell you what, we'll go to the store, come home, then I'll prep the food while you shower, but not start cooking until you're out."

"Deal!" My smile cannot be contained. Compromise at its finest, folks.

I get a kiss as a reward for my exuberance, choosing to melt against him like I should have been able to when I first saw him. Right now, in this instant, it's hard to remember why I made such a big deal about everything.

I would say I'm a lover, not a fighter, but I'm a lawyer and that just wouldn't be true.

We go to the store and I follow Derek around as he picks out ingredients for dinner. He doesn't buy anything that is pre-prepared; he only gets stuff you legitimately have to cook. I can honestly say I have no idea what he is making. I don't even recognize the name of some of the ingredients. He stays true to his word, though. He doesn't let me out of his sight. If his arms aren't around me, we are walking hand in hand. It is almost as if he thinks if he wasn't touching me I would disappear. Needless to say, it is the most enjoyable grocery shopping experience I've ever had.

Arriving home, I help him get the bags in before flying through a shower, going as fast as humanly possible, so I can get back to Derek. I almost twist my ankle slipping on the tile because I am moving too fast, but it's worth it. I do the bare minimum to be presentable before going back out there, including putting on a cute but comfortable outfit of yoga pants and a bright occasion t-shirt and blow-drying my hair. I say a prayer of thanks that I didn't kill myself to get back out to the kitchen quickly. Derek is looking all masculine and domestic chopping something, and my mouth literally starts to water.

Heaven help me. I am but a woman. "Is this what you've planned for us tonight?" I ask out of curiosity.

Derek glances at me as he continues the food prep. "Pretty much. I figured you would want to spend the day with the family tomorrow since you haven't seen them in a while, but I wanted to have you all to myself tonight."

My stomach flutters. "Pool tomorrow?"

"Yep, and don't even pretend you have to work," he says, pointing a knife at me in warning.

I swallow a snarky reply and instead smile sincerely. "No more pretending."

That's a big promise to make. I wonder if he knows that? I wonder if he knows that me hiding from him was as much for him as it was for me? Because if he sees me all the time, full tilt, it'll be the truest test of his feelings. Because then he would know me and know what it is like to truly be with me. The smile and wink he gives me seems a small indicator of what he's truly asking for.

"You ready for that?" I ask, keeping my tone casual.

He grunts. "Bring it, Princess." His unwavering confidence makes me think he doesn't know exactly what he's asking for.

I smile mischievously. "You asked for it."

He fires up a pan and starts sautéing something, seemingly unconcerned with my warning. "I have. Repeatedly. Thank you for not making me ask again." He matches my serious tone with a promise to rise to my challenge.

He adds a few vegetables to the pan and moves on, "So tell me, how did you finish the audit early?"

"I told the auditors I wasn't working Friday, that they had to finish. We worked through lunch Thursday and stayed till eight at night, but we got it done. In my client's favor, I might add," I say proudly.

Derek gives me a pleased smile. "Of course it was. Congratulations, you've earned it."

"Thank you. My firm is so grateful they are keeping my caseload light for the rest of the summer." Mostly because I demanded they do just that, but I don't feel the need to share that little tidbit. Not that I don't feel entirely justified in the request, because I am. The whole point of moving back home was to work less, not more. I just don't want Derek to know exactly how demanding I can be. In case he's missed that tiny fact so far.

"What are you gonna do with all that free time?" he asks as he sprinkles herbs over whatever he's sautéing.

"Oh, I'm sure I'll think of something," I say with a playful smile.

Watching Derek cook is like watching a professional wrestler ballroom dance. It seems disconcerting and out of place due to their size and general countenance, but so mesmerizing you can't look away. He chops, he seasons, he sautés, he does the flippy pan thing all while moving around my kitchen with the grace of a jungle cat.

"What's that?" I ask, pointing.

"Salt," he answers.

"It doesn't look like salt," I counter.

He tosses me a look over his shoulder. "It's flakey sea salt."

"What are you doing now?" I ask next, perched at the bar watching him.

Am I trying to be annoying? Short answer: I don't have to try.

Derek talks as he continues cooking, telling me what he is doing while he is doing it. Adding his growly voice to the whole scenario made me wonder how much I could make if I videoed this and put it on the internet. I bet I could retire early and buy an island.

I set the table while he finishes up and have fantasies of a thousand future dinners just like this one. Derek presents our plates with a flourish, setting something in front of me that is both beautiful and smells delectable.

"This is pasta aglio e olio," he presents proudly.

The first bite is heaven. I have no idea what kind of pasta this is, and I probably couldn't repeat any of the words he just said, but it tastes like what I imagine hopes and dreams taste like. I cannot stop the moan of pleasure that escapes my lips.

"Good?" Derek asks shyly.

"Dear Lord in heaven." I didn't exactly form the words, they just slip out. I'm okay with it, though. It's the only acceptable response. Derek smiles, pleased.

"Seriously...wow. Where did you learn to cook like this?" I ask with an awe that is not dramatized for effect.

He shrugs awkwardly. "I don't know. I just messed around with it I guess."

I narrow my eyes. "An ex taught you, right?" His eyes flick to mine in surprise and I laugh. "It was!" I believe I see a blush crawl up his neck.

"I may have picked up a few things from someone I used to know."

I laugh again, enjoying the reddening of his cheeks. "Was this the thing?" I giggle. "Your biggest asset?" His face gets redder and I give more fully into the giggles. "Your ex taught you how to cook and now you use it to impress other chicks?" I lose myself to an outright belly laugh. I'm not sure why I'm finding this so funny, other than I have tangible proof that big, bad Derek Masters is a mere mortal like the rest of us.

"Just to be clear, I may have originally learned a few things from someone I used to know, but since then I have developed my own interest in cooking," he protests rather grumpily.

"Is that right?"

"Keep it up and I'll never cook for you again," Derek growls playfully. I immediately quiet. "Well, there's no need to get dramatic."

"Be quiet and eat your dinner," Derek instructs, trying not to grin.

I would hate for this to set a precedent that he'll think he can boss me and I'll listen, but the dinner is really good, and I genuinely want to eat more. That's my story and I'm sticking to it.

* * *

Derek

I don't know if Maddy realizes it, but every time she takes a bite she moans. It's the sweetest compliment I never knew I needed. "I've never cooked for anyone else before," I admit after a few minutes of eating in companionable silence.

"Really?" she asks gazing at me in surprise. "Never?"

I shake my head. "Just you, Princess."

Her stunned expression irritates me. I keep telling her I've never really dated, but for some reason, she keeps not believing me. She has it in her head that I'm taking her through some predesigned dating checklist that I've honed with all these different women who have come before her.

"Is it really so hard to believe?" I can't keep the irritation from my voice.

She's apparently so into her meal she doesn't recognize my growing agitation. "I dunno. I guess I just find it hard to believe a man like you wouldn't use these moves on anyone else," she replies lightly.

I take a deep breath and try to stay calm. "Well, that's the point isn't it, Maddy?" Her head comes up and her eyes meet mine in surprise. She finally catches my tone. "The point is that you're the only one. I don't have "moves". I don't have some dating checklist I'm taking you through. I'm genuinely trying to know you, and let you know me."

Her eyes are wide now. My tone may have been a little more frustrated than I originally thought. "Why are you mad?" she asks carefully.

"I'm not mad, Maddy, I'm just..." I blow out a breath. "You keep trying to make me out to be something I'm not. I'm not snowing you. I've never cooked for anyone before because I've never wanted to. I want to cook for you. I want to keep you safe. I want to know you without all the walls and arguments."

Well, not completely without the arguments. She's cutest when she's arguing. She stares at me, and I can see the conflict in her eyes. She wants to argue but she can't; she knows I'm right. Her face softens. "You're right. I'm working on it. I promise. I'm getting there."

"I'm okay with that. I'm okay with a process. Just remember, you're not the only one that's been hurt in the past, Mads."

Something flickers in her expression as if she's seeing something for the first time. She takes my hand and squeezes. "So you'll cook for me again, right?" she asks with a pleading smile.

I pretend to consider it. "I guess that's something I could do."

She smiles brilliantly. "Good, because I don't know what this is, but I think it's what dreams are made of."

I chuckle, highly pleased she's enjoying the meal.

"So, as long as we are clearing the air..." she starts hesitantly.

I glance up as I put more pasta on my fork and watch her study her plate. "Yeah?" I prompt before I take a bite.

Her eyes flick up to me and then back to study her pasta. "Well, I just noticed that earlier, when I asked you to discuss things with me prior to taking them into your own hands, you didn't really say anything."

My lips twitch in a half smile. Perceptive.

I put my fork down and take a breath because this could go either way. Maddy is beautiful, exuberant, and wicked smart with a heart the size of Texas. She is also stubborn. Real stubborn. She's got this female independence thing that can sometimes put her at odds with me taking care of her, which is not because I think she needs me to take care of her, but because I want to be the one to take care of her. It doesn't seem like too much to ask to me, but Maddy is bound and determined to stand on her own with no help from anyone.

Maddy is a firecracker, ready and willing to cut you down if she disagrees with you. The fact that she's sitting here twirling her pasta instead of snorting fire and telling me exactly what she wants me to know tells me she is trying. She wants to make it work. If she is trying, I can too. I consider my own stance and try to determine the best way to go about this conversation.

"You're right. I didn't say anything," I admit carefully.

She raises her eyes to mine. "You weren't planning on telling me you had no interest in agreeing with me?"

I sigh. "It's not that, Maddy. I'll make an effort to talk to you first." I raise a hand to stop her from interrupting when I see my first words upset her. "However, if we disagree as it relates to your health or safety, I'm always going to take whatever precautions I feel are necessary whether you like it or not."

Her chin comes up and her eyes squint. Hello, lawyer Maddy.

"So, you'll 'make an effort' to talk to me first and if I don't tell you what you want to hear you're going to do what you want anyway?" she accuses.

I mean, I probably wouldn't have phrased it like that but...yes.

"To keep you healthy and safe? Yes. All-day long," I say with certainty. I am willing to compromise on almost anything, but not on this. Maddy huffs and sits back in her chair studying me. This is digressing quickly, and I need to figure out how to make her understand in a better way than apparently I am currently doing. "Look, Maddy, this is what I do. My job, my calling in life, is to serve and protect. I will compromise with you on almost anything else, but I won't compromise on this."

Maddy continues to study me. "It's still my life, and my home. I deserve to have a say."

I consider this. "Okay. I can agree to discuss things with you prior to taking action in an attempt at reaching a compromise, except in emergency situations."

Maddy nods. "I can agree to that. As long as I feel like you are listening to me when it comes to my own life."

Is this what progress looks like?

"Did we just agree to compromise like adults, without yelling?" Maddy asks, catching my grin.

"Yes, we did," I confirm, standing to lean over the table and kiss her. "Done?" I ask, grabbing her now empty plate at her nod.

"Here, let me do the dishes since you cooked," she says, coming up behind me at the sink. She wraps her arms around me from behind and pulls me away from the running water.

"If you insist," I say moving back to the table to get the rest of the dishes.

We make quick work of the dishes and settle on the couch to watch a movie. To my surprised delight, I don't have to coax Maddy near to me; she settles close into my side immediately. After weeks without being able to hold her, I don't intend to let her go anytime soon. Today could have gone better, but for all that happened, I can't help but feel like we made significant progress.

Chapter 15

Derek

The next morning, I show up at Matt and Brittany's bright and early. If my guess is right, it's pancake day and I know Maddy will be over soon, seeing as how the only thing she has in her kitchen is the sink.

"Hey! You made it for pancake day!" Brittany cheers when I come into the kitchen.

"Where's Grady?" It's unusual for him to not meet me at the door when he hears my bike.

"In his room cleaning up. He got in trouble this morning," Matt supplies, entering the kitchen.

"Really?" I ask in surprise. That's not like Grady.

Brittany sighs as only a parent can. "He's going through a phase."

I bite back a grin because I'm pretty sure kids are always in some kind of phase.

"Good morning family!" Maddy calls airily as she enters the house.

She comes right to me, wraps her arms around me, and kisses me. I smile when she pulls back. I could get used to this Maddy without all the holding back and pushing away. "Morning, Princess." I go to kiss her again, but I hear gagging to my left and Brittany starts to push me away.

"Enough, geez, it's eight in the morning." Brittany hugs Maddy. "Gosh, we missed you."

"Speak for yourself," Matt grumbles. "I was getting kind of used to having leftovers and quiet."

I grin because I know Matt missed Maddy way more than he'd ever tell her, but as a brother I understand the requirement to pick on your little sister.

"He asked about you almost every day," Brittany finks, pulling back and ushering Maddy to her chair at the table.

"It was not every day! I can't believe you just sold me out like that," Matt objects, offended.

Brittany rolls her eyes. "Yes, heaven forbid your sister knows you missed her," she teases.

"Exactly!" Matt agrees.

I chuckle because it's fun to not be the only one who sticks to the international code of older brothers with younger sisters. "B, you need to get a bigger table. I need a chair to pull up," I mutter, searching for an acceptable chair.

"I know. We are thinking about getting one this summer. Here, get the chair from the desk in the living room," she instructs, pointing.

Maddy glances around. "Where's...." She is immediately cut off by a streak of little boy in Ninja Turtle pajamas screaming her name and flying into her arms. "Aunt Maaaaddddy!!!!"

She laughs jovially and pulls him up into her lap, hugging him and showering his face with kisses. "Miss me?"

"Don't leave again!" he yells as he presses in closer.

Little sucker doesn't even notice I'm in the room. "Morning, Grady," I murmur as I put the extra chair next to Maddy's and pat his leg.

"Hey, Uncle Derek," Grady answers shyly, still clinging to Maddy.

Maddy and Grady put their heads together and are having some kind of whispering conversation that's difficult to understand but appears to be very serious.

"Grady, did you finish cleaning your room?" Brittany asks pointedly as she begins placing food on the table.

"Yes," he replies mournfully against Maddy.

"Yes what, Grady?" Matt corrects from the kitchen.

Grady buries his face in Maddy's shoulder and answers, "Yes ma'am."

Maddy continues whispering softly into his ear for another moment before Grady finally kisses her cheek, climbs down from her lap, and goes to his own seat. Finally, not separated by a seven-year-old, Maddy straightens in her chair and I drop my arm across her shoulders, pulling her in to kiss her temple. "What was all that about?" I ask curiously.

She eyes me scornfully. "Grady, what do snitches get?"

"Stitches," he says seriously from across the table.

I resist pinching her, but can't stop my grin. These two.

"When are we going swimming?" Grady asks pitifully.

"After breakfast, silly goose. You have to eat before we go," Brittany replies with a teasing tone.

"Here we go," Matt presents proudly as he sets an overflowing plate of pancakes in the middle of the table.

We all take turns filling our plates, pausing and saying the blessing before digging in. It's quiet for several minutes as we eat, then Matt says, "What if we went to Mom and Dad's today instead of Gran and Pop's?"

One of Brittany's shoulders lifts and drops as she considers this. "Are they home? Would they mind?"

We usually swim at my parents' house down the street, but Maddy and Matt's parents have a pool too. Our parents have a beach house they go to for most of the summer, but we usually have free reign of their pool without them there. Without them expecting to see us, it's just as easy to go to Matt and Maddy's parents' pool.

Maddy snorts. "Please, they are always home. They would love it.

Good idea, Matty," she praises.

This is a little more awkward for me, because, while I've met Maddy's parents, it's always been as Brittany's brother, never Maddy's boyfriend.

"You mind texting Mom?" Matt asks Maddy.

I nudge her, adding, "And make sure it's okay that I come."

She glances up at me in surprise. "Why wouldn't it be?"

"I don't know. They haven't really met me as your boyfriend." I feel three pairs of eyes watching me curiously, with Grady blissfully unaware and uninterested in the conversation. I'm focused on eating my pancakes and ignoring their stares because I'm fairly certain two of the three have nefarious intentions as it regards this particular topic of conversation.

"You know they love you, right? They'll be fine with it," Maddy says with obvious unconcern.

It's true, her parents do love me. Still, different context. They might like me as Brittany's brother but not Maddy's boyfriend. I've never really been known as the kind of guy you bring home to mom.

"I guess I'll need to do that background check then," Matt murmurs with an amused grin.

Brittany smirks in a serves-you-right kind of way.

Maddy rolls her eyes in irritation. "He's a police detective, Matt. He's already had a background check. Don't be stupid."

"Aunt Maddy, we aren't allowed to say the 's' word," Grady corrects seriously.

Maddy blushes. "Sorry, Grady."

Despite Matt's smug look, I glance triumphantly at Brittany. She knows I'm saying "my girlfriend is better than your husband" without words. Brittany gets a wicked glint in her eye that transforms my look into a warning glare.

"Right, but lawyers can sometimes access sealed juvenile records, right, Maddy?" Brittany suggests, blatantly tattling on me.

I point at Brittany. "Just for that, I'm teaching Grady that thing I agreed I wouldn't teach him till he was older."

She appears confused for a second before her expression clears with understanding. "Derek," she growls.

I shake my head. "Too late."

Maddy holds up her hands. "Whoa. Okay. Wait. What?"

Matt looks at me curiously too. "Come on, what'd you do?" he pries.

I glare at Brittany and consider helping Maddy in her crusade to get Grady to play the drums. I attempt to pass it off. "It's not that big of a deal. I just did some stupid kid stuff."

"Well now, I think you know that's not gonna cut it," Maddy chides playfully.

"I bet he stole a car," Matt says to Maddy, watching me in interest.

She shakes her head. "My money's on breaking into the school and vandalizing something."

"Why would I break into school when I hated it there?" I ask indifferently as I put another bite of pancake in my mouth.

"So, what was it?" she presses, punctuating her question with pokes in my ribs.

I grunt in annoyance and cut Brittany another look for forcing me into this. "It's not a big deal, I just got into a little trouble with some friends when we were drag racing this one time."

"In stolen cars. At fourteen," Brittany supplies gleefully.

My glare turns menacing. "Shut it."

She winks at me and blows me a kiss in unrepentant defiance. Sisters. Can't live with 'em, can't sell 'em to the circus. Matt eyes me, clearly impressed, and Maddy nudges my shoulder.

"I was half right." Matt is apparently very proud of this fact.

"It was a long time ago," I mutter.

"Can we go swimming now?" Grady pleads, still uninterested in the conversation.

"Did you text Mom, Mads?" Matt asks as he continues eating.

"Yep. She says it's fine. I'll let her know we are leaving soon," Maddy says around a bite of pancake, then picks up her phone to text her mom back.

"So," Matt says pointedly to Maddy, "I got an interesting voicemail yesterday."

"I stand by every word," Maddy says flatly next to me. Her shoulders have tensed so I put my hand on the nearest one and rub her neck with my thumb. She immediately responds to my touch, and I have to fight the urge to kiss her again. This technique works for my buddy Chase's dog too. Not that I'm comparing anyone to a dog. I'm just saying the technique can be applied liberally to distressed females of multiple species. It apparently worked so well on his dog, he tried it on his wife and was amazed at the response.

"It's my house, Maddy," Matt argues. "Imagine my surprise when I turn out to be the last to hear about your little friend."

"You weren't the last," Maddy contests defensively.

"You even told Mom and Dad and not me," Matt grumbles in exasperation.

"Well, I had to cancel lunch plans with Mom, so we were on the phone anyway," she justifies.

"Why are you so against a security system? It keeps you safe," Matt challenges.

Maddy stiffens again. "I am against decisions being made about me and my residence without my consent. I am against being handled like a child who can't take care of herself."

I rub the base of her neck lightly in circles with my thumb again. The tension in her shoulders eases.

"Mads, I'm sorry if you think that's what is happening. We are just trying to make sure you are safe. Honestly, it never occurred to me to talk to you about it, it was such an obvious solution," Matt explains sincerely with great patience.

"I like it," Grady pipes in from the end of the table.

"Like what, Buddy?" Brittany asks.

"Aunt Maddy's new door. I'm glad Uncle Derek put it in," he says matter of factly while playing with his fork in a puddle of syrup on his plate.

"Why is that, Bud?" Maddy asks curiously.

Grady looks up and says, "Cause I don't want the bad man to get you."

I could kiss this kid. Maddy practically crumbles into a puddle of mush.

"And because it's cool that I got my own code to open your door whenever I want. It's like a secret spy door," he finishes with a smile.

Maddy laughs. "I'm glad you like it." She turns and looks at me. "I like it too. Thank you."

Well, halle-freaking-lujah.

"Anytime, Princess" I grin. I'm locking away the fact that Grady is the key. She can't resist him. This is incredibly valuable information. Information that, of course, I'm planning to use wisely, but also to my advantage should I need it.

"You've been quiet, Brittany," Maddy prompts.

"I'm with the guys on this one."

Maddy cocks her head. "I maybe overreacted," she finally admits.

Matt breaks out in laughter. "That's a first! Maddy admitting to being overdramatic?"

Brittany glares at him and says, "She acknowledged it, no need to rub it in." She stands and claps her hands together. "Okay, Grady, go get your suit on. I'll clean up breakfast and get some snacks and lunches together."

"I'll clean up the dishes, you just get yourself together," I instruct, putting the borrowed chair back in its place. We'll be here all day if Brittany doesn't start getting herself together now.

We all go separate ways: Maddy going home to change and get a bag together; Grady going to his room to get his suit on; and Matt going to change and put a bag together for them all, which leaves me and Brittany left in the kitchen, Brittany ignoring my suggestion to get herself together.

"You're annoying, you know that?" I grumble as I rinse off dishes and put them in the dishwasher.

"No less annoying than you are." She stops what she's doing and puts her arms around me. "You know I love you, though. And you know that none of the stuff from the past matters now."

"Love you too, B," I murmur fondly.

"Aw! You really do love each other!" Maddy says as she snaps a picture of us with her phone, arriving back from next door.

"Of course we do," I say feigning offense, then nudge Brittany away playfully. "Now get off me, you pest." Brittany playfully punches me and goes back to assembling snacks.

"Mom says Dad will grill, so don't go crazy on the food," Maddy shares as Brittany works.

I finish loading the dishwasher and Brittany finishes up, so I move to help Matt load the car while she gets changed. Maddy is on Grady duty, keeping him entertained while we get everything in the car. This kid just can't stop moving, especially if he's even mildly excited about anything.

"Ready?" Matt asks as we get back into the house from loading the car.

We hear three different cheers of "Ready!"

"Aunt Maddy! Ride with me!" Grady insists, excitedly tugging on her arm.

Maddy looks from me to Grady with consternation, but I'm not willing to give her the opportunity to choose wrong. "Sorry, Buddy, Aunt Maddy rides with me. We'll follow you on the bike," I say decidedly, taking her arm and leading her to where I've parked it.

"Come on, Buddy, let Aunt Maddy and Uncle Derek have their fun," Matt says while opening Grady's car door and ushering him in before closing it and eyeing us sternly. "But not too much fun."

I ignore Matt, instead focusing on Maddy, pleased that she's beaming up at me. "Thanks for the assist. I really wanted to ride with you," she confides. I grin and kiss her gently before handing her my jacket.

She shakes her head and holds up the jacket I bought her in Atlanta. She shrugs it on, and it reminds me I need to check on when the helmet I ordered for her is arriving. I missed having Maddy on the back of my bike the last three weeks. She has this way of taking things I love and making them better. Or taking things I hate and making them awesome. It's tempting to just ride away with her, enjoy the open road, and take her somewhere we've both never been before. But I guess spending the day with our family is almost as good as having her all to myself. Almost.

Chapter 16

Derek

When we get to her parent's house, I get off the bike and tug her into my arms roughly. I missed her, and with everything that's happened, I never got the chance to show her that properly yesterday. I take her lips and grasp her face in my hands, pouring all my emotions into the kiss. I don't stop until I hear a giggle and a throat clear beside me.

"It looks like Uncle Derek is trying to eat Aunt Maddy's face," Grady complains with disgust from beside us.

I pull away from Maddy and, to my approval, she looks dazed. I grin and wrap my arm around her waist as we follow Matt and Brittany toward the house. "I missed you, Princess," I say in her ear, giving it a nuzzle before we hit the front steps.

"I can't believe you did that in my parents' driveway," she whispers in what I think is supposed to be a scolding tone but comes out more impressed than scolding.

"Did what?" I ask innocently, holding her tight.

She nudges me away. "You stop that, Derek Masters." She takes a deep breath and fans herself. "Gracious."

I snicker and let her go, taking pity on her as her mom opens the door and ushers us in. I am enveloped in her mother's hug while Maddy says,

"Mom, you know I've been seeing Derek."

I don't know what I expected, but a wide smile and being pulled into a second enthusiastic hug wasn't exactly it.

"Derek, how are you son?" Cal, Maddy's dad, asks as he nudges his wife aside and offers me his hand.

I shake his hand, grinning. "Good sir. How are those fish biting?"

"Good, real good," he says, pleased.

I help Matt unload the car, carrying everything to the backyard where the pool is. No offense to my parents, but I wouldn't mind permanently relocating our summer swims. Matt and Maddy's parents are wealthy, with Cal being one of the most premier lawyers in town. They have a lot of land attached to their massive estate home, with a back porch designed for entertaining complete with an outdoor kitchen and large dining table. Their pool is easily twice the size of Mom and Dad's, and they have a hot tub. I could definitely get on board with the lifestyle of the wealthy if it means a hot tub with a giant TV mounted above it.

When we haul in the last load from the car, I'm unsurprised to find Grady and Maddy already in the pool. Brittany is chatting with Grace on a lounge chair, and Cal in the pool playing with Grady and Maddy.

"Derek! What are you waiting on?" Maddy calls to me.

"Yeah Uncle Derek! Come play with us!" Grady joins in eagerly.

It's moments like these that make my stomach clench in regret for the years I was wrapped up in myself, unwilling to spend time with my family for fear of getting too close at the risk I wouldn't be able to protect them should I ever need to. Years spent doing all the wrong things trying to fill the void. I was such an idiot.

I strip off my T-shirt and appreciate how Maddy's jaw goes slack when she sees me. I bite back a haughty smile and head for the pool. No more wasting time.

* * *

Maddy

My parents are in the pool. In the pool. Both of them, at the same time.

This is significant. They've never been in the pool at the same time since they bought the house. Mom never wants to get her hair wet, and Dad is usually too busy in the yard or at the grill. Watching them now, Mom with wet hair plastered all over her head and Dad suggesting ordering pizza so he doesn't have to get out and grill, well, it's surreal. Awesome, but surreal.

"I feel like we've stepped into another dimension," Matt says quietly beside me.

"Right? It's weird. Pizza?" I ask in disbelief.

"They are like different people," he says incredulously.

"I guess Grady just has that effect on people." Right then, Grady bursts into giggles and launches himself at our dad, who is pleased beyond measure to catch him.

"You know when the adoption will be final?" Matt asks suddenly.

"My goal is by his birthday. I just have to get a date with the judge," I reply.

Matt nods absently. "Good. That's good."

His tone sounds calculating. "Why?" I ask suspiciously, turning to him.

He shakes his head and gives me the side-eye. "Just wondering."

Matt knows I can read him. He only ever avoids looking at me full on when he's lying or keeping something from me. "Matt?" I press, peering into his face.

"Would you for once in your life leave it alone?" he insists irritably.

I huff. "You should know me well enough to know the answer to that question."

"Geez. Don't say anything. Not to Derek, Mom and Dad, no one." He turns his back to the rest of the group and eyes me seriously. I nod in agreement, dying to know what is going on.

"Brittany's pregnant," he whispers.

He opens his mouth to say something else, but I don't hear it because I squeal and tackle him in a hug.

"Seriously, you had one job," he grumbles, standing and wiping the water off his face.

"What's going on over there?" Mom calls, the group now watching us curiously.

"Sorry! I saw a wasp," I call back. When everyone goes back to their activities, I turn back to Matt, who has a grim expression on his face.

"Not another word, Madison. We want to wait until after Grady's birthday and the adoption is final to tell him and everyone else," he warns seriously.

I nod and press my lips together, even though my body is dancing in excitement of its own accord.

Matt grunts, shaking his head. "It'll be a miracle if this stays secret until we are ready."

I expend great effort to calm myself. "I promise, Matt, I won't say a word," I offer sincerely. "I'm really happy for you. You're a great dad."

He smiles affectionately. "Thanks, Mads. I'm happy too."

"Maddy, honey, order the pizza, would you?" Mom calls to me.

I grin to Matt. "We have officially entered the twilight zone." He chuckles as I get out of the pool and grab my phone.

We spend the entire day with Mom and Dad swimming, taking a break to eat an embarrassing amount of pizza before spending the rest of the afternoon in the water. After playing with Grady for a couple of hours, Brittany and I climb on pool floats and sequester ourselves to the deep end in an effort to relax. It takes everything in me not to freak out and ask her about her pregnancy, but I exercise great self-control since I promised to respect Matt's request to not say anything. I can understand how another pregnancy might be a big deal for her given the circumstances of her first.

Mom and Dad, now dubbed Meema and Papa, eventually take Grady inside for a Lego break and us couples take the opportunity to try out the hot tub.

"No offense to Mom and Dad, B, but I vote we come here every weekend," Derek says contentedly, settling me under his arm and relaxing back into the warm jets.

"It's hard to argue with a hot tub," Brittany agrees, leaning into Matt's side.

"We can come over here in August when football starts. While the girls are in the pool, we could watch the game," Derek adds, gesturing to the big screen TVs mounted under the porch.

"For someone who was nervous about coming here today, you sure are comfortable," I tease.

Derek pinches me lightly as Matt speaks up. "It's not a terrible idea. Mom and Dad would love it if we were over more."

"We're here every weekend and you're acting like we never see them," I argue, rubbing the place Derek pinched.

"I'm just saying, I think they would like to see us more than just after church every Sunday," Matt explains.

"Speaking of spending time, Derek, did you invite Maddy to the beach house with us this year?" my sister-in-law asks.

"What exactly were we speaking of that has any relation to inviting Maddy to the beach house?" Derek asks dryly.

"Spending more time with our parents," Brittany replies haughtily.

In the spirit of solidarity, I turn to him and sniff playfully. "Obviously."

Derek moves to pinch me again, but I dodge him. "No pinching, that hurts," I protest, turning big eyes to him and pouting teasingly. "You don't want me to come to the beach with you?"

He rolls his eyes in exasperation. "I didn't know I was supposed to ask you," he says more to Brittany than to me.

"Mom and I just assumed you were," Brittany explains with an indifferent shoulder lift.

All eyes settle on Derek. He frowns at the attention but turns to me. "Maddy, do you want to come to the beach house with us this year?"

"Well, I would hate for you to feel pressured..." I huff playfully but stop when Derek starts tickling me.

"Stop!" I squeal, breathless.

"See? Settled. She's coming," Derek tells Brittany easily.

"You two are adorable," Brittany says with a dreamy smile.

"Intimidation tactics are not adorable, Brittany," I mutter in faux reprimand.

"Since when is tickling an intimidation tactic?" Matt guffaws.

I spare him a glare. "Traitor."

Derek pulls me close and kisses my temple. "You'll come right?" he asks in my ear.

I smile at him, whispering back, "Yeah, of course I'll come." Then, more loudly to the group, I announce, "Y'all aren't leaving me home alone!"

The matter settled, Matt gets up and pulls Brittany up with him. "Time for you to get out." Hot tubs are a no-no for pregnant ladies.

She groans, "Five more minutes."

Matt gives her a look and she follows him out of the hot water without another word of protest. They walk hand in hand into the house to find Grady.

"What was that about?" Derek asked curiously, stretching out luxuriously into the freed-up space.

Someone needs to acknowledge the position I am in and give me a medal of freedom or something. I have this colossal secret that I am over the moon excited about but am bound to silence. Darn me and my incredible skills of observation and persuasion. For the first time, I am not proud of the fact Matt is so easy to crack. Since I don't want to lie, I deploy a distraction technique. "I don't know, but don't look now, we are alone in the hot tub." I lean into his lips, kissing him slowly.

Derek pulls away. "If you are trying to distract me from the fact that Brittany's pregnant, I already know."

"How do you know?" I ask in shock.

"I notice things. It's kind of my job," he says obviously.

"How long have you known? And how could you not tell me?" I accuse, punching him playfully in the shoulder.

He grabs my hands. "It's not polite to spill other people's secrets. Since I now know you know, I figure it's an okay subject between us," he explains lightly.

I just stare at him. It's all I can do. How can one person be so fascinating and infuriating at one time?

Chapter 17

Maddy

The next Friday I am running late, but aren't I always? This time I didn't lose track of time; I legitimately could not get out of a meeting with a potential client who would not stop talking. The week has been a good one. Most nights were spent at Brittany and Matt's dinner table, but there was a mid-week date with Derek to dinner and putt putt. We wanted to get a last visit in to mini-golf before school let out today and summer break officially started, certain to ensure the local attraction will be constantly busy until school starts again. We had an amazing time, laughing and playing. Putt putt is officially one of our favorite activities. I won, of course. Again. Not that I'm keeping score.

I love that Derek has started having dinner with us at Matt and Brittany's throughout the week, which makes family dinner an event every night. If he gets delayed by a case or gets pulled to cover another shift, he calls me when he gets home and we talk on the phone. We have settled into a routine. It's steady. Reliable. Like Derek.

I still push aside feelings of discontentment, however. All the time we spend together is starting to not be enough. It seems like the more time I spend with him, the more I want to spend with him. I recognize this as the sign of addiction, but am powerless to do anything about it. It's terrifying the amount of time I spend thinking of him, texting him, looking at pictures of him on my phone, and daydreaming about plans for the future. Seriously, I have a problem. I'm in a never-ending cycle of obsession, fear of the obsession, fighting the impulse to hide in fear because of the obsession, self-soothing to prevent hiding, and then I'm back to obsession again. They say apathy is what's killing our generation, so it's not even technically my fault. I'm simply making up for an entire generation's lack of action. So there's that.

Tonight, we have plans to go to May's with Brittany, Matt, and Grady for what promises to be a delicious, filling meal, though I'm holding everyone up. I ditch my plans for a shower when I get home, promising myself at least a change of clothes and a spritz of something fruity to cover the smell of the day. I mentally pick out my outfit, going casual in jeans and a cute top and sandals, desperately hoping I have the time to change before we leave.

When I pull into my driveway, I say a prayer of thanks that Derek isn't here yet and no one is standing in the yard waiting on me. I check the time and mentally assign each of the five minutes I have to a task, then calculate the odds of me being anywhere close to on time.

I run into the house, ditching my heels and ripping off clothes as I run back to my bedroom. I dress like the wind, but unfortunately, I am only halfway through my spritzing and hair plan when I hear a grumpy, "Madison!" called from the front of the house.

Uh oh. Full name. I wonder what I did this time.

"Two minutes!" I call and chuckle at myself. I'll be lucky to get out the door in ten minutes. I'm not intentionally lying, just very optimistic. Too optimistic. Okay, I'm lying. I finish my hair and refresh my makeup, spritz myself one last time, and throw on shoes, jogging to the front of the house winded. Seven minutes isn't bad.

"Okay! I'm ready," I call as I skid to a stop in front of him, hoping my charming smile will rid him of any hard feelings that I'm late once more. I lean in to kiss him, but he steps back away from me, glaring. I frown. Alright, I'm not that late. "What?"

"Do you know your front door was wide open when I got here?" he accuses, visibly upset.

I look at the door, then at him. "I sometimes forget to close it when I'm in a rush," I say like a child caught with her hand in the cookie jar.

Derek's eyes slide closed and he pinches the bridge of his nose as if he has a headache. "Madison," he starts.

I fight a grin; I love it when he says my name. Especially if I ignore the context and he's all growly like he is now.

"I set up a state-of-the-art home security system to protect you from psychopaths who are literally threatening you and you don't even bother to shut the door?" His volume and urgency go up as he progresses through the sentence until he is almost yelling at me.

I tug on his arm and gaze up at him, trying to mimic Grady's puppy dog face. "Just one psychopath. And we haven't heard another peep from him."

"Maddy," he replies in frustrated seriousness, "I need for you to take this seriously."

I drop my puppy face attempt. "I am. I was just in a hurry. You know I have issues with being on time," I say defensively.

"Shutting the door doesn't add any time to your process. It's literally just shutting the door behind you as you fly through it," he growls in argument.

"I promise I will make an effort to shut the door from now on," I say irritably. I really don't see why he's making a big deal about this. He's acting nuttier than a pecan pie.

He eyes me with suspicious, narrowed eyes. "There are devices that ensure the door closes whether you close it or not. Don't make me put one on your door."

I step back and cross my arms, now officially annoyed. "Are you seriously threatening me? I said I would shut the door. What is the big deal? You're being way too intense about this."

"You said you would make an effort, which I'm coming to understand is lawyer-speak for 'I'll do whatever I want to do,'" he accuses harshly.

I ignore the fact that he's not wrong. "I am not giving you lawyer-speak. I am trying to compromise with you and your ridiculous need for control over my home security." I'm very close to yelling.

"It's not about control, it's about keeping you safe from an active threat, and I would very much appreciate you making an effort to do the most basic thing you could do, which is shut...the... front...door." Each word is emphasized in angry exasperation.

"I said I would make an effort," I yell.

"You didn't mean it. I can see you rolling your eyes at me and thinking I'm crazy in your head," he says knowingly.

Again, he's not wrong. And it's infuriating.

"That's fine. If you want to think I'm nuts, I don't care, but I will keep you safe. If I have to do that despite your own lack of concern, then I will," he insists with underlying warning.

"You are yelling at me about a door." I switch tactics. "You get that, right?"

"I think it's ridiculous too. I have never known anyone in my life so bound and determined to be so stupid with their own personal safety," he yells in utter frustration.

"Hey, guys were you planning on us going to dinner anytime soon?" Matt asks from the door.

Derek blows out a breath and I sigh. "We'll be right there," Derek mutters.

I was all ready to start yelling about his "stupid" comment, but Derek cuts me off. "The guy bought a gun," Derek says softly.

"What?" I ask in surprise, trying to place his meaning.

"Doyle, the angry father. He bought a gun. We flagged him in the system and got notified this week that he bought a gun," Derek says as he watches me carefully.

"Why didn't you tell me?" I ask numbly.

"Because I don't want to scare you but I need you to take this seriously. It could be nothing, but it could be something."

Okay, so maybe he isn't acting nutty. Maybe his crazy security measures make me feel a little safer in light of this scary and disturbing news. Maybe, and I would deny this in front of a court of law, maybe I'm glad he forced all this on me, even though I didn't see the point at the time. No matter what I think of his methods, the bottom line is that his intentions are purely to keep me safe, and I can't fault him for that. I guess I can understand why he's so upset about a door.

"Thank you for protecting me," I say as I put my arms around him and bury my face in his neck. He holds me tight, and I know there's nothing in the entire world that can get to me while I'm in his arms.

"Seriously guys, are we going to dinner or what?" Matt asks, clearly hangry from the door.

"Coming right now," Derek says, pulling away from me and leading me out the door. He kisses me roughly before putting the helmet on my head and helping me onto his bike behind him.

I snuggle in, pressing up close as we ride out to May's, taking comfort in the strength of his back. The security system apparently has an app that goes with it that I refused to let Derek install on my phone, but maybe I'll have him show me how it works now, although part of me rebels at the thought of proving him right and doesn't want to give him the satisfaction of my asking.

I can admit when I'm being petty and childish. Well, most of the time. I might just wait a week or so before downloading that app. I don't want to get too carried away with the whole "damsel in distress" vibe. After all, he should have told me about Doyle sooner. For now, I'll just be thankful and take more care with my own safety. I don't even know why I keep pushing when I know this is a hot-button issue for him. Well, I kind of know why. Because I just can't help myself.

* * *

Derek

Finding out that psychopath bought a gun was the worst part of my week. I found out on Wednesday, so I took her out to dinner and putt putt that night hoping to distract myself. In reality, I found myself scanning the perimeter and looking for tails all night. I almost pulled my gun on a little kid who crawled through the bushes to surprise us on one of the holes. It was then I realized I needed to calm down. I put Matt on guard watching the neighborhood and did what I could to make myself feel better, including some things that straddle the line of inappropriate invasion of privacy. Hopefully, Maddy will never need to know the lengths I've gone to in the name of her safety. She'd get so mad she'd probably chop my head off.

When I got to her house and found her door wide open, I thought my worst nightmare had come true. He got to her. He had her. I was immediately frantic, almost having a heart attack right then and there.

Thank God it was just Maddy's carelessness. This time.

Feeling her tight hold on me as we ride out to May's reignites my desire to lock her up where nothing bad could ever get to her. I fight a grin. Maddy would never have that. She's so obsessed with making sure her independence isn't trampled on that if she even thought I was telling her what to do, she would do the opposite just to spite me.

Hence, the ineffective use of the security system and a front door left wide open.

When we arrive at May's, I help Maddy off the bike and pull her in for a kiss before we follow the rest of the family up to the restaurant. I ignore Brittany and Matt's eye rolling at our display. We greet May when we walk in, and I introduce her to the whole party. She guides us to a comfortably large table. It's nice that our family is growing. First by Matt, then Maddy, and now a new baby, which is apparently still a secret. Not sure how long Brittany thinks she can keep this thing to herself, though. It's bathing suit season and she's gonna start showing soon. She's at least two and a half months along already.

"Mom, I thought only mommies and daddies kissed?" Grady asks innocently as we sit in front of our menus.

Brittany eyes me in irritation before attempting to explain the finer points of male/female relationships.

"Bud," I interrupt my sister's clumsy explanation from across the table with my arm draped around Maddy, "when a guy likes a girl, he has to show her, and there's no better way to do that than by kissing."

Brittany glares at me. "Thanks, Derek," she spits sarcastically.

I wink at Brittany, still collecting on what I owe her for spilling about my juvenile record.

"So I should kiss Alison?" Grady asks me as he works out my words for himself.

Hmm. Alison. This is the first I'm hearing of a girl.

"No!" Brittany shouts too loudly. "No kissing anyone but family until you are much older, Grady. Kissing is only for adults." Brittany makes him agree multiple times that he won't kiss Alison before fixing me with an icy stare. I smile at her, finding the whole thing highly amusing.

"This is the first I'm hearing of Alison," I state curiously, actively trying to annoy Brittany.

Matt leans forward from the other side of Grady. "From one man to another, watch your step, bro. Alison's days are numbered."

Brittany cuts her gaze to Matt. "Yours will be too if you don't watch it."

Matt grins and leans over Grady's head to kiss her. "I love it when you go all mama bear."

"Is someone going to tell me who Alison is?" I ask again just to watch Brittany's ire go up.

"She's my girlfriend," Grady explains simply without looking up from coloring on his kid's menu.

"No, she's not." Brittany emphasizes, again too loudly. I can't stop my rising laughter.

Grady looks up. "She's my friend and she's a girl," he says with an unconcerned shrug. "So she's my girlfriend."

The kid has always been an extremely logical thinker. I mean, you can't say he's wrong. Brittany lets out an audible sigh, and thankfully our waitress comes to take our drink order before any other comments can be made.

"Brittany is a little sensitive about the 'A' word. Grady is almost obsessed with the girl," Maddy whispers in my ear. I glance across the table in amusement. That's so Brittany. Personally, I'm happy for the little guy. He gets his game from me.

Maddy nudges me and looks at me in disapproval when she sees the pride on my face. "He's seven."

"Never too young to start with the ladies."

She frowns. "We'll talk about this later," she promises in a tone I'm sure is supposed to be threatening, but I just think is cute. So cute I kiss her, right at the table.

"Gross, Uncle Derek, not at the table," Grady says with a disapproving frown.

"Yeah, Uncle Derek, not at the table. In front of everyone," Brittany says, pointing to Grady over his head so he can't notice. I consider asking Grady when he's going to stop wearing swimmies purely to antagonize Brittany, but it looks like Maddy is staunchly team mama bear, and I think Maddy's been antagonized enough for one day.

"What are we doing after this?" Grady asks, now bored with the adult conversation.

"How do you feel about going to a night baseball game under the lights, Buddy?" I ask, glancing also at Brittany and Matt.

Grady's face lights up. "Cool!"

I survey the table. "Sound good to everyone?"

"It's early in the summer, are they playing?" Brittany asks.

"Pre-season. I got discounted tickets from the station," I explain. Night tickets this early in the season are always pretty easy to come by.

Brittany looks to Matt. "Sounds fun to me."

Matt nods in agreement. "Yeah, great idea."

I look at Maddy and she smiles. "Sounds great."

"We going to Meema and Papa's tomorrow?" I ask. I'm not sure if we are on some kind of rotation or what the deal is about which pool we are going to. It's May in Georgia. We are spending the day at someone's pool; I don't care whose it is.

Maddy speaks up first, immediately forming a plan. "Yeah, let's do that if that's okay. We'll do theirs the next two weeks, then Grady's birthday at Gran and Pop's. Then when Gran and Pop go back to the beach house, we'll go back to Meema and Papa's until beach week."

We all agree to the tentative plan. "Brittany says you played baseball in school, Derek?" Matt asks.

For the rest of dinner, we talk about baseball, college memories, and our antics when we were younger, our table erupting in a chorus frequent laughter. We tell sibling stories on each other and listen to Brittany attempt to explain to Grady the awkward situations we found ourselves in. I can't say when I've had more fun.

We are signing the checks when I look around the table at the smiling faces of my family. My gut drops as I realize this is what I've been missing. All those years I pushed them away and ran after other things, it was this I was searching for. I feel incredibly humble with the new understanding of how God has blessed me after returning to my faith. Even through my rebellion and mistakes, God loved me and is now giving me everything I was looking for that I never knew I needed.

"You look serious," Maddy observes as she tugs on my arm while we walk out the door of the restaurant to the parking lot.

I look down at her face, questioning if she's ready to hear my words. I should wait a little longer given what's happened today, but something's telling me to lay it all out. "I'm just realizing how much God has blessed me. I'm feeling incredibly undeserving right now."

Maddy's face softens. "Completely deserving, I think."

"I didn't know how much I needed this. You. Them. All of you in my life. The fact that God provided you despite my disobedience." I shake my head in disbelief, pulling her in for a hug. "I love you, Maddy," I whisper in her ear as I hold her tight.

She pulls back and looked in my face. "I love you, Derek."

I smile and kiss her, deep and slow until I hear Matt and Brittany start to grumble. I hold her for a minute before letting go and getting on the bike, handing her my jacket and helmet without another word. No way I let her wear her own jacket tonight. Not when mine had lost all trace of that spray stuff she wears. When she gets on behind me, she immediately takes her favorite position against my back, leaning into me, arms holding me tight. I marvel at what's just occurred between us, a new layer added to our relationship. That was surprisingly easy. I totally expected Maddy to freak and run at the seriousness of my words, but I couldn't be more pleased she didn't.

Chapter 18

Maddy

"I wish you would stop teaching my son how to spit sunflower seeds," Brittany says irritably to Derek. "It's gross, and you could at least be paying attention to the game."

Derek ignores her, bending low to critique Grady's latest try. I grin and take a picture of them, then take another of Brittany scowling at them. She grins and winks at me, telling me she isn't really as upset as she seems.

Derek straightens and puts his arm around me. "Take one of us."

We put our heads together and I snap a selfie of us. We both beam at the camera like a couple in love.

Because we are. A couple. In love.

Love.

Derek told me he loves me, and I said it back. I didn't have time to freak out or even make the conscious decision to say it back. The truth just slipped out unbidden, like it wouldn't or couldn't be contained. It's just as well I don't overthink this. We said no more pretending, and I'm standing by that. Gulp.

He kisses my temple before he stands. "I'm taking him to the bathroom," Derek announces. I slide over to steal Grady's seat next to

Brittany while they are gone.

"It wouldn't be fun if I didn't complain a little bit," she justifies to me.

"I totally agree. So what do we need to do to prep for Grady's birthday?" I ask, not at all interested in the baseball game taking place in front of me.

"Same as last year. Pool party. Super easy. Before that, though, you have a big thing to take care of," she says seriously, but with a grin peeking through.

"What?"

Brittany leans her head into mine. "Derek's birthday," she murmurs on the sly as if she's sharing a secret with me and giving me an impossible mission all at once.

"What?" I ask in surprise, pulling out the calendar on my phone. "He told me his birthday is in October."

"I'm not surprised. He hates his birthday. He tells people it's at all different times during the year so no one can pinpoint it and force him to celebrate," she shares easily, tattling on him.

"Are you sure you want to out him like this?" Matt asks from the other side of Brittany. "If he hates his birthday, maybe you should let him be?"

"Matthew Calhoun Gregory Knight, you hush your mouth this instant! No one, and I mean no one, in my family goes without a birthday being celebrated," I scold vehemently.

Matt holds up his hands. "Had to get it on the record." He retreats, puts an arm around Brittany, and goes back to watching the game.

I return my focus to Brittany. "Spill. I need the date and anything traumatic that ever happened to make him hate his birthday."

Brittany smiles. "May 7th. He hates being the center of attention. Except there was maybe this one time when I accidentally caught the curtains on fire with his birthday candles, but I don't think that's it."

Entering his birthday in my phone, I immediately start making plans. The big day is next Tuesday. I appreciate the heads up, but Brittany could have told me a few days earlier so I could come up with something awesome. I immediately send messages to clear my calendar at work for Tuesday so I can spend the entire day popping up in Derek's life unexpectedly. If he doesn't like being the center of attention, that's fine, but the two of us are celebrating, and it will be magnificent.

"I need another water, then we will go into hyper planning mode. Want anything?" I ask as I stand.

"Bottled water," Brittany requests.

"Me too," Matt adds.

I walk toward the concession stands, running through options in my head of things Derek might like for his birthday. I freeze and my blood turns ice cold when I see Derek amid the crowd with a woman clinging to his arm with both of hers, pressing close to him.

Fight or flight, fight or flight, fight or flight. I battle hard to fight my instinctual runner behavior.

It turns out my body knows better than my mind. While my mind considers the options of pulling the woman's hair out for daring to touch my man versus running to literally the farthest away I can get (Washington? Alaska?), my body remains frozen to the ground, forcing the crowd to spill around me like a rock in a river. True, Alaska is further than Washington, but I doubt my shopping habit could be supported in Alaska. Also, I've never really resorted to violence. I'm a "fight with words" type. It goes with the lawyer thing.

While my thoughts spin, my blood heats to boiling as I watch this woman hang on Derek with her fake tan and skimpy clothes. My anger quickly switches from her to him. How could he touch another woman when we said I love you to each other moments ago? Trevor's face flashes in my mind.

I start to turn away from them, but stop in my tracks, my mind clearing instantly. Derek wasn't touching her. He was attempting to extract his arm from her grasp and back away. Every time she touched him, he moved further away from her. His head was swiveling back and forth, and he was pointing behind him, clearly trying to get away from her.

I huff a bit of laughter and take a deep breath. Okay, that was a scary ten seconds when my mind went to crazy town. How could I think that of Derek? He definitely isn't a Trevor. Derek would never betray me like this. Derek has been nothing but respectful and loving to me, edging us toward the line but never allowing us to cross it. None of his actions make me think he would cheat on me. I feel ashamed of myself for letting my mind immediately think the worst of him, even if it was for just a few seconds.

I watch now in amusement as his uncomfortable situation grows worse when she notices Grady and starts fawning all over him. I let this go on until it looks like Derek might actually lose his cool with this chick. When I approach, she is babbling about how much she loves kids and how much they love her. I slip my arm around Derek's waist and take him in a long, hard kiss until bottle-blonde abruptly stops talking.

I pull back when it's clear the message has been received and wink at Derek before turning to baseball Barbie. "Hi, I'm Maddy," I say, extending my hand.

She shakes my hand tentatively and replies back, "Kimberly."

"So nice to meet you, Kimmie. I see you've met our nephew, Grady. Thanks so much for looking out for my guys until I could catch up to them. You have fun now, we need to get back." I pull Derek and Grady away from Wonderbra and back toward our seats.

Derek blows out a relieved breath. "Thanks, I kept trying to get away."

"So I saw. She certainly had you trapped."

"Tell me about it. Wouldn't shut up," he grumbles.

"Friend of yours?" I can't help teasing.

Derek glares at me. "Is that who you think I'd be friends with?"

"I don't know. I've never met your friends," I say with playfully innocent eyes.

Derek glares. "Maddy," he starts grumpily.

I giggle and peck him on the lips. "Hush, I'm teasing you. Lighten up, old man."

I usher them to the seats, then turn to head back to the concessions just as an arm snakes around my stomach, holding me in place. "Where do you think you are going?" Derek demands in my ear.

"Just to see some friends," I tease. He growls and I laugh. "I was on my way to get drinks when I had to stop and save you. I'm going back for my stuff."

"I'll go with you."

"You sure you want to risk it?" I ask slyly.

He rolls his eyes and points forward. "Let's go. I don't want to miss the next inning."

"Okay, but if I have to save you again..." I continue teasing.

He grins mischievously. "I kind of like it when you save me. Maybe you should remind me how it goes."

I narrow my eyes at him. "But you aren't in danger now."

His eyes sparkle with humor. "Maybe I'm in danger of a heart attack and you should give me mouth-to-mouth."

I throw my head back and laugh. Loud. People stare, but I don't care. "You can't be that corny, Derek Masters," I say through my laughter.

Chapter 19

Maddy

Today, this Tuesday the seventh of May, is the anniversary of Derek's birth. He doesn't know I know that. I have taken the day off work to pop up in random areas of his life and surprise him. I've been doing recon since Brittany told me about his birthday on Friday. Little questions at random times since then have ascertained what time he gets up in the morning, what he has for breakfast, what's his favorite lunch, what's something he's been wanting and hasn't gotten himself yet, and what would he do on a perfect day. I'm certain Derek thinks I have lost my mind with all the questions, but I don't care.

The fact that I'm standing outside his house (that I've never been to before) at four thirty in the morning holding balloons, a blueberry muffin, and wearing a dashing multi colored party hat may assist in convincing him I'm completely sane.

I ring the doorbell incessantly, like a five-year-old hyped up on sugar, until I hear grumbling and the lock twisting. When the door flies open, I have to remind myself to breathe. Derek is sporting basketball shorts and nothing else, has bed head, and wears a grumpily confused look on his face.

"Happy Birthday!" I cheer, excitedly bouncing up and down. Maybe

I'm too loud give how he grimaces and flinches away from me. I don't give him a chance to recover, however. I simply fling myself into his arms. After all, I haven't seen him since Sunday and my serious Derek addiction says it's been long enough. He lets out a small "oompf" when I collide with his chest, but he chuckles and holds me tight.

When I step back out of his arms, I hand him the balloons and the muffin. "These are for you!"

He looks just as confused as when he opened the door, only his eyes are a little more open and awake, "Thanks, Princess."

Grumbly morning voice...swoon.

He looks from the muffin to the balloons, then to me and the door. This is pretty much where my plan ends, so I'm left standing awkwardly in his doorway staring at him in anticipation with a huge smile that only mentally unstable patients give.

"Come on in," he says, gesturing inside with his muffin hand.

I walk into his house and wander around, eyeing the bare walls, empty rooms, and state-of-the-art kitchen.

"So, uh, what got you up this early?" he asks hesitantly.

I grin. "I thought we could go to the gym together. That's what you do right? You get up at four thirty to go to the gym?" I gestured to my brightly colored leggings and tank top. Actually, I triple layered tank tops to ensure I achieved both the desired colorful effect and to make sure nothing slips out while I am exerting myself.

He looks bewildered. "Um, yeah. That's what I do. I, uh, well, okay. Sure, let's go to the gym. I'll be right back."

He leaves me in the open living room/kitchen/dining area while he retreats into a room off a short hallway, which I assume is his bedroom.

"Hey, Derek?" I call from the living room while he's in his room getting changed.

"Yeah?" he calls back.

"How long have you lived here?" I'm curious as to the bareness of the place. I mean, this is more than just bachelor empty. He has nothing but a recliner and a TV. No kitchen table, no chairs, no couch, nothing on the walls. Nothing.

"I don't know, a couple years," he answers.

My brows shoot up. Wow. No wonder he always comes over to Brittany and Matt's house now. This place is sad. When he returns, he's dressed in a different pair of basketball shorts, a tank top, and tennis shoes, looking fully awake.

"Why?" he asks.

I grimace. "It's so empty."

"Yeah, I never spend much time here," he says with an unconcerned shrug.

He holds the door open for me and I put on my leather jacket as he climbs on his bike and lets it roar to life. The sun isn't quite up yet, so it's still kind of dark, and we ride through the mostly sleepy town. It's like riding through a dream world.

He pulls into a kickboxing gym. I'm thrown for a minute because this is not the type of gym I had pictured in my head. I should have known Derek would be more into a real sport than fancy machines.

He eyes me nervously as we approach the building, then opens the door for me.

"So what's your normal routine? Is there like an elliptical somewhere I can get on and watch?" I ask looking around. There are no ellipticals. There is a big boxing ring on one side of the large open space, flat mats in the middle of the floor, and punching bags along the wall to the other side. Along the back wall are free weights and a couple of treadmills.

Before he has a chance to answer, I hear a loud whistle from the back of the gym. "Hel-lo to you, beautiful. What can we do for you this morning?" A guy dressed similarly to Derek drawls this out as he approaches from the back with a predator-like look on his face.

"Maddy, Ty. Ty, Maddy," Derek growls, stepping partially in front of me.

The heavily muscled guy guffaws. "She's with you? Hey, Frank," he calls toward the back, "get out here, you need to see this!"

Ty turns toward me again and leers at me, looking me up and down until I officially need a shower. "Nice to meet you, Ty," I say coolly, inching further behind Derek.

"Well, what do we have here?" An older gentleman comes toward us from the same place Ty emerged.

"D brought a chick with him," Ty fills in with amusement.

Derek glares at Ty and Ty smirks.

"I'm Maddy," I say, offering my hand.

Frank takes my hand and bows in front of it. "Pleasure is all mine, dear. Frank Winters. Welcome."

I like Frank. He is older, mid-seventies at least, with soft white hair. He doesn't appear frail like older people sometimes do; he looks fit with a trim waist and biceps filling out his T-shirt.

"What's the occasion, Derek?" Ty asks.

Derek tries to stop me, but is a moment too late. "It's his birthday!"

Ty's eyes glint and he laughs. "No joke? I thought your birthday was in December." He lightly punches Derek on the shoulder.

Derek grimaces at my proclamation but tries to play it off. I forgot in my excitement how much he hates people knowing about his birthday. I mouth "sorry," and he smiles indulgently.

"Derek, you go through your routine. I'll get Maddy settled with me," Frank offers. Without waiting for a response, he takes my arm and leads me away. I follow him to some bleachers on the side of the gym and watch Derek start on a treadmill on the far wall.

"So Maddy, dear, tell me about yourself," Frank invites warmly as we sit.

"I'm a lawyer. I moved back to town last December," I say as I watch Derek run. He watches us back warily, ignoring some other guys who've come from the back to harass him about his birthday.

"And how long have you been with Derek?"

"Oh, um..." I think back, "a few months now I guess." I look at Frank, who is watching me with interest. "So Frank, tell me about yourself," I say, parroting his words.

Frank smiles. "I've been running this gym for sixty years now. Not much else to tell."

"Is there a Mrs. Frank?" I ask in interest.

Frank smiles fondly. "Not for quite a while. The cancer got her."

"I'm sorry to hear that." I put my hand on his arm.

"Do you have any interest in kickboxing, Maddy?" Frank asks, although I'm certain he already knows the answer to the question.

I grin sheepishly. "Actually, when Derek said gym, I thought he meant a Planet Fitness or something. This makes sense, though. He likes to fight, and he has a fighter's body. So I guess, to answer your question, I do now," I say with a tilted smile.

Frank chuckles and winks at me. "Derek's pretty good. He used to be better before he got his life right. He had all this anger that he channeled with his fighting. Now that he has the Lord, he doesn't need the fighting like he used to."

I nod along, dividing my attention from him to watching Derek, who is now moving toward the weight machines.

"He's been coming to my gym for close to fifteen years now, did you know that?" Frank asks lightly.

"I did not know that. It must have been interesting watching him grow up."

"Interesting to say the least."

I'm not going to lie, my interest in Frank is waning more and more as I watch Derek's muscles ripple with each weight he lifts.

"You know how many women he's brought around to the gym?" says Frank suddenly, interrupting my train of thoughts.

I glance over at Frank in surprise, who is peering at me with curiosity. "No, how many?"

I can't imagine Derek wanting to bring women here. I know he had quite a few snuggle buddies. As he keeps insisting, he never dated, so I don't feel right calling them girlfriends. With Ty's warm welcome, I can't imagine this would be a place he'd want to share with one of them.

Frank eyes me steadily. "None. Not one. And he has had a lot of girls." I notice he's raised an arched eyebrow for emphasis.

"What are you trying to tell me, Frank?" I ask pointedly.

"Nothing," he grins. "Just saying I've known Derek through the good and the bad, and in all that time, you're the only woman I've ever seen him with."

"You probably never would have known I existed if I hadn't shown up at his house like a birthday lunatic and invited myself to his gym," I point out.

Frank's head tilts. "Maybe, or maybe he can't focus on his reps because he can't take his eyes off you."

My eyes glance from Derek to Frank. "I think both those things can be true. What's your point?" I smile.

"I don't really have one. I'm just an old man, rambling away at a captive audience," he says with a crafty look.

I laugh. "Frank, you old fox. I don't believe that for a second. You may be old, but you have the experience of a man who has spent his life with his true love."

Frank's eyes twinkle. "Maddy, my dear, I think we will be great friends," he declares, standing and pulling me up with him.

He walks me over to where Derek is punching a bag and says, "Son, Maddy here wants to start training."

I try not to gape at Frank. That is definitely not what Maddy said.

"You'll need to bring her here every morning. She and I are starting slow today," Frank instructs, walking me toward the treadmill. Derek stares at Frank and me as we amble to the machine, looking just as suspicious as I felt toward Frank.

Frank points to the treadmill. "Light jog for ten minutes. Then we will get started with your warmups."

"Um..." I start, but Frank stares me down with a "don't mess with me stare", so I do as I am told. Seven minutes later, he checks my progress and makes me speed up, insisting my light jog is too light. After that, he walks me through alternating high knees, side-to-side shuffles, jump roping, light jumping jacks, squats, alternating reverse lunges, and alternating reverse lunges with a knee. By the time we were done, I am panting embarrassingly and in serious need of a water break.

"Are you trying to kill me, old man?" I ask Frank, gasping for breath.

He raises a brow with amusement. "These are just the warmups, my dear. Step up, time to start your first round." He gestures to a flat mat on the floor. "Okay, we are going to start with the first basic combination: jab, cross, hook, uppercut."

I stare at him dumbly.

Frank smiles patiently. "Like this." He comes around and shows me the moves, positioning my arms in precisely the correct form.

"You could have just said Derek doesn't like flabby women," I grumble as he adjusts my stance yet again.

Frank laughs loudly. "Oh Maddy, dear, you are good for my heart."

I smile despite myself and catch Derek's eye. He's getting ready to enter the ring with Ty and he winks at me.

"Focus, Maddy, you are almost as bad as Derek is." Frank pokes at my shoddy form.

I smile unrepentantly. "Can you blame me, Frank?"

"Do three more reps and we will stop and watch," he baits with an incentive I can't refuse.

Suddenly, I am the most focused I have ever been. Getting through the reps as quickly and painlessly as possible becomes my only goal. As Frank promised, as soon as I am done, he leads me to the bleachers to watch Derek and Ty kickboxing. He explains everything that goes on as I stare.

"Ty gets cocky because he's bigger, but Derek is a better fighter. See? Watch how Derek is observing him. Ty is showing him everything he's going to do before he does it. See how Derek easily blocked that and followed it up with an upper? I'll bet Derek does a roundhouse in the next thirty seconds to knock Ty out and impress you or I'll sell my gym."

I grin widely. I kind of hope Derek does the roundhouse, not just because I would be impressed, but also because Ty is annoying and could probably use getting knocked out. Sure enough, three moves later, Derek ends the fight with a roundhouse that drops Ty, and it is gloriously beautiful.

When he steps out of the ring, I immediately jump up from the bleachers and run into Derek's arms, not caring at all about his sweaty body. Besides, I am pretty sweaty too. "That was really impressive," I say as he sets me down and puts his arm around my waist. I'm suddenly marginally embarrassed by my display, which was maybe too enthusiastic for onlookers in his super-serious gym.

"So, what do you think?" Derek asks, wiping his face with a towel.

I glance at Frank and back at Derek. "It's great! Can I come back?"

Derek looks surprised but happy. "Sure, anytime."

He tugs me toward the door as some of the guys gather around him, wanting him to introduce me, but he isn't quick enough to make a clean escape. I meet a few of them before Derek glares, pushes them all away, and declares we have to go.

I smile dreamily at Derek as we walked toward the door. "Thanks, Frank! See you tomorrow," I call, waving.

Frank waves back with a pleased smile on his face. "See you

tomorrow, dear."

Derek searches my face curiously. "He didn't put the moves on you, did he?"

I throw my head back and laugh. "You don't really think that!"

Derek gets on the bike and murmurs grumpily, "He was touching you a lot when you were on the mat."

I laugh and hug him tight as I climb onto the bike behind him. "He was showing me correct form, you goof."

"That's what they all say, Princess," he mutters as the bike springs forward.

Pulling up at his house, Derek helps me off the bike and leads me inside and straight to the kitchen.

"Water?" Derek asks, opening the fridge. I nod and gape when I see what's inside.

"What is all that?" I ask in disbelief.

"What?" he asks in confusion.

I point. "Your fridge is packed. I've never seen a fridge so full. What is in there?"

He shrugs. "I don't know, stuff."

"Are you one of those foodies who tries to recreate things you've had in restaurants or seen in movies, but who tries to make it better than them?" I ask watching him carefully.

"I told you I like to cook; I have stuff to cook with. It's not a big deal. Your fridge is just freakishly empty," he defends.

"Hey, don't pick on my fridge. I prefer to think of it as clean," I justify.

"So was the muffin my breakfast or do you want me to make us something?" he asks with an excited glimmer in his eye.

If watching Derek cook is ever an option, I'll pick it every time. No question. "I would love for you to make something, but only if you want to. It's your birthday, we'll do whatever you'd like."

Derek grimaces. "About that, can we not share with anyone else about it being my birthday?"

I blush. "Yeah, sorry, I got excited and forgot how weird you are about people knowing it's your birthday."

"What do you want for breakfast?" he asks, surveying the contents of the fridge.

"Whatever you want. Whatever is your favorite. I've had your cooking. I guarantee I'll like whatever you make," I say confidently.

Derek gives me a devious grin before jolting into action. "Anything you're allergic to? Anything you absolutely hate to eat?" he asks as he grabs things from cabinets, then pivoting to root through the fridge.

"Nope, all clear."

Now is when I would sit at the kitchen table and watch the master at work only there isn't one. Instead, I stand in the far side of the kitchen and watch, offering to help until he just ignores me. I finally push myself up to sit on the counter.

I'm expecting omelets. Maybe a scrambled egg with some bacon. I don't know why I expect this, other than they are normal breakfast foods. It's clear I need to recalibrate my expectations where Derek Masters is concerned. I'm cat-like curious when he makes some type of sauce in a blender and puts it aside.

"Is that biscuit dough?" I ask in surprise as he turns out a big, white, blob onto the counter and starts pushing and pulling at it. I don't know if I've ever had made-from-scratch biscuits before.

"Sort of," he answers mysteriously.

"Are you going to tell me what you're making?" I ask, completely drawn in.

"Of course," he says, then turns and winks at me, "when we sit down to eat."

I smile and watch as he cuts biscuits from the dough, then slides them in the oven. Next, he slices tomatoes and pulls green leaves for what I assume is some type of salad? Finally, slices something that looks like cheese and does something to the eggs I've never seen before. That's when I get a tinge nervous.

I stay quiet, watching as much as I can see from my perch. He keeps his back to me most of the time, particularly blocking my view of him plating. I assume it's for the grand reveal, so I stay where I am and don't ask any other questions. "I feel bad you are going to all this trouble on your birthday. I would cook, but I'm a terrible cook."

"HA! I knew it!" he exclaims loudly as he plates, not turning around. Before I can scold him, he continues, "I enjoy cooking. It's no trouble, it's a treat."

He turns, and with a flourish I didn't know big, bad Derek Masters possessed, presents the plate to me as if I were at a five-star restaurant. It is...magnificent. "Wow." I breathe, holding it close to examine it from all angles.

"That, is caprese eggs benedict, with fresh basil and tomato, home-made mozzarella, poached egg, and homemade hollandaise on a made-from-scratch toasted English muffin."

My mouth drops open. "You make your own mozzarella?" How did I not even know that was even possible?

Derek can't suppress his pride. "It was a little project I worked on while you were in Atlanta." He picks up his own plate and sits on the counter across from me. "Come on, try it."

I pick up my fork but can't bring myself to cut into the deliciousness in front of me. "It's so pretty," I say with a frown.

Derek laughs. "It's to be eaten. Come on, try it."

He has that look again, the one just like Grady's when he shows you something he is so proud of. First, I take a picture of my breakfast with my phone because this is art. Then, I reluctantly cut into it and watch the yolk of the egg run perfectly down into the English muffin. The first bite is bliss. Pure bliss.

Homemade mozzarella is absolutely the way to go. I'll never want store-bought trash again. "Dear heavens," I groan as I chew the first bite. My eyes slip closed and I relish the flavors.

When I open them, Derek is watching me with a huge smile. "Good?"

"My goodness, Derek. You are gifted," I say, hurriedly putting another bite on my fork.

He smiles, pleased. "I'm glad you like it."

"Like it?" I question around another mouthful. "Cook for me the rest of our lives. Please." I groan a loud mmm. "Frank must have known," I say as I take another bite. Of course, Frank knew if Derek would be cooking, I would need to burn the calories. Is Frank all-knowing?

"What?" Derek asks in confusion at my mention of Frank.

"Nothing. This is amazing. What is this sauce? Is it made of angel's wings?" I ask, bathing a bite of English muffin in a golden sauce.

Derek chuckles. "No, hollandaise sauce."

"We should put it on everything. Everything," I say earnestly before shoving the bite in my mouth.

"Want another one?" Derek asks, noticing I am unashamedly picking up the leftover sauce with my finger and licking it off.

"No thank you, don't want to be too full for lunch," I say with a wink.

Derek eyes me suspiciously. "What are your plans for lunch?"

I shake my head. "It's a surprise, so don't make plans."

"What exactly are the plans for today?" Derek asks as he takes my plate.

"Oh! I'll do the dishes, here, give me that." I snatch the plates away. "Well, first was the breakfast muffin, then the gym, then you go to work, then I pick you up for lunch, then we go to lunch and you receive a birthday surprise, then you go back to work, then we go out for dinner at a special restaurant where you receive your birthday present," I recite eagerly. Took me all weekend to put all this together. I'm incredibly excited about it.

"Here's the thing, Princess," Derek starts hesitantly, leaning on the counter near where I'm rinsing dishes and putting them in the dishwasher. "I'm not real big on surprises."

I smile brilliantly. "Oh, don't worry, I am. It'll be great! I promise!" I ignore his implication intentionally. I know he hates surprises. That's why his surprises were carefully crafted with him in mind, and why I told him about them beforehand without springing them on him like a birthday ninja, as I have been known to be in the past.

"These surprises..." he starts cautiously.

"Don't even try it," I say, zipping my mouth shut and tossing away an imaginary key.

Derek smiles uncomfortably and raises his hands in defeat. "No, I'm not, I just want to know. They aren't public surprises are they?" he asks tentatively, looking somewhat afraid of the answer.

I smile sheepishly. "I promise, other than my slip up this morning, no one else will know it's your birthday unless you want them to."

He blows out a relieved breath. "Thank you."

"Honestly, it was five in the morning Derek, what did you expect? I promise I planned the entire day with your birthday aversion in mind." I turn and point at him seriously. "But you better thank your lucky stars that Brittany spilled because if you had let your birthday pass without telling me, I would have been so mad." I make my warning clear.

"Why?" he asks, simultaneously amused and curious at my vehemence.

I start his dishwasher and gape at him. "Because it's your birthday. Your day. You get one day a year to celebrate being you, and this is it. I want to celebrate you. I want to spend the day making you feel as loved and adored as you make me feel every day. If I missed it, I would have felt awful, absolutely terrible because I love you," I explain passionately.

Derek's gaze softens as he approaches, caging me between him and the counter with his arms. "You give me more than I deserve," he murmurs, his face close to mine.

"Respectfully disagree," I reply immediately.

My stomach dips as he kisses me. My arms come up around his neck so I can pull him as close to me as I can. We make out in the kitchen until we are both panting, and it's clear he is having to physically hold himself back from pouncing on me.

"I should go and let you get ready for work," I say sadly, making no effort to let him go.

Derek groans with reluctance. "I guess I should let you go." He kisses me again, and again, until we are making out once more.

His ringing phone jolts us from just beyond oblivion. He sighs in annoyance and steps back to grab it from the counter without leaving my lips. I hold him tight as he answers, kissing his neck all the while.

"Masters," he answers gruffly, his arm around me and one hand moving up and down my back.

I hear Brittany on the other end. She and Grady are singing him "Happy Birthday." I smile and continue nuzzling and kissing him until Brittany asks, "How's your day going so far?"

Derek makes a contented noise. "Couldn't be better, B. Thanks for getting with Maddy."

I beam at him; I can't believe he actually thanked her!

"Wow!" I hear Brittany exclaim in surprise. "You must be having a really good day so far."

"Maddy went to the gym with me, then we came back here and had breakfast. It's been great. Thanks again for calling," he adds, starting to nuzzle my neck again, fast losing interest in the call.

"Have a good day, Derek! We love you!" Brittany chimes brightly before hanging up.

Derek drops his phone on the counter and goes back to my lips. After a few minutes, his phone rings again.

I giggle at his irritated growl. "I really should go. Neither one of us is going to get anywhere if this vicious cycle continues."

Derek grunts in agreement, kissing me a last time before answering the phone. "Masters." He holds the phone away from his face and kisses me again, whispering, "Thanks again. See you for lunch."

I wave as I leave him standing at his front door.

Chapter 20

Derek

My freaking birthday.

I've hated my birthday since the first grade when Donny Sylvester had the same birthday as me and proceeded to beat the crap out of me for it. It seemingly got worse every year. In second grade, Brittany accidentally lit the curtains on fire with my candles; we had to evacuate the house and I didn't get my presents until three days later when the literal smoke cleared. Third grade I had the one and only case of the flu I've ever had and spent the day in the hospital hooked up to an IV receiving fluids. Fourth grade my Mom was going through some sort of plant-based diet fad, and you can imagine what that meant for my cake. My birthdays never got better. A broken bone here, a soul-crushing embarrassment there; eventually you just learn to hate the day. I stopped acknowledging my birthday, figuring birthdays were for some people and not for others. I've lived blissfully as a non-birthday person ever since with no regrets.

Then I wake up to Maddy ringing my doorbell like a junkie trick-or-treating at four thirty this morning, and, just like that, I become a birthday person.

Her passionate speech about celebrating me on my birthday because she loves me cracks my heart wide open and makes me want to mourn for all the birthdays she was never in my life. Similarly, I mourn for each birthday she celebrated without me.

I'm whistling as I walk into work, earning more than one strange look. I get it; I never come into work whistling. As a general rule, I hate whistlers. Why do whistlers always think other people want to hear whatever tune is in their head? It's obnoxious and annoying. But not today. Today I'm a whistler.

"Masters, you got a second?" Barnes asks me.

I like Barnes. He's a good cop. Gonna be a detective soon if he keeps doing what he's doing.

"What's going on, Barnes?" I ask, gesturing to the chair beside my desk.

"I'm taking the detective's exam in a few weeks and I want to ask if I could put you as a reference?" he asks nervously.

"Absolutely. I'll gladly be your reference. I'd be happy to be your partner while you train, too, assuming you pass the exam," I offer.

Barnes smiles. "Thanks, I appreciate it."

It feels good to do good things. It's a good day. I woke up and saw my girl first thing this morning, she watched me take out jerk-face Ty, I cooked a rockin', awesome breakfast. I sigh. Yeah. I can do this birthday thing.

I do paperwork at my desk for most of the morning, taking it easy since it is my birthday and I don't have an active case. At twelve on the dot, Maddy comes floating into the station in the prettiest dress I've ever seen. It's a bright blue with blues and greens sprinkled throughout, and although it's casual, it looks like she just walked off a runway. I swear I don't know how she does that.

"Hey, handsome. Having a good day?" she greets when she gets to me.

"Better now."

"Come on." She tugs on my hand. "I have a surprise waiting," she whispers eagerly.

I love that she's respecting my birthday rule and containing her excitement when she so clearly wants to shout from rooftops. "Sally, I'm headed to lunch," I call to the front desk. She waves us off with a smile.

Maddy is doing the thing Grady does when he gets super excited; both fidget and can't keep still. She takes us to her car and reaches in, presenting me with a small bag. "Birthday surprise number one," she says as softly as she can considering the amount of enthusiasm behind it.

I gaze curiously in the bag. "Thanks, Princess." She has gotten me the new pair of designer sunglasses I wanted. "How do they look?" I ask after I put them on.

"So handsome," she says dreamily.

I smile and lean in for a kiss. She only lets me have a quick one before she's pulling back and saying, "Okay, in the car. I'm driving."

My brows lift. "Oh yeah, why's that?"

She puts her hands on her hips. "Because you don't know where we are going, and birthday surprises two and three are in the car."

I roll my eyes, which thankfully she can't see since I have my new sunglasses on. Apparently arguing with Maddy about birthday protocol is out of the question today.

"Come on, get in." She rushes me around the car.

"Are you going to tell me where we are going?" I ask as I follow her instructions.

She grins wickedly. "Absolutely, when we get there," throwing my words from this morning back at me.

I chuckle. The little pest.

When we pull up to the marina, I am confused.

"Don't worry, I'll get you back in an hour. Although Chief owes me a favor, so if you want it to be longer, it can be, I'm sure," she boasts with a wink.

"Why does my chief owe you a favor?" I ask suspiciously, but she pretends not to hear me as she grabs a big basket from the back and starts hauling it toward the water.

"Okay," I start, taking the basket from her, "how about since we are here, you tell me where we are going now, and maybe even what's in the basket."

She eyes me for a moment before breaking into a huge smile. "We are taking out my Dad's boat for a picnic. Surprise!" she squeals and bounces up and down. "I'm so excited!" She skips past me and trots down to a small yacht. A freaking yacht. I mean, a small one, but still. I hope she's not expecting me to drive this thing.

"Um, Maddy?" I start hesitantly.

She's not paying attention to me in her delight. "Come on, hurry up. Set the basket there and I'll untie her so I can get her out in the open water."

I breathe in relief. Good, I don't have to drive.

Suddenly, she stops in consternation. "This is good right? No one else is here. You don't mind boats, right? I thought it would be fun and different for your birthday. Special but just for the two of us."

She looks so uncertain, it breaks my heart. With a broad smile, I take her in my arms. "It's perfect. Thank you," I say with sincere gratitude for everything that's led to this moment.

She smiles proudly. "Good. Sit, relax. I'll get her out and we'll find a little spot to sit for lunch."

I set the basket down but follow and watch as she works the boat like I'm sure she's done all her life. She's so capable that suddenly I'm revisiting that old feeling of insignificance, that there's nothing she can't do. I smirk, except cook apparently. I do have that.

She maneuvers the boat out into the water and drives up the river until we are in a scenic spot. I'm captivated by her dress whipping around her legs, her wind-kissed cheeks, and her dark brown hair flying all around her face.

"This spot okay?" she asks, but all I can do is nod. I can't look away from her. She smiles and does something that I assume is dropping the anchor. Finally, she stands in front of me, work done. "Okay, third birthday surprise." She makes a sound I assume is supposed to be a drumroll. "I got your favorite from May's!" she exclaims.

"May's isn't open for lunch," I say, eyeing the basket.

She lights up even more, which I didn't think was possible. "I know. But I called yesterday and when she heard it was for you—I didn't even mention your birthday by the way—she said I could come and pick it up."

I pull her into my lap. "That was very nice. Thank you."

She beams, very proud of herself. She stands and starts unpacking the basket, and I'm amazed at the spread we have here. May really went all out.

I groan in rapture with the first bite. "So good."

She glows. "Isn't this great?! I just knew it would be."

"It's pretty great. I've never had lunch on a yacht before."

"I'm so glad you like it. And technically, it's not a yacht. It's a speed boat. It's not big enough to be a yacht," she says matter of fact.

I grunt. "It looks like a freaking yacht."

Maddy giggles and proceeds to tell me the difference between a speedboat and a yacht, and about each of the different boats her parents owned when she was growing up. I know next to nothing about boats, so I only understand every third or fourth word she says, but I'm enjoying listening to her talk. She's so expressive and lit up with life and enthusiasm.

"So what's the plan for tonight?" I ask when she pauses to take a breath.

"Pick me up at six. I'll tell you where we are going from there. And I'll give you your present when we get where we are going," she says mischievously.

"Present? I thought the sunglasses were my present?" I ask in confusion.

She's gleeful. "No silly, the sunglasses were a birthday surprise you got to go with your other birthday surprise." She gestures around the boat.

She then explains the birthday surprise—I mean experience—present tier system. I should have been taking notes because there's no way I will remember this when her birthday rolls around. I'm just enjoying listening to her talk. She transitions from my birthday to Grady's at some point. There's a breeze blowing, the sun is glistening on the water, and Maddy is curled up next to me talking about plans for the rest of the summer. The boat rocking, with Maddy in my arms on a bright summer day, is as close to my happy place as it gets.

After what feels like mere minutes, Maddy jumps up and starts cleaning up. "I should get you back."

"Let's not rush back. Come sit with me." I hold out my hand and, when she puts her hand in mine, I tug her down on my lap.

"I don't want to get you in trouble on your birthday," she says against my neck.

"They're fine." I need to stay focused. There's something I've been wanting to bring up and I don't want to miss my chance again. I am feeling her lips brush against my neck and getting distracted. Today, right now, I'm counting on this moment to be the one that changes my birthday luck for good. "You said you have a light summer at work, what about after that?"

She looks at me in confusion. "What do you mean?"

"I just mean what are you thinking for your future?" I clarify.

"I don't know. I want to stay here. I like the new firm, and I want to keep the lighter caseload if that's what you're asking." She pulls away to see my face.

I nod along but know I'm screwing this up. She's not seeing where I want this conversation to go, so I decide to state it plainly. "What about us? You see us in your future?"

Understanding dawns, like she sees exactly what I'm getting at. She smiles. "I love you, Derek. Of course I want you in my future."

"I love you too, Princess."

That's what I needed to know. I knew she was mine and I knew she wanted me too. I knew she felt the same for me that I've felt for her since she first stood in her house and yelled at me. I didn't mind convincing her to give it a chance; I didn't mind putting a little pressure on her to push her past her fears. But I need to know now she's with me. I need to know she's past her fears and can say to herself, and to me, that this is what she wants. Now that I know that she's with me, I can proceed with the next phase of my plan.

If it were up to me, I would demand she marry me next week, but that's not Maddy. Her knowing she's for me is not the same as being ready to jump in with both feet. I can tell that even though she loves me and is enthusiastic about spending time with me, she is still consumed with fear. She needs more time to know I'm not going anywhere, to make sure those fears are gone for good. I will be coming for her, though, and she's just told me everything I need to know to seal the deal.

After a little longer just drifting on the water, Maddy takes us back to the marina and then drives me back to work. I have to say, she's gifted at birthdays. The rest of the workday crawls by and I count down the minutes until I can get home and get ready to pick up my girl. I don't even care about the rest of my birthday celebration; I just want my day to begin and end with her.

Happy birthday to me.

Chapter 21

Maddy

I'm early. Can you believe it? I can't. I absolutely cannot. But I didn't work today, and I've had nothing else to do but get ready for Derek, so when you look at it like that, it's awfully hard to imagine how I could have been late.

I take extra care in picking out my outfit of dark jeans and a bright pink and yellow ruffle top, something I know he hasn't seen me in yet and that will go great with my leather jacket. After I'm dressed, I take my time with my hair and makeup, playing around until I get it just right. I spritz myself, triple check that Derek's birthday present is wrapped and good to go, and then I...I don't know what to do with myself. I've never been early. So I pick out my shoes, go back and check my hair again, and fix a few I find out of place.

I am on my second makeup check when I hear a bang from the front of the house. I smile; it must be Grady again. I leave the bathroom and start up the hall toward the front door.

"Grady, is that you? Did you ride your rollerblades into the door again, silly?" I stop at the sight of the man standing just inside my door, pointing a gun at me.

I scan the room, making sure Grady is in fact not in the house, before

185

looking at the man as objectively as possible. He is not wearing a mask, so he wants me to see his face. He is holding a gun on me, so he intends to kill me. A glance toward the door tells me he forced it open, which means the police should be notified any minute by the intrusive security system Derek forced on me. Thank God.

I stand frozen in place, and my only thought is that after this, Derek's never going to let me celebrate his birthday again. Weird. Shouldn't my life flash before my eyes or something?

"Ms. Knight," the man says evenly, "Do you know who I am?"

I nod carefully. "Mr. Doyle, the defendant in a custody case I worked on a few months ago."

"You took my kids from me," he states menacingly.

Okay, I see what everyone meant by calm being scary now. I'll never doubt Macy or Derek again.

I shake my head. "No sir. The judge did that, I pled my client's case."

He inches closer. "No, the judge did exactly what you told him to do. I was there. You told him exactly what you wanted, and he did it. And I lost my kids."

I shake my head no even though he's right. I mean, technically, I did tell the judge what I wanted, and he did it. But that was likely to happen because Mr. Doyle didn't have representation. "Have you thought about hiring representation and contesting the settlement?" I ask carefully.

"I don't have money for that. That's why I didn't hire anyone to begin with. I was a good dad. I just want to see my kids," he says in calm desperation. "You told the judge I was an alcoholic, an unfit father. You told the judge to restrict visitation, and he did. You took away my kids, Ms. Knight."

I don't regret that, even now. He is an unfit father, clearly, even more than I originally thought. My mind races. Any judge would have come to the same conclusion, but if this man thinks he didn't get a fair shot, I do have a suggestion that could help him. "I could recommend a public defender for family cases like this one...." But, Mr. Doyle is shaking his head, so I stop talking. I can see he's already made his decision.

"I'll never get my kids back. Not now. This is all I have." He steps closer. "You don't have kids." Then he cocks his head, remembering. "Who is Grady?"

My eyes slide closed as my mind races to determine Grady's schedule. Matt and Grady are out fishing today, but they should be getting home soon. Hopefully, Grady won't want to come over. Matt and Brittany let him come over whenever he wants by himself. The thought of him getting hurt in this situation causes my throat to close with fear and my eyes to tear up.

"Who is Grady?" Mr. Doyle asks more persistently.

"My nephew," I whisper.

Mr. Doyle nods. "And he comes here a lot? I mean, he must if you thought it was him coming through the door and not your brother or your cop boyfriend."

It's disconcerting how much he knows about my life. Does he know about the security system?

"Does he?" he asks again.

"Yes, he comes here a lot," I say, trying to stay calm.

"You must be close," he assumes.

"Very," I whisper as a tear falls down my cheek.

"What if someone took him away from you, Ms. Knight? Would you be upset?" he asks, inching toward me.

"I would be devastated," I admit along with another tear.

Should I keep him talking or try to incapacitate him? I'm not sure what Derek would want me to do. I only had the one kickboxing lesson, and I'm not sure I can take him down. He's way bigger than me. Then there's the gun. What if I go at him and he shoots me? Should I just stay here and keep him talking? Where are the police? Shouldn't they be here by now? How long has it been? Because it feels like it's been three days.

"Multiply that by maybe a thousand to understand losing your own child, and then multiply that by three because I have three kids. You took my kids away from me, Ms. Knight. Don't I have a right to be devastated?" he insists.

I take a calming breath and try to explain. "Sir, I did not take your kids. I'm so sorry for your loss, but that was the judge's decision. I just pled..."

He cuts me off. "Your client's case. Yeah, I know. Sure felt personal, though, when you called me an alcoholic in court."

My eyes slip closed. This isn't looking good for me.

"Are you wondering what's taking the police so long to get here?" he taunts.

My eyes fly open and I gaze at him, stunned.

He grins. "I cut the line before I broke the door. They aren't coming, Ms. Knight."

I swallow. Well, isn't that just my luck. Derek and Macy were completely right. He is calm and deliberate and knows exactly what he's doing.

Crap.

* * *

Derek

I leave work early to get home and get ready for dinner with Maddy. I'm pulling on a new shirt and wondering what the odds are of her being early for once when my phone dings. I see the notification is from her security system and immediately pull it up.

The hard line has been cut and the front door broken. Thank God I set up her system to run primarily off Wi-Fi with the hard line as a backup.

I simultaneously pull the video feed I have of her living room and call the station. Cold fear pulses through me as I see a man holding a gun on Maddy. I jolt into action, grabbing my gun and keys, heading for the door.

"Barnes." Finally someone answers at the station.

"Barnes!" I bark. "Doyle—the angry father—is at Maddy's with a gun. I need backup."

I give Barnes Maddy's address and listen for a 10-4 before hanging up, burning rubber out of my neighborhood to get to Maddy. I knew installing the security system was the right move. Even though I told her there were cameras, I am pretty sure she had glazed over by the time I explained them, so I know she probably doesn't remember they are there. After the guy bought the gun, I went a little nutty, obsessively watching her feeds and getting alerts on my phone anytime she went in or out of the door.

If she knew I was keeping that close of a watch, she'd be furious, so I kept this little fact to myself. Keeping an eye on her with the security system, and the tracking app I put on her phone, and the trace I put on her car...well, you never know, just in case. I may have gone a little overboard, but in my defense, when a psychopath with a gun is threatening your girl, you do what needs to be done.

Thankfully I show up at her house the same time the first squad cars are pulling in, so I meet them outside and show them the feed I have of her living room. The street is bathed in red and blue, and the officers crowd around one car to form a plan of action.

"It looks like they are still talking for now," one officer says.

"He's just noticed the lights and is moving to the window," another updates, pointing to my phone screen.

"We need to get her out now," I growl through clenched teeth.

"Green, Perry, notify the neighbors to stay in their homes. Masters, stay back. We'll have Coleman handle this," Barnes directs as he takes charge of the scene.

"I don't think so." My fists clench, and Barnes puts his hand on my shoulder as Coleman approaches Maddy's front door and knocks on it. "I'm not standing out here doing nothing while Maddy is in danger," I yell at Barnes. "I'll go in through the back."

"Coleman can handle this objectively. You're too emotional and you know it," Barnes yells back, continuing to block my path.

I don't know where it comes from, but I start swinging. Barnes goes down with something that crunches under my fist. I keep hitting him until two other officers pulled me off and away from everyone else, forcing my arms behind my back. I stop struggling after a minute, taking deep breaths to calm my anger.

"You good?" the first asks.

"Masters, get it together man," the other says.

"Where's my phone? I want to watch the feed," I grind out, ignoring them.

The officers exchange a look, and I let out a noise of frustration that gets one of them moving to get me what I want.

"Here. Green got the feed from the security company to our system, so they are monitoring the situation with that," Officer Berry says as he hands me my phone.

I can see Coleman got in the house, but it looks like the police presence has thrown Doyle, forcing him to improvise. Doyle looks more erratic, now holding the gun against Maddy's head. My eyes slip closed, and my blood runs cold at the sight.

When calm guys lose their control, things can turn bad quickly. I feel my face flush with anger at not being able to charge in there and get her away from him. I look around for an ambulance, just in case he gets a shot off at her. Thankfully, two have already arrived, and Barnes is in the back of one having something done to his face. I'll have to think about that later.

I walk up to the line of cops in the front monitoring the situation "Why aren't we sending someone to the back door?" I demand.

Sergeant Smith holds up a hand. "Sit down and stuff it, Masters, or we'll lock you down."

I glare at him, but he doesn't care. I know better than to force it with Sergeant Smith. His version of locking me down is most likely sending me to the hospital myself. I go back to watching the feed, but the more I watch, the angrier I get. I can't watch her having a gun pointed at her and just stand here not doing anything.

It's torture.

At the same time, I can't look away. I can't stop watching to make sure she's okay, at least for another moment longer. All it would take is a little bit of pressure on the trigger and that psycho could end her life so easily. I don't stop my roar of frustration before scrubbing my head and picking up the phone, pasting my eyes to its screen again.

I feel someone come up beside me, but I ignore him. There isn't anything on earth that matters more than what I'm looking at right now. I clench a fist in frustration. "I can't do anything," I say through clenched teeth. I look around briefly for Green. Hitting something again would help, I think.

"Pray, Derek. You can't physically do anything, but you can pray for her," Barnes says from beside me.

I look at him, taking in his blackening eyes and what is probably broken nose. He's right. I can't protect Maddy from this, but God can.

I grunt in acknowledgement. "Thanks, Barnes. Sorry about your face," I grumble.

"Don't worry about it," he says reassuringly, taking up post by my side.

* * *

Maddy

"I could have made this quick. Painless. But you don't deserve that. You should know how much pain and agony you've put me through. You deserve to feel the same pain I feel. That's justice, Ms. Knight. You think your job is getting justice, but you don't even know the meaning of the word," Doyle spits at me, officially starting to unravel.

Okay, but my job isn't justice. That's the judge's job. I don't tell him this. He seems to be ranting a little bit, and for whatever reason, I find it comforting. Like however long he keeps talking, the bigger the odds Derek will get here and find us. Although, he doesn't usually get here early because I'm always late.

Dang it. Why can't I be more punctual?

Suddenly, the room floods with blue light, and Doyle's eyes bulge. He moves to the window and peaks out. Thank you, God, for boyfriends with stalking tendencies. I promise to never complain about his overprotective nature again.

Well...for at least thirty days. I can definitely promise thirty days.

"How did they know? I cut the line," Doyle says to himself. He stares at me, then back at the police, then at me, seemingly confused. His eyes dart around like he is searching for something.

Then there's a knock on the door.

Doyle comes up behind me and presses the end of the gun to my temple. I close my eyes. It wouldn't take much for him to end it all right here, right now.

"Go away!" he yells.

His cool detachment is officially lost. The cops seem to have thrown him for quite the loop.

"My name is Coleman. I'm just here to see if we can't get this worked out," comes the shout through the door. "How about you let me in so we can talk? I'm unarmed." Coleman pushes on the door without waiting on a reply, and it swings slowly open. "Don't shoot, I'm just here to talk. I'm unarmed," he says with his hands up.

As someone with a gun to their head, I have never been more opposed to the diplomatic process.

Doyle backs us up, putting more pressure on the gun resting on my temple.

Coleman slowly enters the house, hands up. "Doyle, right? I'm Coleman," he says, slowly lowering his hands. "Why don't you take the gun from Ms. Knight's head and we'll talk?"

"No. Stay there. I don't want to talk. She took my kids, and I want her to pay. I'm prepared to end it here," Doyle tries to say this calmly, but his voice is shaking. Being pressed against his body, I can tell he is sweating profusely.

"I know things seem bad now, Doyle, but if you shoot Ms. Knight, things will get infinitely worse and you'll certainly never see your kids again. You don't want that, right? Let's end this here. We'll all go home, and you can retain visitation with your kids."

Doyle shakes his head, removes the gun from mine long enough to wipe the sweat from his brow, and then presses the weapon against my temple again. "I'm never seeing my kids again. My ex will see to that. This is all I have. All I have is justice."

Coleman inches closer. "This isn't justice, Doyle. Ms. Knight was just doing her job, same as any of us. Things aren't as bad as they seem right now. But you have to help me out and drop the gun. We can figure the rest out later."

"This is all I have. All I have is the gun and this." He presses it harder against my temple. "Getting justice is all I have."

"Mr. Doyle, please put down the gun. I promise we will work everything out, but we can't do that if you don't drop the gun," Coleman insists.

Is it just me or does this conversation not seem to be going anywhere? My eyes widen as I hear a roar from outside. If my guess is correct, either a mountain lion has a splinter in its paw or someone told Derek he couldn't come barreling in to take control of this situation. Coleman glances at me but quickly returns his attention to pleading with Doyle, who is becoming antsier and antsier behind me.

"No, no, no, no, I'm staying here. You should leave now. Let me finish. This is all I have. Go now," Doyle commands Coleman with rising panic.

To my horror and shock, Coleman turns to leave. I open my mouth to protest, but Coleman spins back around with his gun pointed at Doyle.

The gun lifts from my temple, then my ears are ringing from shots fired, and I'm being pulled to the ground by Doyle.

Oh no! Was I shot? I can't be shot! It's Derek's birthday, and I can't get blood on this top!

* * *

Derek

I pray. I watch the screen as Coleman negotiates with agonizing slowness. I watch and pray and lose my breath in a rush as Doyle points the gun at Coleman. Two shots go off, and Maddy and Doyle both drop to the ground.

No one can hold me back this time. I clear a path as I run into the house, ignoring the shouts from fellow officers at my back. Coleman is bending over Maddy, and I lose my heart as I look at her lying motionless on the floor.

I drop down beside her. "Maddy?" I look down her body for blood but don't see any. "Maddy?"

Her eyes open and she smiles. "Hey! I was just thinking about you."

I let out the breath I've been holding since the second I saw that man holding a gun on her and take her into my arms. "Are you okay? Are you hurt?" I ask as I hold her close.

"I'm really sorry about your birthday dinner. I was ready early and everything," she insists against my neck.

There is a flurry of movement around us now as the paramedics pick up Doyle and take him out of the house, escorted by officers. I hold Maddy tighter. "I love you, Madison. I love you so much. You're okay?"

She nods and holds me just as tight as I'm holding her. "I love you, Derek. Is he...is he...?" she asks, clearly not wanting to follow her train of thought.

"He'll be fine. In jail. For a long, long time," I mutter, glancing at where the paramedics are taking him on the stretcher.

Her body shudders and I hold her closer. "Are you hurt, Maddy?" I ask again, just to be sure.

She shakes her head.

"He shot at me and missed, but mine hit him. Paramedics still want to look at her, though," Coleman says to me from behind Maddy's back.

"I'm so sorry about your birthday. Promise me you won't hold this against me for all of time," Maddy pleads earnestly, desperately.

"Promise," I whisper, my birthday being the very last thing I want to discuss right now.

"It's your birthday? Hey, happy birthday, man!" Coleman jovially exclaims.

I glare at him and he gets the hint, getting up and walking away to give us some space. I pull back to look into Maddy's face for any signs of shock. "You're sure you are okay?"

"I'm fine. I'm real upset about your birthday, though," she says with a pout.

For the first time tonight, I grin.

"Get up and let the paramedics at her, Masters," Sergeant Smith directs gruffly. I stand, helping Maddy up. I do another once over of her body to make sure she's whole and stay as close as possible as the paramedics ask her questions and perform rudimentary tests to ensure she's not going into shock.

"Masters, we have a concerned neighbor out here, says he's her brother," calls an officer from the door. I nod and wave Matt in.

He loses no time. "Maddy? Thank God! Are you okay?" he asks worriedly as he crushes her in a hug, which is borderline awkward because I still have my arm around her, but I'm not letting go. Not for anyone.

"I'm fine. Just a little scared, that's all. By the way, how did you know?" she turns and asks me. "He said he cut the outside line to the system."

"The primary is Wi-Fi. I got a notification the line was cut and the door was busted into," I explain easily.

"You get notifications on your phone for my security system?" she asks with confusion, then sighs. "I don't know why that surprises me."

"Sure worked out tonight. Almost had a heart attack when I saw that guy holding a gun on you." I hold her a little tighter at the memory.

"How did you see that?" she asks with bewilderment.

I point up "Cameras."

She follows my finger and looks back at me with huge eyes. "You have cameras in my house?!" she shouts.

"I walked you through the entire system when I put it in. You don't remember?" I ask innocently, even though I know the answer. She can't be upset about this. There was a man with a gun on her. The security system saved her life; she can't possibly be mad about that.

"No! You didn't tell me about the cameras! Is there a camera in my bedroom?" she screeches.

"No, of course not. Just right here and in the doorbell. Maddy, I went over all this with you," I repeat.

Her eyes narrow. "You saved that for last knowing full well I stopped listening," she accuses.

I raise my hands in surrender. "How was I supposed to know you weren't listening? You said it wasn't awful. I thought you were okay with it."

"You've been checking those cameras like a legit stalker, haven't you?"

"I have been monitoring your security system since there has been an active threat against you, yes," I say carefully.

"Oh. My. Falafel," she gasps. "You are a crazy stalker boyfriend, and while I'm okay with that right now, in thirty days we are having a very serious conversation about basic human rights."

I roll my eyes. "You can't possibly be mad about this. That system saved your life tonight."

"Don't you tell me what I can and can't do, Derek Masters!" she argues with a finger in my face.

I smile. I can't help it. Arguing Maddy is my fourth favorite Maddy, right after Lawyer Maddy. She almost died tonight, and her arguing with me like she always does is the most precious thing in the world.

Matt looks back and forth between the two of us. "Okay, well, looks like all's good here. How about you two pop over and see Grady and Brittany when all this calms down, will ya, Mads? They're worried."

She nods but doesn't look away from me as Matt leaves the house.

"You aren't really mad about this," I say, taking her into my arms.

She sighs in surrender. "I know. It felt good to yell a little, though." She holds me tight and buries her face in my neck. "Thanks for being a crazy stalker boyfriend."

"Anytime, Princess." Then I kiss her. A lot. Because she could have died, and I almost never got to kiss her again.

After a few minutes, some of the crowd starts to clear out of the house, and it gets a little quieter. "You wanna stay with Matt and Brittany tonight?" I ask when I finally pull away from her lips.

She shakes her head. "I'm fine to stay here."

After another minute of just holding her, I let out a small laugh. "You were early, huh?"

She groans. "First time ever. I can't believe you missed it. And we missed your birthday dinner."

"Let's go over to Brittany's and see them, then we'll go pick something up and bring it back here. The guys should be done by then," I suggest.

She nods and leans into my side as we walk slowly over to Brittany's, stopping to chat with several officers who ask after Maddy. The force is like a family, and since Maddy's mine, they're her family too.

"Glad you're okay, ma'am," Barnes says respectfully.

"Thank you." Then she does a double-take. "Goodness, what happened to your face? Are you okay? Did a criminal do that?" she asks in concern.

Barnes smirks. "No ma'am, not a criminal."

"Come on, Maddy, let's get going," I insist, pulling her toward my sister's house.

Barnes chuckles and waves as we walk away, and I determine to buy him lunch or something for his trouble. Or at least for not selling me out. I like loyalty.

"Derek?" Maddy says lazily at my side.

"Yes?" I reply, kissing her temple.

"Please tell me you did not break that man's nose," she asks casually.

I stiffen. "Well, I haven't heard for sure it is broken...."

Maddy pulls away and glares at me. "Derek, how could you!"

I tug her back against me because not touching her is not an option. "He's fine. You saw him, and I've already decided to buy him lunch this week."

"You broke his nose, Derek, not his favorite ballpoint pen," she says in exasperation.

"What does that mean?" I'm genuinely confused about her point. I wonder if I should take her back to the paramedics. She isn't making much sense tonight.

"It means you broke the man's nose. You should do more than take him to lunch," she says as if should be obvious to me like it is to her.

"Lunch is more than sufficient. Frank broke my nose once and all I got was yelled at for not ducking." I argue logically.

"I think getting your nose broken at a kickboxing gym is different than a coworker breaking your nose for no good reason," she returns sarcastically.

"Fine, what do you want me to do?" I ask, giving in to her.

She glares at me again. "Well how am I supposed to know? But it should be more than lunch."

I open Brittany's front door. "We aren't talking about this anymore."

"Don't you tell me what we will and won't discuss," she says menacingly. Well, I'm sure it's supposed to be menacing. It's not.

"Geez, are you two still bickering? Can we not just enjoy the fact that everyone is safe?" Matt asks in annoyance.

"That sounds like a great idea." I say, reluctantly letting Maddy go so Brittany and Grady can hug her. Doesn't stop her from glaring at me over their shoulders, though. I grin in return. She can be as irritated with me as she wants as long as she's okay.

I sit down on the couch next to Matt with a sigh.

"You okay?" Matt asks quietly while the girls talk.

"Better now," I say, rubbing a hand down my face.

"Rough night," he says in understanding.

"You could say that."

"You really break that guy's nose?".

I glance at Matt and shrug. "Eh...."

He nods. "I get it."

"Try explaining it to Mads for me, would you?"

Matt chuckles. "Nope, not my department, my friend. That's all you. She'd argue about the sky being blue."

"Sometimes it's not blue, Matty," our girl says as she comes around the couch and plops down between me and Matt. "Sometimes it's pink, or orange, or purple. You can't make a blanket statement like 'the sky is blue' and just expect everybody to be okay with it."

Matt cuts her an ironic grin. "Ah yes, how could I forget. You are so right."

Brittany sits on Matt's lap while Grady crawls up on Maddy's lap. "I'm glad the bad man didn't get you, Aunt Maddy. Uncle Derek saved you," he says sincerely.

"Yep, Uncle Derek saved me," she agrees, snuggling him close.

"Has anyone had dinner? I'm starving," Brittany speaks up from her husband's lap.

I smirk. Brittany's hungry all the time now. Good thing Grady's birthday is in a couple weeks and we can all let the secret out.

"Can we have pizza?" Grady pleads.

Matt looks over to me and Maddy. "How does pizza sound?"

"Like manna from heaven," Maddy gratefully answers.

I nod in agreement. "Sounds good. I'll order."

A little less than an hour later, we are all sitting on the living room floor eating pizza. Grady is up past his bedtime, a movie's on that no one is paying attention to, and we are laughing hysterically as Maddy animatedly relays her experience at the gym this morning.

Happy birthday to me.

Chapter 22

Maddy

You would think having a gun held to your head would be the roughest part of the month. That things would pretty much go uphill from there. Unfortunately, the whole gun thing is nothing compared to the cleanup. To be more precise, the actual cleaning part is easy. A little blood here, a bullet hole there, bing, bang, boom, all cleaned up.

There is tension, however, surrounding the replacement of the door and the repainting after the bullet hole repair. Tension may be an understatement. Things are said, feelings are hurt. It is maybe the most significant thing to happen in my relationship with Matt since he ripped the head off my favorite teddy when we were six and nine.

"What is your aversion to a little color?" I ask in frustration as we sit at his kitchen table arguing for the thousandth time.

"I just want it back how it was. You are making this infinitely more difficult than it needs to be," Matt argues.

"It's not that hard to pick a different color. Why does everything have to be so bland?" I shout in frustration.

"Neutral colors are calming, good for resale value, and allow you to decorate with whatever colors you want," Matt returns calmly.

This has been his argument from the beginning. It's getting old.

"But I have to live there. We aren't going to be selling anytime soon. And I don't understand what your issue is with the door I picked out."

"I'm not spending two thousand dollars on a door. We are getting the one that's the same as the one that was there. I liked the original door," Matt insists obstinately.

"But it's boring. And I said I would pay for the door."

Matt lets out a frustrated grunt. "Maddy, enough. I'm tired of your whining."

"I'm not whining!" I yell.

"You are whining like you did that day Mom and Dad took us to Six Flags," he grumbles.

I open my mouth to respond to this ridiculous accusation but am interrupted. "Okay, separate corners you two," Brittany says as she comes between us.

"She's being unreasonable," Matt cries.

"He's being boring and stubborn," I say petulantly.

"You're both being unreasonable," Brittany says with a look of disappointment. "Take a break from fighting over it. Grady wants someone to play with him," she says with a nudge to Matt.

Matt takes the hint and walks back to Grady's room, leaving me alone with Brittany. We sit down with a huff on the couch. "Be honest, you can't approve of the boring door and neutral colors," I say to her.

Brittany grins. "Nope, I'm not getting in the middle. Although, I think you should remember that Matt is very particular about his house."

"Why? What is the big issue? I mean, if he hates it or if I move, he can change it back."

"We talked about it a lot while he worked on it. He asked my opinion on a lot of it. I think he thinks of it as something we did together," Brittany shares quietly.

Matt can be pretty sentimental. I don't know whether to be appalled that Brittany shares Matt's taste in decorating or find it sweet that Matt is so protective of their shared project. Okay, maybe both. "Fine. I'll give in. It is his house, I guess," I say grudgingly.

"We'll go shopping and find some super pretty and colorful things to put on your walls," Brittany offers.

"Sounds terrific!" I say with a smile. Although if I'm honest, I'm questioning her judgment more now than I ever have before.

"Hey, guys!" Derek calls as he walks through Brittany and Matt's door.

"Hey," Brittany greets.

"Hey, handsome," I say heaving a sigh, still mourning the loss of the sunburst orange-colored walls I had picked out.

"What's going on?" he asks as he drops down into a chair across from us.

Brittany fills him in with a long-suffering tone. "I just broke up fight two hundred and fifty-seven between Matt and Maddy about the repairs for the house."

"Paint or door?" Derek asks knowingly.

"Both," I groan. "But I have agreed to forfeit for the greater good."

"A sacrifice you're making gracefully, I see," he says with a mocking grin.

I glare at him playfully. "What can I say? I'm a giver," I crack.

Derek and Brittany's laughter dies down as Matt and Grady come into the living room from his room.

"Uncle Derek!" Grady cheers and hugs him.

"Hey, Bud."

"Glad you're here. Maybe you can talk some sense into Maddy," Matt says bitterly.

"No need. I concede. It's your house, you choose." The words are harder to get out than I expected.

Matt's brows lift and his eyes narrow with skepticism. "Why?"

I glower at him. "Accept it and say thank you or I'll change my mind and we can go another round."

Matt opens his mouth, but Brittany beats him to it. "Maddy, we appreciate your concession. Matt, you can take it from here. Let's never ever discuss this again. I want agreements from both of you, now." Both Matt and I nod grudgingly. "Good. Okay, what do we want to do for dinner because I'm starving."

I smile because odds are if you are with Brittany for more than two hours at a time, you'll hear those words. Brittany's pregnancy is getting harder and harder to ignore, and Grady's birthday can't come soon enough. I console myself about the walls and the door knowing that I'm doing the right thing, and that we have more important things to look forward to. Grady's adoption will be finalized this week and his birthday party will be next week, which also happens to be the first anniversary of meeting Derek. There's too much to look forward to for me to be focused on Matt's obstinacy.

I determine to take any further aggression I have with Matt out on Frank during our next morning training session and join the discussion about dinner.

Chapter 23

Maddy

I think I hate Frank. Every day I get up at four-thirty and meet Derek at the gym, and every morning Frank takes me through what he calls "basic training", which doesn't feel basic at all. In fact, the fact that my entire body hurts and he keeps calling it "basic" is mildly insulting. My court-appropriate suit feels like a vice around my arms and shoulders, the areas that are the sorest.

"Why are you limping?" Brittany asks as we walk down the hallway of the courthouse.

"I'm not limping," I protest.

"You are. You're limping," Matt confirms beside Brittany.

"I am not limping," I say, straightening my walk. A smiling Derek waits for us outside the judge's chamber doors, looking hot in a suit. Geez, I love his smile. I especially love it when it's for me. I beam back at him.

"Hey, your limp is better," Derek greets cheerfully.

Matt and Brittany crack up beside me as I frown at him. "I. Am. Not. Limping."

Derek remains silent. Wisely.

I turn to Matt and Brittany. "Ready?"

They both nod excitedly. I look down at Grady, "Ready for this, Bud?"

"Can we get ice cream after this?" he asks, ignoring my question.

I smile, a proud aunt. I love that he is always ready for ice cream. Court appearances can wait. This kid just wants a snack.

Now that we are all here, the judge's clerk sees us into his chambers. The judge swears us in, and I introduce the judge to Matt and Brittany, explaining that Matt wants to adopt Grady. He asks Matt a couple of questions to make sure he understands the adoption is permanent. Then the judge declares the adoption approved and moves to sign the adoption decree.

"Can we get ice cream now?" Grady whisper/yells to Brittany.

"Shhh. Not yet," she whispers back.

"Grady, do you want to come bang the gavel, making it official?" the judge offers.

This is my favorite part of the adoption process. Not all judges do this, but Judge Mayweather does, and it's so sweet.

Grady looks to his Mom for permission, then tentatively goes around the massive mahogany desk. The judge hands him his gavel and shows him where to hit.

"Okay, hit it here, and it's official," he says, pointing to the exact spot for Grady.

Grady bangs the gavel, hard. Enthusiastically. Then he looks at the judge with gales of laughter. "Can I do that again?"

The judge grins. "One more time, just to be sure it sticks."

Grady bangs the gavel again and laughs. He returns the gavel to the judge and hops back to his mother, who prompts, "What do you say?"

"Thank you, sir, for making Matt my Daddy." I swear we all tear up at that. After a moment, Grady says, "Oh, and for letting me bang the gavel."

"You're quite welcome," Judge Mayweather returns, standing to see us out of his chambers.

We step out of the chambers and exchange congratulatory hugs and take photos. We make it down the front steps of the courthouse toward the parking lot when Derek breaks the silence. "Okay, I have to say it. I'm sorry, Princess, but you're limping."

I stop, turning on the group. "Of course I'm limping! Frank is trying to kill me. You would be limping too. Every muscle in my body hurts from that torture you psychotically call a hobby. I would, however, appreciate not being told how awful I look limping while it's taking all the strength in my incredibly painful legs to keep me upright," I say glaring from him to Brittany to Matt.

Matt, Brittany, Grady, and Derek look at me warily as if any sudden movements will set me off again. Finally, Matt looks at Brittany. "Ice cream?"

"Yeah!" Grady cheers loudly.

"That place down on the Riverwalk?" Derek asks.

"Ooh yeah, the family place. They have the best ice cream," Brittany gushes. "Such a great family too. I love them."

I proceed to my car without looking back, mentally deciding whether or not I'm done with the human race for the afternoon or if I'll join them for ice cream.

"You need to drink more water," Derek says, snagging me from behind with an arm across my stomach and pulling me against his chest.

"I've been drinking so much water I'm shocked I haven't floated away by now. I think I'm going to spend some quality time in my parents' hot tub tonight," I say grumpily.

"Ride with me," he says, his lips close to my ear.

I groan. "I'm not sure I can get my leg over the bike. Or that I have the strength in my arms to hold on."

I don't hear anything, but Derek's chest starts vibrating against my back. I turn and glare at him. "Are you laughing at me?"

Derek looks all innocent. "Come on, I'll drive then."

I hang my head because that would be awesome.

"You better not tell Frank to take it easy on me," I mutter, putting my seatbelt on as he cranks my car. "He already complains about what a girl I am."

Derek laughs. "He says that to everyone. You're doing great. Just give it another couple of weeks and you'll feel great."

I gape at him. "Another couple of weeks? I thought I would be fine in a few days!"

Derek winces. "Everybody's different."

"Hurry, then. I need ice cream," I moan.

Chapter 24

Maddy

It's mid-May, the adoption is final, the attack has been put behind us, and I'm only experiencing mild soreness from Franks' torture. It's Grady's birthday and, as if I could forget, the excited little boy currently jumping on my bed...while I'm still in it...at seven in the morning who is happily shouting, "It's my birthday!" would surely remind me.

"Grady, Aunt Maddy needs her beauty sleep. These good looks don't happen on accident, Buddy," I say yawning.

"Come on! It's my birthday!" he yells, pushing on my stomach.

"Do your Mom and Dad know you are here?" I ask and consider changing his code on my door.

"Daddy told me to come over. He said you would play with me while he and Mommy slept in a little longer," Grady explains cheerfully.

"Of course he did," I grumble, reaching for my phone to unlock it for the ball of excitement still jumping on my bed. "Here, call Uncle Derek and remind him it's your birthday."

He grabs it from me and continues jumping on the bed. "Uncle Derek, it's my birthday!" Grady shouts into the phone.

"Tell Uncle Derek to come over and make you breakfast."

"Aunt Maddy says you should come over and make me breakfast."

Grady is quiet as he listens to Derek. "Chocolate chip pancakes!" he cheers. "Okay. Hurry, IT'S MY BIRTHDAY!"

I laugh when he hangs up the phone. "Stop jumping, Buddy, come snuggle with me."

Grady drops down and crawls under my covers, squirming and twisting until I find his favorite show on my phone and say, "Here, let's watch this in bed."

"Cool!" he says with excitement.

I chuckle and resolve that when he's a moody teenager, I'm bursting into his room on his birthday at seven in the morning to wake him up and make him snuggle with me. We watch a few episodes of Grady's favorite show on my phone until Derek finally arrives.

"Seriously, I drove all the way over here to make you breakfast and you guys are in bed?" Derek asks from my bedroom doorway.

I grin. "We were waiting for you."

"Uncle Derek!" Grady gets up and runs across the top of my bed, taking a flying leap into Derek's arms. "It's my birthday!"

Derek laughs. "I know, Buddy, happy birthday. Come help me with your pancakes while Aunt Maddy gets up and gets ready for your party."

Grady runs into the kitchen ahead of Derek, and I climb out of bed to get ready. I could be annoyed that I'm getting up earlier than I want to on a Saturday, but you can't argue with pancakes.

I walk into the kitchen and find Grady standing on a stool helping Derek flip the pancakes. It is so ridiculously cute I take a picture.

"Did you stop by the store on the way?" I ask. Since Derek has started cooking for us there's a little more in my kitchen than just bottled water, but it still isn't much. He always has to go by the store first or bring what he needs from home.

"Yeah, quick trip. No big deal," he replies lightly.

I wrap my arms around him from behind and plant a kiss on his cheek. "Thank you."

"Well, isn't this a happy family?" Matt says as he enters the kitchen, Brittany trailing behind him.

"Oh, yay! Pancakes! I'm starving," Brittany cheers. She comes around to kiss Grady on the head. "Happy birthday, Buddy."

"Everybody want chocolate chip? Cause we are doing a big batch of them right now," Derek asks as he pours batter onto the skillet.

All in agreement, Grady abandons his post to run to Brittany and whisper into her ear. She looks concerned and says, "Are you sure?" When Grady nods, she says, "Go ask your Dad."

Grady runs to Matt and whispers in his ear, Matt whispers back, and then Grady says, "I'm sure. Can I tell them now?"

Matt and Brittany looked at each other and nod. With that, Grady shouts gleefully, "I'm gonna be a brother!"

I squeal and scoop Brittany in a huge hug. "I'm so excited!" I yell jumping up and down.

Derek comes around the kitchen bar and hugs Brittany while I move to hug Matt.

Brittany eyes us suspiciously. "You guys already knew!" she accuses.

I freeze, my eyes darting between Matt and Derek, not wanting to sell out Matt. Thankfully Derek saves us. "You're like, what, at least three and a half months along now. You're showing, B. It was hard not to notice," he says obviously as he flips pancakes.

Brittany frowns. "I'm not showing that much. I could have just been getting chubby."

I snort. "Please, with those boobs?"

Derek grimaces. "Eww. Sister," he reminds me in disgust.

I pull Brittany down to the table. "Tell me everything, don't leave anything out. And I thought we were waiting until after his party to tell everyone."

Brittany frowns pitifully. "We were. We wanted today to be just about Grady and the adoption, but he kept asking questions about why

Mommy is so hungry all the time, crying all the time, why is my belly getting hard and poking out. We ended up going ahead and telling him last night."

"I can't wait to tell everybody at the party today!" Grady adds.

"Do all the parents know too?" she asks, glaring at Matt.

"I don't know. I didn't tell them," he says, hands up in surrender.

"I didn't discuss it with anyone," I confirm.

"Except me," Derek says from the stove. "Pancakes," he announces as he places a platter filled with them on the table.

Grady reaches for one, and Matt puts his hand on his shoulder to hold him back. "Blessing."

"I'll say it," Derek volunteers.

Derek isn't much of a talker. I've never heard him volunteer to say the blessing unless it is just the two of us.

"Dear God, thank you for this day, and for the wonderful blessing that our family is expanding. Thank you for Grady, and the joy he brings us all. I pray you bless him on his birthday and help him to have a special day. Bless Brittany and keep her and the baby healthy, and bless the food we are about to eat, to the nourishment of our bodies, and our bodies to Your service. Amen."

Grady drives for the pancakes immediately. I continued holding Derek's hand and whisper "I love you" before giving him a quick kiss.

Derek smiles at me and kisses my hand. "I love you too." When we come out of our love bubble for pancakes, Derek groans and rolls his eyes heavenward. "Are you crying?" he asks Brittany in disgust.

"Just a little," she sniffles. "That was so sweet!"

Derek looks at Matt in bewilderment, who just shrugs in boredom. "It was a sweet prayer."

"This is why I never say anything around you lunatics. You make such a big deal out of everything," Derek grumbles.

"When can I open my birthday presents?" Grady asks around a

mouthful of pancakes.

"Oh, is it your birthday today? Were we supposed to get you presents?" I tease.

The horror on his face is just plain funny.

"When do we open presents on birthdays?" Brittany asks him.

"At the birthday party," Grady answers, heaving a disappointed sigh.

Keeping Grady entertained before his birthday is a herculean task. Derek and I end up taking him to Gran and Pop's pool two hours early just for him to burn off some energy. By the time Matt and Brittany get there, along with Meema and Papa, he has settled from vibrating mania to enthusiastic excitement. I am tasked with helping Brittany man the food tables and I take the opportunity to catch up with her about her pregnancy. "Have you been very sick?" I ask.

"No, not really. I have been really hungry. All the time. Like probably more than I should be at this point. My working theory is maybe because I'm running around on the floor all day," she says, referring to her job as a nurse manager on the oncology floor of the hospital.

"Any weird pregnancy things going on?"

Brittany blushes. "Not particularly weird. Just...you know. The hormones, that kind of thing."

"How excited was Matt when you told him?"

Brittany laughs. "I'm surprised you didn't hear him. I told him when we were out on the front porch swing one night. I thought he was going to wake the neighborhood with all his hooting and hollering. Needless to say, he was very excited," she remembers fondly.

"You know, one of my favorite things has been watching Matt be a dad," I say, looking over to where my brother and Grady are playing.

"He loves Grady like his own. I couldn't be more grateful." Brittany sniffles, and I take that as a sign to change the subject to less sentimental things. Surely, Grady's birthday offers her enough opportunities to cry as it is. I don't really want to be the cause for any more tears than necessary.

"So who's coming today?" I ask in a lighter tone.

"Grady's friends from day camp, that's pretty much it. Five or six kids maybe," Brittany answers easily.

"He's only goes two or three times a week, right?" I can never keep up with this kid's schedule.

"He goes three days a week to day camp, and Matt keeps him the other two. Matt has started on the kitchen reno, so it gives him some time to get stuff done without Grady being underfoot. He saves the lighter projects for when Grady's home and can help," Brittany explains with a loving smile.

"That's sweet! I bet Grady loves it."

"He does. Matt mentioned doing a few other upgrades to other areas of the house to help with the resale value."

I gasp. "Are you thinking of moving?"

Brittany looks guilty. "I don't know. I love our house. I love the cul-de-sac. I love being so close to you and probably, eventually, Derek." She nudges me not so subtly. "But I don't know how many kids we will want. I mean, we are kind of thinking of having a few more, and the house is kind of small."

My heart starts having palpitations, and not the good kind. "I like living beside you. What if I don't get to see you and Grady and the baby every day?" I am verging on tears now and I'm not pregnant. That's how strongly I feel about the topic. No one is more surprised by this than me.

Brittany stares at me in surprise. "I had no idea this was such a big deal to you. I'm not trying to abandon you," she says, her eyes tearing up along with mine. She grabs me in a hug and assures me if they move, they'll find two houses together so we can move too.

"What is happening over here?" Matt asks, eyeing us like he really doesn't want to know.

"I don't want you to move!" I wail, unable to contain my feelings a second longer, tears streaming down my face.

"Dear heavens, it's catching," Matt mutters, walking away to leave us to our emotionally charged hug situation.

Derek starts to head over when he sees I'm upset, but I see out of the corner of my eye that Matt warns him off. Instead, he lingers by the grill with Matt, keeping a solid eye on me and Brittany.

"I really didn't know you felt so strongly," Brittany sniffles.

"I didn't either. It's just been so great. I love living next to you. I don't want to have to drive to your house every day. It would be incredibly inconvenient for each meal. Then we wouldn't have as many meals together. Then I would never see you, and I would miss you," I say, entering another emotional spiral.

We start crying again.

Honest question—are hormones catching?

"Okay you two, guests are starting to arrive, and parents aren't going to want to leave their kids with hysterically crying women," Gran mentions from beside us.

We sniffle a bit and have a last hug before the first kids come up the drive. We greet the parents and point the kids in the direction of the pool. I am not surprised to see Alison, but I'm surprised that her dad brought a date. Brittany met Gordon, Alison's dad, at Grady's birthday party last year. They had a bit of a weird experience when Gordon made it clear he was interested in Brittany and resented Matt in a big way. Since then, my brother and sister-in-law have done their best to keep their distance from Gordon as much as possible even though Grady is obsessed with his daughter.

"Is that...?" I whisper to Brittany.

"Yep."

"Did he?"

"Bring a date to an eight-year-old's birthday party? Yep."

"Weird."

"Yep."

"Is it just me or does she look maybe five years older than Alison?"

Brittany glances at me meaningfully and says, "Yep."

I shudder. Eww.

"Brittany, good to see you," Gordon greets stiffly.

"Gordon, good to see you and Alison. Grady is in the pool, Alison, go on ahead." Brittany points through the gate to the pool. When Grady shouts Alison's name in reverence, she almost succeeds in hiding her grimace. Almost.

Gordon appears similarly pained. "Yeah, that's still going on for us too. Brittany, I'd like you to meet my girlfriend, Kimberly."

Brittany shakes her hand graciously and introduces me. I do the same. I know not all bleach blondes with skimpy clothes and fake tans are named Kimberly, but it's a weird coincidence given my recent experience with Derek.

"Please feel free to stay if you want. We are grilling up some food now." She points to grill where Matt stands watching their interaction like a hawk.

"Actually, Kimberly and I have other plans, but thanks. We'll be back to pick up Alison a little later," Gordon explains, turning to leave.

Brittany nods diplomatically. "Absolutely. See you later."

"Is it that weird every time you see him?" I whisper.

"Yep."

"Ugh."

"Yep."

In typical birthday party fashion, once all the kids have arrived, Derek and Matt finish grilling, and the food is placed on picnic tables on the covered porch overlooking the pool. The kids scarf down hamburgers and hot dogs at alarming rates while happily chattering away. Grady opens his presents, appropriately excited and thankful for each and every gift. After presents, the kids enjoy cake and ice cream, then run around the small side yard until their food settles enough for them to get back in the pool. Gran and Pop have a staunch thirty-minute rule before you can get back into the water after eating. The second the thirty minutes are up, each and every kid goes running for the pool. As soon as they are splashing around, the adults sit under the covered porch watching the kids play and taking their time eating and visiting.

"I can't believe you got Grady a slime kit. That's going to be so messy!" Brittany complains.

I giggle. "I know."

"I think we should let that be a special project for fun Aunt Maddy at her house," Matt suggests.

"Nope. Birthday presents are strictly take home. That's the rule," I say smugly.

"I'm going to need to see that in the book," Matt grumbles.

Just then, Grady comes running up to the porch and whispers in Brittany's ear. I immediately get excited because I know what's coming.

Brittany nods. "Why don't you tell everyone?" Brittany suggests to Grady.

"I'm gonna be a big brother!" he yells at the adults before running back to the pool to tell his friends.

Cheers and hugs are given all around, with, of course, my mother, the queen of all emotions, bursting into incoherent sobs of joy. Matt and I share a look of long-suffering understanding. Grady and his friends play for another couple of hours until their parents eventually arrive to pick them up.

When all the kids have left, Matt, Brittany, Derek, and I get into the pool with Grady. We play ball and then a new game Brittany and I have created called "Brittany and Maddy relax on floats in the deep end while Matt and Derek entertain Grady." Brittany and I have been chatting for a little while, enjoying our relaxation time when she says, "We should do a girl's night soon. It's been a crazy few months."

"Great idea! We can try that new restaurant the guys are sure to hate," I suggest, picturing us ordering a wonderful meal.

"What would we hate?" Matt asks, splashing me with water.

"That new Asian fusion place downtown," Brittany answers.

"Correct," Derek nods.

"Yeah, we would hate that," Matt agrees.

Derek props his arms on my float and drifts us away from Brittany and Matt, who has taken a similar position on Brittany's float.

"Where's Grady?" I ask in curiosity, but not enough to lift my head and look for him.

"On the porch with Mom and Dad eating more cake and playing with his presents," Derek answers lazily.

"Good call on the huge NERF gun and megapack NERF bullets."

I hear Derek chuckle. "You know Brittany and Matt will get us back for this, right?"

I open my eyes and am momentarily blinded by the sun. I turn my head to look at him. "You mean with our kids?" I feel my ovaries leap to attention at the mere thought of having Derek's babies. I love Derek, and, little by little, day by day, as he proves his love for me, I have more and more faith that he isn't going anywhere and this could be forever.

Derek nods. "I think we should start thinking more strategically. They will take great pleasure in repaying us when the time comes."

I nod seriously. "You're right. We should be smarter. More strategic. Maybe we should draft a tentative action plan and forecast to determine possible implications."

"Or, and I'm just throwing this out there, we could try to not intentionally antagonize them," he suggests with a straight face.

I wrinkle my nose and glare at him. "That sounds a bit drastic, don't you think?"

Derek laughs and kisses my nose.

I lay my head back on the pool float and close my eyes again, sighing in contentment.

"What do you want to do tonight, Princess?"

"Will you cook for me?" I ask sweetly. As I believe I've stated before, whenever Derek cooking is an option, I always choose that option.

"I suppose I could whip something up," he says, playing with the fingers on the hand he's now holding. "What about after that?" he asks.

I crack an eyelid and eye him curiously. "Is there something you want to do tonight?"

He shrugs casually. "I thought maybe we could go for a ride."

My eyes narrow. "To anywhere specific?"

Derek's lips twitch. "Oh, I don't know. Wherever you want to go to show off your new helmet."

I gasp and sit straight up, slipping off the thin float and into Derek's arms. "Really?" I ask excitedly.

Derek grins. "Yep. Came in yesterday afternoon."

I squeal, wrapping my arms around his neck. "I can't wait to see it! Is it sparkly? Did you bring it? Is it a pretty color? Can I see it? It's not a full face one, is it? It's like yours, where it's just on top, right? Because my hair would never be the same if I had to wear one of those full-face things."

"I did bring it, it is sparkly, it's pink, which I hope you think is a pretty color, and, no, it's not a full face one. It's one like mine because I know about your hair."

"Oooh! I can't wait to see it! I love pink!" I can't contain another squeal.

"I know. And you love sparkles," Derek states proudly.

"I do!" I cheer. "I really do!" I kiss him and relax into his arms

"Hmm. Where can we go to show off my new helmet? Is there a biker bar in the area?"

"I don't think so. Why don't we take a drive and then go downtown for some dessert?"

"And you'll cook for me?" I ask to double-check because that's the most important part of the plan.

"Yes, I'll cook. I've actually been thinking about this recipe for...."

I'm not proud of this, but I stop listening. It honestly doesn't matter what he cooks. I'm positive it'll be delicious. I won't understand most of what he says anyway. I just like listening to the sound of his deep voice, being held in his arms, floating in the pool. Bliss. It's bliss.

"Mads?" Derek rumbles in my ear.

"Mmm." I'm too relaxed to form words.

"Does that sound good?" he asks.

I force myself out of my cocoon of contentment. "Of course, you know I'll love anything you make."

"That's sweet, Princess, but I was asking about plans for tomorrow," he chuckles.

I smile, my cocoon of contentment sucking me back in at his chuckle. He has a great snicker, chuckle, laugh, smirk, and grin, but his chuckle is my favorite. "Oops."

"Does that mean you don't have an opinion about what we do tomorrow?" he asks in amusement.

"Mmmm" I respond, slipping into serenity. I couldn't care less about our plans for tomorrow. I don't care about anything but being in his arms, listening to his voice right now.

"Would you like me to stop talking so you can relax?" he asks.

My eyes pop open and my head jerks up at the suggestion. "Gosh no! Half my serenity cocktail is the sound of your voice."

"Serenity cocktail, huh?" he says smugly.

I smile like the cat that got the canary, because from where I'm sitting (in the canary's arms) I did. "I highly recommend them."

"What's the other half?" he asks, playing along.

"Roughly, the recipe is two parts being in your arms plus one part your eyes to an equal part of your voice, mixed with a dash of the knowledge that you love me. Shaken, not stirred," I explain, laying my head back on his shoulder.

"Is that right?" he asks in amusement.

"That's right. Could you walk me through that thing you are thinking of cooking tonight again? I could use another drink." I relax with a contented sigh.

Derek chuckles. Ah, sweet symphony. "Absolutely, Princess." As Derek speaks lowly in my ear and I sink back into his strong arms, my serenity cocktail kicks in.

I think that's my favorite thing about Derek. I thought for so long that I would never fall in love again. I had been hurt, had put my trust in the wrong person, and been betrayed in the most humiliating way possible, and as a result I didn't feel safe to trust my own judgment. I pushed Derek away to protect myself, afraid I would be hurt again.

But Derek's persistent. Bless his heart, when he knows what he wants, he just keeps going till he gets it. For some reason I'll never understand but forever be grateful for, he wants me. In the process, before I even knew what was happening and how, it was taken out of my hands as to whether or not to love him. I just did. I couldn't help it. It's not a thing I chose. I just gave in to it. I let it have me. I let him have me for better or for worse. Part of me was worried once I stopped holding back that he wouldn't want me anymore, but the opposite was true. He stopped holding back too, and it turns out, we are pretty perfect together.

At some point, the longer we are together, there will come a time when something big happens. I will have to choose our love over anger, bitterness, resentment, or hurt feelings. It's inevitable in any relationship. I don't doubt what my choice will be. Not for a single second. I know with certainty no matter what we face, we will do it together, and I will always choose him. Choose our love. Right now, in Derek's arms, I know. I know without a shadow of a doubt he will choose me too. He's proven it to me over and over again. He chose our love in the very beginning and never stopped choosing it. He just waited patiently for me to catch up.

I open my eyes and smile, "I love you, Derek."

"I love you, Maddy," he replies tenderly.

Epilogue

Christmas Day

Maddy

"Maddy, you have to share," Derek growls above me.

"Says who?" I challenge.

"The law of common decency."

I huff. "The law of common decency doesn't apply to babies." Shows how much he knows.

Derek glares at me. "It applies especially to babies."

I roll my eyes and say defiantly, "I waited my turn. It's my turn."

"You barely let Dad touch her before snatching her away. I haven't gotten to hold her at all. You know Mom and Dad and Meema and Papa don't get to see her as much as we do. You should let them spend more time with her," he says reasonably.

I ignore him.

"Maddy," Derek prompts, patience lagging. After another minute, Derek sighs and reaches for me. "Give me the baby, Maddy."

I sigh and sniff her head one last time, speaking softly into her ear. "I guess I have to let you go for now. It doesn't mean I don't love you more than everyone else loves you, it just means that Uncle Derek is getting growly like a bear and I don't want him to be mad at me." Derek huffs above me. "I'll come rescue you soon," I promise in a whisper to her.

I surrender the baby to Derek and watch in amusement as both our mothers pounce on him and whisk her away from his arms. They know better than to try that with me. There was a bit of a skirmish half an hour ago when I got her away from Gran, so after that, they've given me my space.

Lily Grace Knight, a perfect baby girl, was born on November 14 to Matt and Brittany. She has downy, light brown hair, a dimple in her chin, chubby cheeks, and the cutest fingers and toes you've ever seen. I fell in love the moment I saw her. Needless to say, I've spent as much time as possible at Matt and Brittany's soaking up her tiny baby magic.

During the Thanksgiving holiday, our parents' monopolized much of baby Lily's time, leaving me with diaper changes and a few minutes here or there when she wasn't sleeping. I vowed Christmas would be different, strategizing to ensure I got the same amount of hold time as everyone else. Admittedly, though, I may have gotten a tad aggressive in my efforts.

Derek's right, I have been selfish, but it's really just to curb my disappointment. Derek and I have been blissfully happy for months. He has long since dispelled my previous fears and insecurities with his consistent love. We talk about the future all the time, but he hasn't mentioned any specific plans. I thought he was maybe giving me the time that I fought so hard for in the beginning, so I patiently waited. For a couple of months. After that, I started getting antsy.

I had hoped he might propose over Thanksgiving, but that didn't happen. Coupled with not being able to spend any time at all with Lily, Grady was the only bright spot in the entire day capable of curbing my despair. In my disappointment, I had convinced myself Derek was saving it for Christmas, using my Christmas gifts as an opportunity to propose and start our life together.

Yet, here I sit. In my parent's massive living room with all our family around. Decorations filling every stable surface, Grady on the floor playing with his mountain of toys, all the gifts opened, Christmas dinner eaten, with no ring. No plans for the future.

Not even a baby to take comfort in.

I glare at Derek. Baby comfort snatcher.

My backup plan, should this have happened like it has, is to convince myself that a ring is coming New Years, but I don't want to think about that right now. I'm not sure I can face more disappointment.

"Come on, Princess. Don't be mad. I promise you'll hold her later. I'll kidnap her for you if I have to," Derek reassures, coming to sit next to me on my parents' loveseat.

Huh. Loveseat. Even the furniture is mocking me.

Am I making too much of this? That's possible. I mean, we are happy. Mostly. I just want more. I need more. I'm tired of saying goodbye every night, having to wait all day to see him. It's not enough, and it's all his fault.

Derek puts his arm around my shoulders and tucks me into his side. "You okay? You look down."

"I'm cranky," I hesitantly admit.

"How can you be cranky? It's Christmas."

I eye him, not appreciating his disapproving tone. "I can be cranky whenever I want."

"But why would you want to be cranky?" he presses.

I open my mouth to argue with him and close it again. He's teasing me. I can tell by the amusement in his eyes and the grin threatening his usually stoic face. Normally it would be charming, but I'm not in the mood. "Go away," I demand, shifting away from him.

Derek chuckles. "Come on, what's the matter? Didn't Santa bring you what you wanted?"

I resist Derek's uncharacteristically good humor. Because no, Santa did not bring me what I wanted. And that's certainly not something I want to discuss with Derek. I know he wants a future with me; we talk about it all the time. If he doesn't want that future now, then I guess I'll just keep waiting. Impatiently. Resenting every single day we aren't together.

Derek stands and takes my hands, pulling me to my feet. "Come with me."

"Where? And why? I was comfortable," I grumble.

"There might be one last gift for you, but if you are too cranky...."

I perk up in curiosity. "Another gift?"

Derek nods, taking me through my parents' house to the backyard. "Maybe. Only if you want it."

"Who wouldn't want a gift?" I ask, not appreciating that he wants me to work for this when he knows I'm not in the mood.

"I don't know. Who would want to be cranky? It's a crazy world out there," he answers in amusement.

"Why are we outside? It's dark and cold," I say, looking around cautiously.

"Maddy," he growls.

"Derek," I copy his tone.

He sighs and stands in front of me, taking my face in his hands. He stares at me for a moment before he kisses me, claiming me in that all too familiar way he's had since the very beginning. By the time he pulls back and stares into my face again, my mood has brightened considerably. So has the yard. My parents' porch is covered in twinkle lights and there are flowers everywhere.

Oh dear Lord, it's happening. It's happening! My hands start shaking and my heart starts pounding. The lights are so pretty, and the flowers are so fragrant and gorgeous. Derek is staring at me. I should focus. I don't want to miss anything.

Is that a trellis? Have my parents always had a trellis? Or did Derek bring this in? Because a trellis proves a hefty commitment to setting the scene. Crap, focus. Focus. Derek is still staring at me. "Derek?"

"From the moment I saw you, I knew you were mine. You are a beautiful, intriguing, intelligent, infuriating woman, and I love you. I love your independence. I love how you can't help but argue about everything, even when you agree. You are this unstoppable force that came into my life and turned it upside down, and I love you for it."

"I love you too," I whisper. I can't help it. The words just slip out. This is happening. My entire body is frozen, but I couldn't not say those words.

He nods emphatically. "You do. You love me. You love me like no one else in the world has loved me, teaching me what love and family are all about. You are so brave, fighting past your fears and insecurities to love me." A hand cups my cheek, "Do you remember on our second date you bet I would run screaming by fall?"

I nod. I do remember that. Tears I have no control over fall down my face.

"I've known for a long time you were mine. For a while now, I've known that you knew it too, but I wanted you to be sure. To see that I'm not going anywhere. To see that I will spend my life loving you and making you happy." Derek takes a breath and drops to one knee. "I told you that night I would collect at Christmas, and I always keep my word. Marry me, Madison."

Just like Derek to make a question more of a command. I can't begrudge him that, though; I love it about him. I love it because it usually gives me the opportunity to bicker with him if I'm in the mood, but there will be no bickering tonight.

"Yes" is barely audible as I throw myself on top of him, pressing my face into his neck.

"I love you," he whispers to me.

"I love you," comes out garbled and muffled as I press myself closer to him and cry some more. He holds me tight, then lifts us back to a standing position.

"Did she say yes?" I hear Mom ask in a loud whisper near the door.

"I think so. She may have just tackled him," comes Brittany's overly loud whispered reply.

"Can we go out yet?" Grady asks in a normal voice.

"Shh, no, close your eyes!" Brittany admonishes.

"Daaad," Grady whines.

"Trust me, Grady, you don't want to see it," Matt says to him.

Derek and I can't stop our laughter when we finally part. He takes my left hand and puts a stunning ring on the fourth finger.

"Like it?" he asks tentatively.

"It's gorgeous. Best Christmas present ever," I say, kissing him. "Just what I wanted."

We stare dreamily at each other for several moments before we hear a soft whimpering cry from the doorway. We turn and look at our family, both sets of parents, our siblings, and our niece and nephew, gathered watching us with goofy smiles on their faces. Well, Lily can't smile yet, but she would if she could.

My heart explodes with joy and I throw my hands up squealing, "We are getting married!"

I hear Derek chuckle behind me as Brittany and I run at each other, colliding in a tight bear hug that catches Grady in the middle.

"Ugh, you're squishing me," Grady complains as he squirms out from between us.

"Finally!" Brittany squeals.

"I know, right?" I shout, maybe in her ear. I let her go. "Look! Isn't it pretty?" I shove my ring excitedly in her face.

She grabs my hand. "Dang! Who knew he had such good taste?" she teases.

Derek wraps his arm around my waist. "She's only saying that because she helped me pick it out."

Matt pulls me in a side hug from the other side and protests, "Hey! You knew and didn't tell me?"

"I know it was you that spilled to Maddy about the pregnancy," she says knowingly.

Matt glares at me. "I didn't tell her!" I protest.

We separate from Brittany and Matt to hug our parents. Naturally, my mother is incoherently sobbing.

"Okay! Everyone inside for hot cocoa and another round of dessert!" Mom instructs loudly, despite having just been crying. It's shocking how she can just turn her tears on and off like that.

Each of our moms takes one of my arms and guides me inside, chattering excitedly about wedding plans. I turn back to see Derek watching with a grin on his face. "Help," I mouth. His grin widens and he winks at me.

When we all get back into the kitchen, Grady is already two cookies deep into second dessert, and Brittany blessedly distracts our moms while Derek tugs me down on his lap. Ah, my happy place.

I sink into his arms and relish him nuzzling my neck. Matt sits across from us and snags Brittany, pulling her into the same position. I look around. Lily is currently cooing in Dad's arms while Pop makes faces at her. Our moms are bustling around the kitchen, pulling desserts out and happily batting ideas for the wedding back and forth. They have become surprisingly close friends since Matt and Brittany got married. Grady is trying to convince Brittany that two pieces of pie and a piece of cake would be best washed down with Christmas fudge. Matt and Derek are making plans to take out the remote-control helicopters they got as gifts today.

I look down at the sparkling ring on my finger, envisioning Christmases like this for the rest of my life.

"Happy, Princess?" Derek whispers in my ear.

I nod, looking dreamily in his eyes. "Blissfully happy."

"You ready or do you want to stay?" he asks.

"Stay," I say quickly. "Let's stay and visit some more."

He nods, although I think he wants me all to himself.

"Besides, you promised to kidnap Lily for me later. I'm cashing in," I say with a playful nudge.

He groans. "You want me to take her away from our dads?" He says it like I've asked him to climb Mount Everest for a block of ice.

"You were the one that was all like 'I always keep my word'," I say imitating him.

"Fine, but I'm holding her first," he says as he pats my leg before I stand to let him up.

He doesn't know this, but he's only getting to hold her long enough to give her to me.

"Aunt Maddy?" Grady asks.

"Yeah, Buddy?"

"Is Uncle Derek going to move in with you now?"

"Yeah, after we get married," I feel safe in saying.

He sighs in relief like this is something that has been truly bothering him. "Good."

"You like that idea?"

"Yeah. We can always live next to each other, right?" he asks.

Derek catches the end of Grady's words as he reaches me with baby Lily and winks at me. I settle my little niece in my arms before taking my position in Derek's lap again, looking at Brittany and Matt when I say, "Of course we will, Bud. Always."

Matt and Brittany smile in agreement, and Derek kisses my temple.

"What if we need to get a bigger house?" Matt asks, and I'm sure it's just to be argumentative.

I roll my eyes, assuming he understands that we just covered this.

"Then you need to find two houses side-by-side or buy a really big lot to build two houses," I say staring him down. Brittany's with me on this, and between the two of us, I'm not worried. Besides, I know he's only bringing it up the same way he brings up me being at his house all the time. Because he loves it.

"Actually," Mom speaks up as she places pies on the table, "that's something your father and I wanted to talk to you about."

Matt and I exchange worried glances. It's never good when Mom has something to tell us and it's especially bad when she brings Dad into it. Throw in real estate? This could get ugly.

"We were going to buy a house for Matt and Brittany as a wedding gift when they got married," Mom says, and I watch in amusement as Matt winces and Brittany's eyes bulge and mouth drops open. "But they seemed so happy in their house. Then, you moved just next door, Maddy." Mom shrugs, continuing, "It just wasn't the right time. However, your Dad and I kept an eye out, and we found two houses just down the street from here."

Matt and I trade knowing looks.

"Mom, you live in the woods. You and Dad own all this land. What do you mean you found two houses just down the street?" Matt asked flatly.

Mom's face turns guilty and she looks to Dad for assistance. "We built them," he explains shortly.

"You..." Brittany starts in shock.

"...Built us houses?" I shout in disbelief.

"Without consulting us?" Matt finishes with a frown.

I look at Derek and he's staring at me with his stoic face. I look back at Matt and Brittany, who are staring at each other.

"Not exactly without consulting you," Mom argues gently.

"What?" Matt asks in confusion.

Mom's eyes twinkle. "Remember when I showed you girls the floor plans of my friend Ellen's place? Well, it was really for your houses. I took very good notes of all the things you said you would change and want in your own houses. Of course, they aren't done yet, so we can still change things."

My mouth drops open. The CIA ain't got nothing on Grace Knight. "Mom, you can't be serious. You can't give us houses," I sputter.

"Land too," Dad says with a nod.

"It's part of your inheritance, you're just getting it early," Mom justifies.

"But you built us houses," Brittany says stubbornly.

"Without asking us first," I remind her, "or even asking us what we wanted."

"I did though!" Mom argues. "I just couldn't tell you it was for you."

Derek puts his hand on my neck and rubs the base with his thumb like he does when he's trying to ease my tension. His touch always instantly calms me, and I think it's so sweet when he does this. It lets me know he's with me and has my back.

"They built us houses," Brittany says to Matt somewhat numbly.

He nods and looks at me helplessly. I shrug. "At least we can live next door to each other forever now."

Matt rolls his eyes. "That was my one chance to get away from you."

I smile. "Never getting away from me now, Matty," I taunt.

He grimaces, but I can see his grin.

"So, are we just...okay with this now?" Brittany breathes.

"What are you gonna do, Britt? It's done. It's kind of perfect. You guys need more space, we need a place with a little more color." I shrug, "We get to stay together. Everybody wins."

"If you don't stop about the colors I painted that house," Matt threatens.

"All beige! Who does that? It's like a sanitarium," I say emphatically.

Brittany looks at Derek. "You're awfully quiet."

I turn and look at Derek. His face is not giving anything away, but his eyes, his eyes tell me all I need to know.

"Thank you, Grace, Cal. That's very generous of you," he acknowledges to my parents. He looks at me. "I'm okay with it."

Mom claps her hands together in ecstasy. "It's settled! I can't wait to show you the plans. We can get started tomorrow. Now, we'll need to go over floor plans and have you approve. They've already begun building, but I'm sure they can move some walls around...."

Mom chatters on about house plans while Brittany looks at Matt as if she is contemplating some kind of murder-suicide situation. Not because my parents are building us houses, but if I know Brittany, it's because she doesn't care at all about floor plans and colors. Matt tugs her closer, whispering into her ear. Dad snagged Lily from me when I was distracted by the news of the houses, so I relax against Derek and settle into my happy place.

I'm pretty sure Grady snagged the pie and cake he wanted and washed it down with not one piece of fudge but two. He wanders to the living room, no doubt to get back to his Legos.

I'm not listening to Mom anymore. I don't think any of us are. We simply are sitting around in stupefied silence, glancing back and forth between each other and thinking the inmates have taken over the asylum. I snuggle closer to Derek and breathe him in. As long as Derek seems okay with asylum living, I'm okay with it.

"I love you," I whisper.

"I love you," he rumbles against my ear. "You know I'm going to need to design our home security, right?" he warns softly.

"Yes, crazy paranoid detective, I know," I answer with resignation.

"Just as long as we're clear," he replies, pleased.

"We're clear. I'll even throw in the kitchen," I say as I settle under his chin.

"You're just saying that because you want me to cook for you at each meal," Derek returns with amusement in his voice.

I snort softly because Mom is still talking and, technically, we are listening. "Of course I do. Just so we're clear, I want you to cook for me. All the time, in fact."

He grins.

"We're getting married," I whisper in his ear dreamily.

His grip on me tightens. "Yes we are, Princess."

"You sure you can love me forever?" I tease. I already know he can.

"I certainly can, but I believe it was you who was supposed to declare her undying love to me today," he rumbles lowly.

I grin at his reference to our second date. "I didn't already do that?" I joke.

My perfect Christmas gift shrugs. "I don't remember. Why don't you remind me?"

I settle in to remind him, sure that this will be a recurring conversation throughout the course of our lives together.

* * *

Thank you for reading Maddy and Derek's story! I hope you had just as much fun reading it as I had writing it. Keep reading for a SNEAK PEEK of book 3.

Reviews are like warm hugs and if you love warm hugs as much as I do, please consider leaving a review for Shut the Front Door.

For more Oak Street Series exclusive content like bonus scenes and short stories such as Barnes and Shelly's Adventure, join the Least Boring Email list here:

lm-karen-author.mailchimpsites.com

Sneak Peek!

The Oak Street Series is concluded with book three titled: Everything. Grady is all grown up and his story ties Oak Street all together. Keep an eye out for the final book in the trilogy, to be released in November 2021. Continue reading below for a preview.

To be the first to recieve new release information, Oak Street series exclusive content like bonus scenes and short stories like Barnes and Shelly's Adventure, subscribe to LM Karen's Least Boring Email. I promise you'll never find the words, 'committee', 'donations appreciated', or 'volunteers needed' in this newsletter. It's strictly for fun.

Sign up here: lm-karen-author.mailchimpsites.com

Everything: Oak Street Series Book Three

Chapter 1

Alison

I hate sitting at bars. Who wants to sit with your feet dangling like a paper doll?

Admittedly, this may not be an inconvenience for most of the population. As I am significantly shorter than the majority of Caucasian American females, it is an inconvenience for me. You would think after a minimal growth spurt that stopped at 5'2, a lifetime of ridicule, and the odious nickname of Tinkerbell; I would have acclimated to my size by now. Yet, it still annoys me.

I make the leap down from the stool at the bar to the floor and edge my way through the crowd of the busy restaurant to the restroom. The restaurant is similar to the majority of trendy restaurants in downtown Atlanta. Modern, flashy, and overpriced with a frivolous fusion menu. Thankfully the restroom is spacious and empty, the quiet allowing me to collect my thoughts.

I observe myself in the mirror as I wash my hands. Side note- why are bars always sticky? I idly wonder if people who sit at bars are generally more likely to be messy eaters and if there would be any benefit to doing a study to find out. My light blonde hair is still held proficiently in a bun at my neck, no hair slipping free. I push my black framed glasses up my face and inspect the lenses in the mirror. Blemish free. Perfect.

I check my watch and notice I have been waiting for thirty minutes. Allowing the customary fifteen minute grace period to accommodate Atlanta traffic, Mark, my date for the evening is still fifteen minutes late. I decide to wait for fifteen more minutes before going home. Home would be preferable to proceeding with this date anyway.

I stifle an impatient sigh. My former nanny and surrogate mother for all intents and purposes, Denise, insists that I go on at least one date a month. I would refuse, but I don't refuse Denise much of anything. She was the only good thing my father ever gave me, with the notable exception of tuition money for my undergraduate, graduate, and doctorate degrees. She was one of the only people in my life to truly care for me in a maternal way throughout my growth and development, always a source of love and support when I needed it. I am required to call Denise every Sunday night at eight pm on the dot, much like I assume other mothers require of their children. The only exception, of course, being when I am visiting her which I am scheduled to do at least once every two months. Date reports, as I prefer to think of them, are due at the end of every month. I arrange these dates as efficiently as I can from a professional dating website to take place in the middle of the month, to account for last minute cancellations and reschedules. However, this month's date was required to be pushed to the last week in the month due to a microbiology research conference I attended in California last week. Denise has always strived for my contentment and I know it would make her feel better if I were settled with a spouse. It is for her sake alone that I allow her to lovingly nag me into these dates and subsequent date reports. The only way for me to cope with them is to think of them clinically, like any other monthly chore, similar to changing an air filter or having your oil changed.

My only objective for the dates is to get through them with minimal effort, getting home and in my pajamas reading my favorite book by ten. It's terribly troublesome to possibly miss my date report this month due to an unexpected cancellation. I have always made it a point to never miss a deadline. I check my phone again to determine that I haven't missed any messages.

I take a deep breath before venturing back out to the popular restaurant and begin to edge past the crowd back to the bar. I hadn't gotten many steps before I heard a high pitched squeal calling my name.

"Alison! Alison McKay!"

My shoulders tense. I would recognize that voice anywhere. I turn and find a beautiful brunette with glowing green eyes bouncing toward me.

"I just knew that was you!" she cries, scooping me into a huge hug.

Although at least eight years younger than me, Lily Knight towers over me. The last time I saw her was my high school graduation day, she was only around ten at that time but already my height. It's been ten years since then, and she's grown into a beautiful young woman. My heart aches unexpectedly, and I am shocked to find myself glad to see her.

"Lily, it is good to see you." I say sincerely when she lets me go.

She squeals exuberantly, "Gosh Alison, you haven't changed a bit. Still so beautiful. How are you? Why did you stop coming around? We all miss you so much." Lily hugs me again and without giving me the opportunity to answer any of her questions keeps talking, "Ohmigosh!" she pulls away from me and takes my arm excitedly, "Grady is going to die when he sees you!" she exclaims, pulling me toward the opposite corner of the bar where I had previously been sitting.

My feet and my heart concurrently and instantaneously stop, my hand pulling away from Lily's. Of all possible scenarios, likely and unlikely, I would have placed seeing Grady Knight tonight as the single most unlikely thing to happen, only short of a meteor destroying earth. I am not prepared. The thought of facing Grady Knight, the only man I've ever loved and therefore the only one to shatter my heart, tonight? On monthly date night? When I have likely been spontaneously cancelled on and left alone in a pretentious fusion restaurant? I shake my head in horror and back away. I feel conclusive in stating there is nothing more abhorrent that could happen.

Lily turns and looks at me in surprise at my abrupt stop, "He's this way Alison, he will definitely want to see you." she says with a worried frown "Are you ok? You look pale... well, even more pale than you usually are. Not that you're normally pale, you just have a naturally alabaster complexion." She finishes with an envious smile.

"I...I am sorry, I have to go." I stutter and turn quickly toward the door, making a run for it before Grady sees me, or I see him.

"Alison McKay." A friendly voice says appreciatively through the crowd. My actions freeze. I inhale a panicked breath as my heartbeat thunders at what I'm sure is an unhealthy speed due to the adrenaline and norepinephrine flooding my system. I force myself to turn around.

The crowd easily parts for Grady as he makes his way to me. He is below average height for a Caucasian American male, but he has a presence people notice. The last time I saw him was our high school graduation day. His light brown hair is the same, but instead of it being shaggy and long, it's neatly cut and combed. The freckles on his face have continued to lighten and his eyes are the same warm brown, but his face is more chiseled. In truth all of him appears to be more sculpted than the last time I saw him.

Deep breath. I can do this. "Hello, Grady." I'm pleased my voice is even despite my insides quaking violently.

He reaches me and covers me in a bear hug. He smells different... but the same. I close my eyes and pretend that a simple hug from Grady Knight doesn't cause my brain to release dopamine at levels indicative of addiction. He releases me with a wide smile, and I look away from his face to find Lily watching me closely. I forgot she was here for a moment.

"Lily said she saw you but I didn't believe her. I can't believe you're here. What's it been? Ten years?" he asks jovially.

I focus my attention on Grady's neck instead of his blinding smile and comforting eyes. It's closer to my eye level anyway, and I need to attempt to keep the hormone flooding to a minimum if I am to retain any natural semblance of sanity through this interaction. "Ten years, four months, and twenty three days." I recite automatically.

Grady chuckles, "I have missed you Alison. Join us, Lily and I were just grabbing dinner."

I mentally correct myself. Joining Grady Knight and his sister Lily for dinner is the single most abhorrent thing that could happen tonight. I shake my head and back away, "I was just leaving. It was good to see you, but I must go." I turn to leave and pray my legs carry me swiftly away before Grady catches my arm. Warmth spreads up and down my arm at his touch.

"No, don't go yet, we should catch up." Grady insists.

I avoid his face again by focusing on his neck, "I really need to leave, I apologize. Please have a lovely dinner." I carefully extricate my arm from his hand and hurry away without looking back.

I furiously swipe at my cheeks as I dash to my car to rid evidence of tears. Sitting in my car, I take deep gulps of breath to try and stop the flow of tears. I recite pi in my head, and when that doesn't work I think through the physical process of crying. My cerebrum registered overwhelming emotions I still can't identify, thereby triggering my endocrine system to release hormones to the ocular area, causing my tear ducts to overflow.

Physically, I can pinpoint what is happening. Emotionally, I am left as if a ship without an anchor. I feel all the feelings, so many I can't begin to sort or understand them all. Happiness at seeing Grady and Lily again, heartbreak all over again upon seeing Grady's perfect face. Aching loneliness for the family I lost the day Grady broke my heart, and longing I've never known before.

Eventually my tears clear and I drive home, fighting the onslaught of memories that came with seeing Grady and Lily again.

About the Author

LM Karen writes contemporary Christian fiction romance. As a long-time lover of words, she can generally be found behind her laptop or with a book in her hand. A graduate of Toccoa Falls College, her heart is in the mountains. She eventually made use of the voices in her head by putting them on the page.

You can connect with me on:

🌐 https://instagram.com/lmkarenauthor

📘 https://facebook.com/lmkarenauthor

Subscribe to my newsletter:

✉ https://lm-karen-author.mailchimpsites.com

Also by LM Karen

Summertime Lilies: Oak Street Series Book One
A sweet and sentimental contemporary Christian romance with a uniquely witty voice.

There are three things you should know about Brittany Masters:

1. She's a single mom and a nurse manager at the local cancer clinic;

2. She has big plans for a quiet summer;

3. She's convinced that fudge pops are the answer to almost all of life's most important questions.

A new neighbor, Matt, making friends with her son while simultaneously pursuing a relationship with her blow plans for a predictable summer right out of the water. A chance meeting at the cancer clinic where she works renews a connection with an old friend that gives her the perspective she's been missing. From quiet nights on her front porch swing in Matt's company to long talks in the clinic with her old/new friend, Brittany's summer is anything but routine.

Summertime Lilies can be found wherever books are sold.

Ebook ($2.99): books2read.com/u/mVgOyM

Paperback ($12.99): https://www.lulu.com/en/us/shop/lm-karen-and-ebooklaunchcom-and-michelle-schacht/summertime-lilies/paperback/product-e6z2w7.html?page=1&pageSize=4